The Stationmaster's Daughter

Amy Myers

© Amy Myers 2005

Amy Myers has asserted his rights under the Copyright, Design and Patents Act, 1988, to be identified as the author of this work.

First published in 2005 by Severn House Publishers Ltd.

This edition published in 2018 by Lume Books.

Table of Contents

Prologue	7
CHAPTER I	8
CHAPTER II	27
CHAPTER III	47
CHAPTER IV	69
CHAPTER V	92
CHAPTER VI	112
CHAPTER VII	130
CHAPTER VIII	153
CHAPTER IX	173
CHAPTER X	184
CHAPTER XI	198
CHAPTER XII	214
CHAPTER XIII	229
CHAPTER XIV	244
CHAPTER XV	262
CHAPTER XVI	273

Author's Note

There are many lost railway lines in Kent, and one of the most beautiful is the Elham Valley Line, which ran from Canterbury to Folkestone. The line was closed in 1947 after sixty years of service; little evidence of it remains, however, except in the delightful Elham Valley Railway Museum in Penne, near Folkestone, in the work of its volunteers, and in excellent books such as Leslie Oppitz's *Lost Railways of Kent*. The loop line to its west, serving Fairsted and Applemere, is fictitious, though for me it is no less vivid than the Valley line itself.

The kingdom of Montevanya is also fictitious, although it has come to assume such reality in my mind that I am puzzled when war histories fail to mention it. I have not attempted to explain the intricacies of Balkan politics during these years except as they affect Montevanya. The latter is strategically placed on the River Danube, and during the period of this novel had the mighty Austro-Hungarian Empire breathing down its neck to its north and north-west, Roumania to its east, and Serbia (later part of Yugoslavia) to its west. The Russian Empire was not far away, and panting for power to its southeast was Bulgaria, beyond which lay Turkey and the last vestiges of the Ottoman Empire. All in all, faced with such fire-breathing giants, the tiny monarchy of Montevanya saw independence as crucial for its survival; its neighbours lusted after it in vain, since a move by one of them would bring down the fury of the others on its head.

Serbia too was independent at the outbreak of the First World War, though its neighbour Bosnia, in which many Serbians by race lived, had been snaffled by Austro-Hungary a few years earlier. Austria longed to keep Serbia in its place, which was, in Austria's view, within its own empire. The murder of Archduke Ferdinand, heir to the Austro-Hungarian Empire, was to give Austria its opportunity.

In writing of Serbia in the period up to and during the First World War one has to make a choice between its former spelling, Servia, and the now familiar Serbia, which was adopted during the war. I have used the latter throughout as being the more sensible choice for today's readership. There are several excellent memoirs by British women about their experiences in Serbia during the first half of the First World War, and in particular Mrs St Clair Stobart's own account (*The Flaming Sword*) of how she led her unit out of Serbia during the retreat was an eye-opener as to the part such women played in the conflict.

I would like to thank my agent, Dorothy Lumley of Dorian Literary Agency, and my editor, Amanda Stewart of Severn House, for their enthusiasm about this project and their constant support throughout its birth, and my gratitude also goes to the Severn House team for turning it so efficiently into printed form.

Prologue

There is a lane deep in the heart of Kent that winds its way into the folds of the North Downs. Along it drove the carriages and motor cars of emperors, princes and kings, of prime ministers and statesmen, and of Kentish yeomen and labourers. All were welcomed at Applemere, provided they had the eyes to see it and the heart to love it.

The spirit that once kindled Applemere still slumbers on in the comfortable — some would say ugly — old house. The pool that gave it its name is not yet glorified into a lake, and is still surrounded by the wild daffodils. The apple trees that overhung it have vanished long ago, but others still flourish in the orchards that surround the house. Even vandals have forgotten Applemere, or if they find their way there are deterred by its very solitariness. What follows is the saga of how Applemere came to be as it was, and how the stationmaster's daughter played her part.

CHAPTER I

1907

I want to rule the world!"

Jennie Trent flung open her arms as she leaned out of her bedroom window and shouted her joy at being twelve years old at last. Not too loudly, for that would bring the wrath of the household down upon her head, a bad start for a birthday. Then she took a deep breath and surveyed the kingdom spread out below her. Not bad. To whit, one smallish but colourful cottage garden, with three cherry trees and her brother Tom making his way back from the Pretty House, as they called it, the privy at the far end. Aunt Winifred had tastefully covered it in honeysuckle and roses, which were now so thick it was almost impossible to see the real purpose of the wooden shack.

Outside the garden lay the lane into the village, already full of life. She could see the sails of the windmill turning and hear the clip-clop of horses' hooves. She could hear a blackbird singing in one of the cherry trees; he — or was it a she? — seemed to be as approving as Jennie was of this promising sunny day; she could smell the lavender even from here, combined with the freshness of the still dewy grass.

Jennie waved regally towards Fairsted village. Right, that was one part of her realm. Now for the other part. She was lucky in having a corner bedroom in the Station House. Tiny it might be, but it gave her that precious second window, and if she unhooked the latch and pushed the window full out she could lean over the sill to see the line.

And there it was. She could see one end of both the up and the down lines, and the signal box. Darling Jack was on his way back to the platform. She waved furiously at him, but he didn't see her. Jack Corby had just become a junior porter now that he was fifteen — well, the only porter in fact. From here, Jennie could even see through the arch of the bridge down the line into the blue and green haze of the distant hills. Their branch — more of a loop really — linked up with the Elham Valley Line towards Folkestone and *boats*. Boats could take you away far across the sea to other countries where the people didn't even speak English.

The up line of their loop linked with the Valley Line and joined it to Canterbury. Just beyond Fairsted the trains disappeared into a tunnel, leaving only a puff of smoke behind them as their huge black bulks vanished into the mystery of beyond. Father said you could get to London that way, but she had never been there. In fact, actually travelling on the train to Canterbury, as she sometimes did, was never quite as thrilling as watching the trains disappear into the black hole of the tunnel. Both directions held unsatisfied questions, which half of her longed to have answered and the other half didn't, preferring to remain safely in Fairsted.

She decided to hang out of this window too and make her declaration once again. "I *am* going to rule the world! So there."

"You couldn't rule a straight line."

Brother Tom was directly underneath the window, jeering at her. She didn't mind. She adored Tom. She adored everyone today, but especially Tom, Dad and

Freddie. Tom, her big brother — two years older than her, golden haired and already tall — was the apple of Dad's eye, as well as hers.

"Anyway," Tom continued, "you're only a girl."

Jennie laughed. "Queen Victoria did it." The old queen had still been on the throne when Jennie had been born, and she could just remember all the fuss there had been when she died six years ago. Fairsted railway station had suddenly acquired purple and white drapings round a huge portrait of the old queen, and Dad had had tears in his eyes. So far as she could recall, the Queen had never visited Dad, so why should he care so much? Jennie had wondered.

"She was an old woman, not a kid like you," Tom jeered.

"I don't mind waiting," Jennie conceded. "Not too long, though."

"Your father does, miss." A grim-faced Aunt Winifred was standing in the bedroom doorway. "He can't laze around like you all day. The 8.04 down's gone, and he's been in for his breakfast these five minutes. So you just get down there."

"It's my birthday," Jennie pointed out indignantly.

"Time enough for that when you're properly dressed." The door banged behind her and Jennie, remorseful at holding up her father, washed in the cold water in her bowl, and quickly pulled on drawers, stockings and chemise. Then she hesitated, wondering whether to put on her best pink pinafore dress now, knowing it would only call down wrath upon her head. Oh well, so what. She quickly pulled the dress on, then crept down the stairs and out to the privy. It might be early August but it was still chilly, and she was eager to rush back inside.

There they all were, halfway through their breakfast — so Aunt Winifred hadn't even waited. Tom didn't even look up, but Freddie, a year and a bit younger than Jennie, grinned at her. "Happy birthday, loopy sister." Aunt Winifred merely sniffed, but Dad put his newspaper down and held out his arms. She promptly rushed into them.

"I'm twelve," she announced proudly.

"And uglier by the day," Tom pointed out.

George Trent cuffed him lightly with his newspaper but Jennie didn't even dignify Tom with a glance. Rulers of the world were above petty revenge, especially today.

"And just why have you got that frock on, miss?" Aunt Winifred enquired.

"It's my birthday." Jennie slid into her seat and removed the cosy from her cooling boiled egg.

"I imagine we're all aware of that, young lady. How do you expect to do the housework dressed like that?"

Jennie was aghast. "But it's my birthday. I can't do housework."

"It's also washing day," Aunt Winifred retorted. "I can't do both. Besides, you don't do the cooking on *my* birthday, do you?"

Jennie said nothing. Aunt Winifred was old, well over thirty, and, although she had birthdays and they all tried to be nice to her then, it wasn't the same. Jennie cheered up. It was silly to sulk. "If I do the housework first, can I put this dress back on for tea?"

Tea, after all, was the important time for birthdays. That's when you had presents — they weren't much, but they meant your family was glad you were alive. And Aunt Winifred would make a cake, too. She wasn't much of a general cook, but she could make the most marvellous cakes. Jennie forgave her everything for that.

Her mother, Aunt Winifred's sister, Alice, had died so many years ago that Jennie had few memories of her. In her mind her mother had been all love and tenderness, and was always like the lovely photograph of her in the family album. Two years later, when Jennie was about seven, Aunt Winifred had come to rescue them. That was how Dad had put it, but to Jennie it was more like being put in prison.

Tom and Freddie managed to cope with her all right, because they were boys. Tom charmed her and Freddie was spoiled as the baby of the family. But for Jennie life seemed a never-ending battle. Aunt Winifred, it seemed to her, was determined to turn Jennie into her double. "Stern Daughter of the Voice of God," her aunt would read out solemnly from her boring old book of Wordsworth's poems. This "stern daughter" was apparently called Duty, and Duty insisted Jennie spent all her time washing up, cleaning the privy, dusting and sweeping, especially in the holidays. True, Aunt Winifred did a lot of it herself, but it was dull, oh so dull, compared with what Jennie could have been doing — helping Dad on the railway station.

"Why is Aunt Winifred always so strict and serious?" she had once wailed to her father.

He had coughed, obviously searching for an answer. Finally he had one. "I believe she was disappointed at Omdurman, my love."

Jennie had gaped at him. "What's that?"

Dad's face went red, however, and he quickly buttoned his lip.

Since then, whenever Aunt Winifred was particularly Winifreddy, Jennie, Tom and Freddie would intone solemnly, once out of her hearing: "Disappointed at Omdurman."

Jennie discovered that Omdurman had been a big battle in Egypt years ago, which Lord Kitchener had won against dervishes, whatever they were. What role could Aunt Winifred have played in this battle, they wondered. A family game had developed, played strictly among themselves, with Tom playing the gallant Kitchener, and Freddie with a tablecloth draped round him playing a whirling dervish (after a little more research had been done into what these were). Jennie played Aunt Winifred either as a Queen Victoria-cum-Britannia urging her side on, or as a Florence Nightingale pleading with them to stop — depending on how close teatime was. She soon became fed up with these female roles, however, and usually took a poker in the fight herself.

"I am Disappointed," she would intone from time to time, allowing Tom to knock the poker from her hand.

"You will be," Aunt Winifred had interrupted on one occasion, "if you don't come to the table *now.*" She seemed puzzled by the meekness with which they obeyed her, but when she left, they collapsed with laughter.

"Do not let us Disappoint her again," Jennie solemnly urged her brothers.

"What are you going to do with yourself today, Jennie?" Dad asked, putting aside his newspaper again to cheer her up when he saw her downcast look.

"Help you?" she asked hopefully. It was not yet hop or apple-picking time, and so she was free to do what she really liked best: collecting passenger tickets, poring over Dad's shoulder as he did the Returns, as he called it, and looking at the tickets to see where the passengers had come from. She made up stories about why they had come to Fairsted if they were strangers, or why they'd been away if they were Fairsted folk.

"After the housework," Aunt Winifred reminded her, then relented a little. "Your Aunt Eileen's coming this evening. You can make up the camp bed in your room for yourself, so she can have your bed. Get things tidy for her, and then you can go."

"Oh!" Jennie flew round the table to put her arms round a rigid Aunt Winifred, who seemed pleased at the attention. Aunt Eileen was Jennie's very very favourite person, as well as Dad, of course — and Tom and maybe Jack and Freddie. Aunt Eileen was the third Harkness sister, and was disapproved of by Aunt Winifred, which had instantly made her a person of great interest to Jennie. Like Winifred, she had never married, for there was never any mention of an Uncle Eileen. There was a sense of mystery surrounding Aunt Eileen and all Jennie knew was that she was a traveller. She talked of the desert and of wonderful, far-off places like Petra or Knossos or the Silk Road, so Jennie could never work out why there was such an atmosphere of disapproval when she came. Instead of sharing a bedroom with Aunt Winifred, Aunt Eileen always slept in Jennie's room. This seemed odd to Jennie, but she loved it. They would talk far into the night — or rather Aunt Eileen would, with Jennie asking questions and urging her on. As her aunt's voice came out of the dark after the candles had been blown out, Jennie could imagine she too had been climbing on camels, bartering in markets, finding rich and wonderful new places and meeting strange and wonderful people. And to think all of this lay just at the end of their down line to Folkestone, and a boat ride away.

Aunt Eileen even smoked a pipe from time to time, to Aunt Winifred's horror and Dad's obvious amusement. Tom could not stand Aunt Eileen, and Freddie was rather scared of her, but she was a magnet for Jennie. If she was coming, this was a *real* birthday, and it didn't even matter that she had to do the preparations for it.

"Can I help Jack in the goods office today?" she asked her father.

"He's going over to the Halt," George answered. "Go with him if you like." He smiled.

Jennie gasped. "*Applemere!* Oh, yes." What a birthday this was turning out to be!

Trains did not normally stop at Applemere Halt, which was an unmanned station just over half a mile away. When they did stop, Jack or sometimes Dad himself had to walk there to take tickets and help passengers with their luggage. Sometimes there were even specials for Applemere, trains hired privately and only carrying passengers for the Halt. On a few glorious occasions the Royal train itself would come, when the King visited or other members of the Royal family.

This did not seem surprising to Jennie, for it reaffirmed her belief that Kent was the centre of England. The King might live and rule in London most of the time, but he *chose* to come here. When he did, nearly everyone in Fairsted would walk to Applemere Halt, the children would wave flags as he stepped down, and Dad would have his buttons brightly polished and nearly bursting off in pride. Once it seemed to Jennie that the King looked straight at her — almost as if he knew she was going to rule the world one day. She had been disappointed at first that he was not wearing ermine robes and his crown, but only a suit and hat like anyone else. The lovely Queen Alexandra had made up for that, wearing the most lovely silk gowns and hat, together with a wonderful smile.

Often foreign people came, and Dad had even mentioned princes and princesses, but she could never get him to tell her more about this. His passengers were entitled to their privacy, he said, just like anyone else. So Jennie knew little about the mysterious people who descended from the trains at Applemere Halt. All she knew was that they were bound for Applemere, the large old house at the foot of the lane leading from the Halt. Though the lane through Fairsted led round in a loop to Applemere, it led nowhere else save the Halt, for it had been specially extended by the owners of Applemere. If visitors to Applemere wanted to approach by road, they drove through the village, but mostly they came and went by train.

The villagers grew used to seeing the pony trap, the brake and the large impressive Albion motor car. "That be for Applemere, annit?" one might remark to another, but mostly they took Applemere for granted now and abandoned curiosity. It was there. It was Applemere.

*

The sun was blazing down later as Jack, Tom, Freddie and herself set out for the Halt. Tom and Freddie had insisted on coming, which surprised Jennie. She could understand Freddie being interested, for he was always tagging along if she and Jack were off somewhere, but she was puzzled that Tom had chosen to accompany them. He was always pouring scorn and mocking whenever Dad mentioned Young Master Michael — and he was the reason that the train was stopping today at the Halt. He was returning from a visit to one of his Etonian friends for the rest of the summer holidays. In a rare fit of anger when Tom made a sneer one day, Dad had turned on him.

"That's enough, Tom. Show some respect will you? He'd be a prince in their country." Then he had turned red as usual when he'd said too much, but even Tom was silenced.

What did this mean? *Their* country? So far as Jennie knew, England was their country. It was generally known that Sir Roger was something at court, working for the King, and that he had a beautiful foreign wife, which accounted for the foreigners visiting from time to time. They had two children: Michael, about Tom's age and away at school, and a girl who had a governess at home, and was a year or two younger. But they were all English, so what did "their country" mean?

As they walked through the fields along the footpath by the railway line, the sun was so hot that Jennie began to feel dizzy despite her sun bonnet. Harsh sun such as this could have a cruel streak to it. It had been on a day like this that two of Farmer Hutchings' cows had strayed on to the line, and there had nearly been a terrible accident — well, for one of the cows it *had* been terrible, and the train itself had come partly off its tracks. Jennie had seen the remains of the cow and felt sick, not just with pity for the animal but because it brought home to her that not everything in life was as beautiful as a summer day in the meadows with grasshoppers and bees and flowers. The cow had been killed by man-made machinery, but nature itself was built on cruelty, so Dad reminded her, and so were human beings. It was their duty to fight cruelty. That word "duty" again. "In every garden there's a privy," Dad would say, "and all the waste of mankind has to be stowed somewhere and dealt with." Behind the spic and span cottage doors of Fairsted, he told her, there were many old and frightened people, and there were the sick and the poor and the violent as well.

"When I rule the world," she vowed to herself today, slashing the com with a piece of couch grass, "it won't be like that. No poor people, no sickness, nothing."

"That's God's job, Imogen," she remembered her mother saying once; she was the only person who had ever used her full name.

"I can help Him," Jennie had pointed out. So far there hadn't been much helping she could do, apart from fetching and carrying for village people and tidying gardens for those who could no longer do so. Helping God seemed far preferable to obeying Him, as Aunt Winifred's Stern Daughter seemed intent on doing.

"What time is it, Jack?" she asked as she saw him looking anxiously at his pocket watch.

Jack Corby was a lad of few words. He was as quiet as her father, though physically he bore little resemblance to him. He was of medium height, but very slender, almost frail looking with his fair hair, pale face and large grey eyes. Yet this was misleading, for he was very tough. "As hardy as a Cudworth 2-4-0," Dad would joke. The Cudworth-designed engines were legendary on the old South Eastern railway.

Trains were his passion, but poor Jack! He had wanted so much to learn to be an engine driver, but the nearest sheds were too far away for him to reach every day. He couldn't be a double homer, lodging overnight under the usual system, because he was wanted at home by his widowed mother, to help look after his younger brothers.

"I wish I could drive engines," Freddie said wistfully, trudging along the path as the up train to Canterbury thundered past, enveloping them in steam clouds.

"Not much of a job." Tom shrugged, glancing at Jack.

"Yes, it is," Jennie told him crossly. She knew how wonderful it was to be on the footplate for a short time, feeling the sense of power as the engine roared along. She had no desire to drive a train herself-just as well, Dad joked — but she wasn't going to have Jack snubbed.

"That's the Kent Flyer," Jack cried in alarm. "We've only got five minutes." He began to run, and Jennie tore after him. She saw Freddie trying his best to catch them up, but she couldn't wait. As she and Jack ran up the ramp to the up platform she could see the signal was already down to clear the train for the next section, and Mr Wilcox, one of Fairsted's two signalmen, was standing by in his box.

The Halt was a lovely station, with only a tiny waiting room that doubled as a ticket office, and then nothing but the platform and fields all around. It made that moment when the black friendly monster came puffing in, so full of self-importance, all the more vivid. She couldn't see Fairsted railway station from here because there was a bend in the line, but she could hear the train already grumbling its way towards them. Hurriedly they crossed to the down platform.

"No one to meet Master Michael yet," Jack remarked anxiously. Normally there was a dog cart or sometimes the carriage or even the Albion motor car to meet the train, and usually his sister too. As Tom and Freddie reached them, the smoke came into sight, and then through its swirls the train itself came in, hissing to a halt with a last triumphant puff. The usual acrid smell in Jennie's nostrils and a fleck of black soot in her eye were all part of the excitement that the train brought with it.

The Trents had all seen Master Michael before, and his sister, though she remained nameless to them. It was the very sense of their apartness that drew Jennie here time and time again, and she suspected that might be why Tom had come too. There was a divide between the Applemere people and themselves, which was never crossed. Their pale faces passed them by periodically, never touching their lives. This boy and girl must have lives of their own, but what were they? *Who* were they?

A carriage door opened and Master Michael descended, wearing his Eton jacket and boater and looking round expectantly. Jack immediately approached him, doffing his cap, his fair hair blowing in the breeze. Master Michael wasn't at all like Jack or Tom, not nearly so good looking. He's like a lizard, Jennie suddenly thought, as tall as Tom, but darker haired and leaner, and his face looked as if a long lizard tongue might slither out at any moment. This thought pleased her and brought *Master* Michael down to size. The girl always looked the pleasanter of the two.

"Twerp," Tom muttered, and Freddie giggled.

"Get my bags," she heard Master Michael order Jack, who promptly leapt into the first-class carriage to remove first a trunk by himself, while Tom made not a move to help him,

then two portmanteaus. Then he went back inside to gather up a collection of magazines that Master Michael had obviously left scattered over the seating.

Michael glanced at Tom, and then, almost as if he divined Tom's reluctance, ordered him: "Give him a hand with that trunk across the line."

Tom stepped back indignantly. "He's the porter, not me."

Appalled, Jennie ran to help Jack herself, while Freddie picked up the bags and struggled across, and Tom stood watching them in one of his belligerent moods.

Jack put the trunk down on the up platform, to Jennie's relief, because it was very heavy. Michael stared at them. "Well, go on. Take them to the carriage. Don't just leave them there."

"No dog cart yet, sir. Nor car."

"Why the dickens not?" Michael cursed Jack as though it were his fault, and then walked to the station gate as if to suggest that Jack was completely wrong.

"I expect they'll be along in a moment, sir," Jennie said brightly.

They weren't, but the girl whom Jennie presumed was Michael's sister suddenly appeared round the bend pedalling furiously on a bicycle. She dismounted in a flurry of skirts and hurried towards her sullen brother. Jennie sympathized. She knew exactly how the girl felt as she'd often been in the same position trying to appease Tom.

"I'm sorry, Michael," the girl said. "Dawkins hasn't returned yet, and the motor car's broken down again."

He more or less ignored her, announcing to the world at large: "It seems no one is particularly interested in my coming home."

"Of course we are." The girl looked increasingly anxious. "Dawkins won't be long."

"I'm not waiting here to be gawped at by villagers," Michael said mutinously.

The girl flushed, obviously more aware of others' feelings than her brother. "Then let's leave the luggage here and walk back. You can have my bicycle, if you like. You'll look after the baggage, won't you?" she asked Jack politely.

"Of course, miss."

Michael looked him slowly up and down and obviously found Jack wanting. "Nonsense," he said. "These kids can carry it home."

"It's far too heavy," the girl said, horrified.

"I'll try, sir," Jack said hastily.

"But *I* won't." Tom had his surliest expression on his face. "Carry your own baggage."

Jennie's heart sank. Why couldn't Tom be his usual charming self? Ninety-five per cent of the time he was, but every so often, when his pride was hurt, he could be really objectionable, just because he thought being one of the villagers was beneath him. He had grand ideas, did Tom. Dad wanted nothing more than for him to follow him into the South Eastern and Chatham Railway, but Tom couldn't see what a chance he was throwing away by refusing even to consider it.

Jack heaved up the trunk but Tom turned round and stalked away, so Freddie took the other end. Jennie was furious. It was letting Dad down, for one thing. In his book Applemere came first, high above Fairsted Manor, where Mr Hargreaves the brewer lived.

"I'll take the rest." Jennie quickly ran forward to seize the portmanteaus. It was less than a mile to Applemere House and, though she'd seen its turrets and gables above the high hedges that surrounded it, the opportunity to go within those gates was irresistible. She hoisted up one portmanteau but, as she bent down for the other, the girl forestalled her.

"I'll balance one on my cycle," she said, "since my brother doesn't seem to want it."

"You'll wobble."

The girl smiled. "Don't worry. I'll push it along."

Jennie felt awkward at first, as she and the girl took up the rear of the short procession. What should she say? Perhaps nothing. Oh, no, she couldn't do that. But she hadn't curtsied. Should she have done? If her brother was a prince, didn't that make this girl a princess? She longed to pour out endless questions, but could manage none of them. They want their privacy, Dad had decreed. Instead, she suddenly found herself giggling.

"What's funny?" asked the girl.

"Your brother leading us all like a band of pilgrims down the lane." Jennie wondered whether she should have dashed after Tom, but for once she wouldn't. He could stew in his own juice.

"I wish Michael had waited for Dawkins," the girl said apologetically as her brother moved further and further ahead.

"I don't," Jennie said valiantly. "It's fun walking along this lane, and the baggage isn't heavy. Well," she added honestly, "not very. And we can rest if we're tired. It's a lovely walk with the ragged robin out."

"The what? Where is it?"

Jennie waved a hand at the pink-flowered banks. "There, the flowers."

"Oh." The girl laughed. "I thought you meant a bird. I call that *lychnis flos-cuculi.*" She caught Jennie's amazed eye. "I prefer your name."

"It's the village name," Jennie muttered. "Like dumbledores."

"What are they?"

"Bumblebees. Don't you learn about things like that?"

"Yes, but not the local names," the girl said wistfully. "My governess comes from London."

"That must be interesting though," Jennie said eagerly. "Does she tell you all about Gog and Magog and Jack the Ripper and Anne Boleyn's ghost with her head tucked underneath her arm?"

"No. She lived in Bayswater till her father died. He was an army man."

"Omdurman? My aunt was disappointed there." Jennie couldn't resist it.

"*What?*" The girl stopped to stare at her in amazement. "What do you mean?"

"I don't know," Jennie laughed, and explained.

"Why don't you ask her about it?"

Jennie considered this. "I wouldn't dare. Anyway, I like my stories." She hesitated. "It's like wondering where the trains go when they vanish into Fairsted tunnel."

"To Canterbury," the girl answered practically.

"Ah, but do they? Perhaps the ones you *travel* on do, but suppose the others, just suppose, the others go somewhere completely different when they're out of sight."

The girl looked at her carefully. "I think I see what you mean. They might sneak round and go to Dover, just for fun one day."

"Or to Iceland, or the North Pole."

"Or Montevanya."

"Where's that?"

"In the Balkans. On the Danube."

"The blue one, like the waltz." Jennie broke into da-da-da song.

The girl laughed. "Not very blue, according to my mother. But there are blue mountains in Montevanya."

"How do you know?"

"I've been there."

At this exciting point, Jennie had to bite back her questions because Michael was shouting back to them: "Here's Dawkins at last." The dog cart approached at a brisk pace, though Michael didn't bother to wait. He simply walked past it, on towards Applemere, while the other four, with Dawkins' apologetic help, got the baggage into the cart.

So Jennie wasn't going to get her first glimpse of Applemere House after all. That was its formal name, but to her it was just Applemere, which sounded so mysterious and wonderful, as though a whole new magical world lay within its gates. As the girl was about to climb up she stopped. "I'm Anna Fokingham." Then, even more hesitantly, "Was that another brother of yours at the railway station?"

"Yes, that's Tom. This is Freddie — " he was busy chatting to the horse — "and I'm Jennie, Jennie Trent." She flushed with embarrassment, remembering Tom's behaviour.

"Brothers can be…"

"Difficult," Jennie agreed, and Anna laughed.

Jennie watched as the dog cart turned and disappeared round the next bend. Freddie began to stroll back down the lane with Jack, but Jennie continued gazing at the empty lane. It was her twelfth birthday, and something marvellous had happened, something so marvellous she would never forget it.

In bed that night it was hard to sleep. Aunt Eileen was still downstairs chatting to Dad and Aunt Winifred, but Jennie was still running through her mind the events of the day. Aunt Winifred, seeing her flushed face, had put her hand on her forehead and declared: "You've had too much sun, my lass." It had been a glorious day, despite the usual everyday little difficulties — even though it had been her birthday. But that, as Dad said, was life. It would be dull if it was all plain sailing, wouldn't it? Most of all it seemed to Jennie that the world had reached out and touched her at last. It wasn't the sun that had caused her flushed face. It was Anna's last whispered words as she climbed up on to the dog cart.

"Would you come to see me one day, please?"

CHAPTER II

1909

"Sometimes I think," Jennie observed, "that there's no happier place in the world than Kent in apple-blossom time." Anna sighed. "It can only be an escape place, can't it?"

"There's nothing wrong with that," Jennie said defensively. "Some people stay in escape places all their lives. And I'd be happy here."

Surely there could be nowhere more lovely than their own special place, hidden away in the grounds of Applemere. They'd discovered it by accident in overgrown woodland, their very own magical grotto, nestling against a high mossy bank and overgrown with wild roses and honeysuckle. From the top of the bank they could see the apple orchards, and all around them were bluebells.

"Perhaps I'll be the very first woman to fly away in an aeroplane when I grow up," Jennie said idly. "What will you do, Anna? When you're out of the schoolroom," she added, since this was a joke between them. What a stupid phrase, yet it seemed very important in Applemere House, which was a strange mixture of formality and the most entrancing peculiarities. Jennie loved it. Where else would you find chamber pots with a picture of the German Kaiser in full uniform painted on them — especially if Anna were to be believed and her mother, Princess Marie, had painted them?

Anna scowled. "I don't have any choice. I'll have to be presented at court after I'm seventeen."

"But that means you're grown up and free."

"You're wrong, Jennie," Anna said dolefully. *"This* is freedom, here with you. After that it will be like prison. I can never choose for myself again. After I'm presented I'll have to live in London every season and obey the rules, not laugh and have fun as we've done, at least until I'm married. And then I'll have to do what my husband wants and I'll have children and never be free again."

She looked so sad that Jennie had to work hard to cheer her up. "You might have a nice husband." Princesses did, after all, and Anna was a princess. She might not look like it now, in her dowdy serge skirt and blouse, but when she was forced to put on evening clothes for family dinners she looked lovely — thin and fair and delicate.

"But I won't be able to marry whom I choose. I'll be lucky if he speaks the same language as me."

"Why?"

"I'll have to marry whomever they think I should marry." She glanced at Jennie. "Don't look so concerned. It might not be too bad, I suppose. It's what I've been reared for, after all." What an odd way of putting it, Jennie thought. As though Anne were a prize mare to be disposed of.

Anna's mother, Lady Fokingham, was really Princess Marie of Montevanya. Jennie had grown so close to Anna that it was difficult sometimes to remember her mother was sister to King Stephen III. Montevanya, Anna had explained, was a small kingdom on the edge of the Balkans, and because of where it was it had an importance beyond its size, and so still ruled itself. As with Switzerland, King Stephen did his best to remain politically neutral in his alliances, although the much larger countries that bordered Montevanya — Roumania, Serbia, and Transylvania — all wanted it, partly because everyone was greedy for such fertile and mineral-rich land, but also because

Montevanya was on the River Danube. Bulgaria and Russia were also very close to Montevanya, and kept a close watch on it. None of these countries dared to swallow Montevanya up, however, because all the others would promptly go to war over it.

Jennie had never been much interested in history before she knew Anna, but now she would pore over the atlas at home, trying to work out which of all these exotic-sounding countries belonged to the Austro-Hungarian Empire, which to the old Ottoman Empire, and which still owned themselves. The Austro-Hungarian Empire was the most powerful, and ruled by the Emperor Franz-Josef in Vienna, who only last year had taken over the countries of Bosnia and Herzegovina. Dad had explained that this was because these places bordered the Adriatic Sea, and Aunt Winifred had added that it meant *trouble*.

Franz-Josef also ruled Transylvania, which was part of Hungary. To Jennie, Transylvania meant Count Dracula and all those creepy stories about vampires that Tom used to scare her with, but she supposed that, to Montevanya, having the Austro-Hungarian Empire on its doorstep was even more frightening than vampires.

"But you're not heir to the throne of Montevanya, Anna, so why does it matter that you marry well?" This still puzzled Jennie.

"Because...oh it's difficult. I suppose whoever marries me has a small stake in Montevanya, even though I live here. So *they* want me to marry one of my Montevanyan cousins, to be on the safe side. But that means I'd have to leave England and Applemere — and I don't want to. I don't, I *don't!*."

Jennie was silent after this outburst. Put that way, Anna's future seemed terrifying. "You won't even be fourteen till early July," she pointed out. "Which means you won't officially be out till the 1913 season."

"This is *out* to me. Being presented will force me *in.*"

Jennie began to giggle and Anna cheered up. "Anything could happen in four years," Jennie said. "Suppose you married one of King Edward's grandsons, then you'd be Queen of England, or nearly; that would be nice."

"But suppose I wanted to marry someone who wasn't royal?"

"Like who?" Jennie persisted.

"Well." Anna laughed nervously. "Jack, for example."

"*Jack?*" Jennie asked incredulously. She knew Anna got on well with Jack but, anyway, it was out of the question because Jack was Jennie's sweetheart, in so far as she had one. She felt close to Jack in a way that she never did with her other friends' brothers, let alone Michael.

"Only an example," Anna laughed, and Jennie relaxed.

"But you wouldn't want to marry someone like Jack. You wouldn't be happy living in a tiny cottage doing the cleaning."

"Sometimes, you know, I think that's just what I'd like to do. Not the cleaning," Anna added honestly, "but I wouldn't mind the cooking, if I could get away from all this. You've no idea what it's like sometimes. If we have formal dining, I'm stuck in the schoolroom with Gillyflower — " their name for her governess, Miss Gilchrist — "or if it's semi-formal I might be stuck next to old men with huge moustaches and beards and told to talk. That's even worse because — "

"So, *Jóa napotata*. Cousin Anna, we find you at last!" The undergrowth and bushes, which they so carefully kept in place to avoid discovery, were brushed aside and before Jennie's surprised eyes appeared two young men who were quite unlike anyone she had seen before. Firstly, they both seemed enormously tall, probably because of their high, feathered caps, and the long boots over their tightly fitting white breeches. Secondly, their uniform jackets were ablaze with colour and embroidery.

Anna leapt up from the grotto like a scalded cat, almost guiltily, as though she had no right to be enjoying herself. Jennie's friend seemed to vanish inside another Anna as she kissed both young men — not kissing as Jennie knew it, but formally on each cheek.

"Good day, Viktor. Good day, Max. I hope you slept well."

"Extremely," said the one who looked the younger of the two and whose eyes wandered curiously to Jennie, who remained decorously behind Anna still in the grotto, wondering whether she should be abasing herself on the ground, or curtseying, or what. They were foreign, and must surely be royal. She jumped as Anna turned round to her.

"Jennie, permit me to introduce Prince Viktor Deleanu of Montevanya. Miss Imogen Trent."

Viktor came forward. He was very handsome in his ornate and peacock-like golden jacket. Like Michael, however, there was something of the lizard about him, she decided. Or perhaps, in his case, a fox. He took her hand but unfortunately this coincided with her decision to curtsey so her hand remained aloft with him. However, when she rose again he actually kissed the hand. "How do you do," was all she could manage. Prince Max looked somewhat more approachable, almost as if he had thought her gaucheness funny, as he also took her hand to kiss it. She managed the curtsey better this time. All she could think of was how romantic they looked. Max even had a lute or some such instrument slung over his shoulder. It was just like Anthony Hope's stories of Ruritania. Perhaps *The Prisoner of Zenda* had been based on Montevanya.

Max must have seen her looking at his lute because he glanced at his brother, and said: "Permit us to sing to you a song of our country."

Jennie could hardly believe this was happening, but Anna pulled her down on to the grotto seat again to listen. Jennie couldn't understand a word of the song, of course, but Anna told her, "It's an old folk song about a girl — "

"A peasant girl," Viktor interrupted, seemingly amused at something.

"With whom a prince falls in love. He takes her back to his castle, but every night she dreams of her native woodland and finally runs away to go back there. The prince loves her so much he abandons his castle and goes in search of her. When he finds her, they remain together in a woodland hut, and he lives the life of a woodcutter."

"At which he is very bad," Viktor added solemnly.

"I think it's a wonderful story," Jennie said stoutly, but Anna stayed silent.

As Jennie walked back home across the fields, she wondered whether she should have spoken at all. She had an idea that in England the King had to speak first, but perhaps in Montevanya it was different. Certainly she couldn't imagine King Edward entertaining her with a lute. She couldn't wait to tell Jack, who might still be on duty in the signal box. The Applemere clock had told her it was three o'clock and there would just be time before the three thirty down had to be signalled, after which he handed over to Jimmy Wilcox. He'd have been working for fifteen hours by then — his usual twelve-hour turn plus overtime. The railway was a hard master, but she couldn't wait to begin herself. Only a few more months and then she too could really become part of the railway instead of just a spectator. Not as a cleaner or barboy — Dad's joke — but in any case she could never have been one of the old barboys who squeezed through the firehole door to clear the firebox of clinker and ashes. She only had to look at a fire for it to go out, Aunt Winifred said.

Her fourteenth birthday, on August 1st, meant that Jennie would be nearly grown up, and she, unlike Anna, could marry whom she liked, and *when* she liked, too. But that wouldn't be for years and years and years. Unless it was Jack, of course. That would be different. She pondered this for a few moments, feeling a shiver of excitement run up and down her spine.

From the foot of the signal box, where she could see Jack standing over the levers, she called up to him; visitors weren't always welcome at busy times. Too late, she saw there was someone else in the box, but it wasn't Jimmy. It was Michael.

Michael looked down at her so furiously when he, not Jack, came to the door that she stammered, "I'm sorry," but then wondered why she was apologizing. Then Jack called for her to come up, so Michael had to stand aside as she entered.

Master Michael was still looking cross. Perhaps Jack had been giving him a lesson on signalling. Yes, of course, how could she have been so silly? Michael must be ashamed of being caught displaying his interest in trains, and Jack was showing him how to do it. It wasn't, now she came to think of it, the first time he'd been here. Last holiday time he'd also been up here. So Michael had a secret passion for trains. What fun! It gave her a small sense of power over him.

Jack was only a junior signalman at present, but so responsible for his seventeen years that Jimmy Wilcox had no qualms about leaving him alone in the box.

"No Mugby Junction this," Dad would laugh. *Mugby Junction* was Dad's favourite book; Charles Dickens was a king among men in his view, and from an early age the great treat for the Trent children was for Dad to read to them during winter evenings. His favourite line was, "Look out! Look out! For God's sake, clear the way!"

Dad was quite an actor and would stride up and down, his lantern in one hand and reading with the other, while Aunt Winifred tried to say, "Don't be foolish, George," but never quite succeeded because she was enthralled too.

"I've been to Applemere." Jennie could contain herself no longer, Michael or no Michael. He didn't approve of her going there, but she had become part of its life now and since his parents encouraged her friendship with Anna, he could not object, though he was careful to keep his distance from her while she was there — and indeed anywhere. "As if I'd give him lice," Jennie had once giggled to Freddie.

"They wouldn't jump on him in a million years," he'd retorted. "They'd freeze to death. You keep them, sis."

"I met your cousins," she couldn't resist adding to Michael, once in the signal box. "Prince Max sang a song to me. Do you play the lute too?"

"Balalaika," Michael corrected her curtly. "And I don't."

Seeing Jennie about to retort, Jack quickly intervened. "The piano's enough for me."

Jennie was instantly remorseful for boasting about Prince Max. Jack played the out-of-tune upright piano in his mother's cottage beautifully. He loved folk songs, and she and his family would often have an evening listening to "The Ash Grove" and "Sweet Nightingale", usually before slipping into music hall choruses. His mother had been a Londoner before she married Sid Corby and still remembered the old songs.

"When are you off duty, Jack?" she asked, to make it up to him. "We could go for a walk."

"As soon as Jimmy's back."

"I'll wait," she said happily.

She could see that Michael didn't like that, and he brushed past her to leave. As he did so, he turned to her and said, apparently casually, "The princes will be here for a week, so Anna won't want you there."

Jennie flushed. "Of course not. I understand." It was Michael who didn't. She knew Anna would want to see her more than ever, to offset the burden of company. It suddenly occurred to her that these would probably be the cousins that Anna feared she would be expected to marry — well, one of them.

Michael had obviously thought of something else to annoy her. "And tell your brother to keep away from her, too. With my compliments."

That shook Jennie. What on earth did he mean? Tom? It certainly couldn't be Freddie, because Freddie never went to Applemere House — but then nor did Tom. Michael was just making mischief. Just then Jack rang the electric bell for the next box down the line to confirm his section was clear and then he lowered the signal for the three thirty to enter. Dad was as proud of the old lock and block system as if he'd invented it himself.

"You can laugh all you like," he'd say solemnly, when they teased him, "but that Sittingbourne accident would never have happened if they'd had lock and blocks going then." Dad had only been eight when a blunderbuss from the seaside had run into a train being shunted on the same line, and he had seen the results. For years Jennie had assumed a blunderbuss was a kind of train, but then Tom, in one of his nicer moods, had gently explained it was slang for a train over which a signalman had made a mistake.

Jennie went down the steps to wait for Jack below, and as soon as Jimmy was back in the signal box Jack hurried to join her.

"Did you hear what Michael said to me, Jack?" she asked as soon as they were away from the station and in the fields. "He told me to tell Tom to keep away from Anna. I didn't know he ever even met her. I can't remember Anna talking about him."

Jack didn't reply for the moment, whistling instead as they walked along by the stream that fed the Applemere pool. Michael called this a lake, but it really wasn't so grand. Lakes were big and organized and this was a pool with wild flowers all round it, almost hidden in the trees and left to its own peaceful natural self with only a little help from the gardener.

Jennie and Anna loved it, and went fishing for sticklebacks and tadpoles, much to Michael's disgust.

Jack put an arm round her shoulders. "We're all growing up, Jennie. Even you. Tom's sixteen and working for the brewery. Life changes, don't it?"

"You mean he's interested in girls, don't you?" she asked forthrightly. "I know that." Several village girls thought Tom was Prince Charming himself. But Anna was different. "Anyway, why shouldn't he be friendly with Anna? There's no harm in it."

"Perhaps." Jack bent down to examine the ground. "Look at this. It's early for poor man's weather glass to be out. Must be a good summer coming."

"You're avoiding the subject, Jack," she pressed him, worried now.

"He's your brother, Jennie. He always has ideas in his head. If he want to see her for the right reason, that's good, annit? She needs friends, and she's not yet fourteen. When she gets a year or two older it will be different. She won't be able to be friendly with him then. She'll have young gentlemen as her friends."

"She likes you, Jack. It's you she talks about, not Tom."

"Me?" Jack just laughed. "Not that way, she doesn't. Anyways, there'd be no point." He tweaked her ear. "No other girl for me than you, Jennie Trent. So just you hurry and grow up, will you?"

Jennie threw her arms round him. "I love you, Jack, you know that."

"Do I?" he said wistfully. "Seems to me, Jennie, you love everybody."

"What's wrong with that?"

"Because you *see* nobody and nothing, and that's a problem."

What did he mean? Jennie puzzled about this, but then soon forgot it as she talked about the great event of the day. "What do you know about Montevanya, Jack?"

"'Tis always a trouble spot, the Balkans. They're all at each other's throats. Half of them are fighting each other, or Turkey, and the other half is trying to be free of that Austro-Hungary."

"Montevanya's independent, so Anna says."

"Doesn't mean it always will be. There's family to be considered. They can stir things up."

"What family?"

"I looked it up once," Jack said. "Lady Fokingham's got some interesting relations. Anna's grandmother, Queen Zita of Montevanya, is a granddaughter of the old queen, Victoria. German by birth, she is, but her sister's married to the Tsar of Russia, her cousin to the King of Roumania, and another is the Kaiser of Germany. What do you think of that?"

"I hope they all come here," Jennie said excitedly. "Especially the Kaiser, though they'd have to change the chamber pots." Jack looked blank until she explained, and then she had to wait until he stopped laughing. Then he calmed down.

"I hope they don't never come here. There's a lot of war-hungry folk around, and Fairsted's better off without them. Let the rest of the world get on with its own battles, say I, and leave us be."

*

Jennie debated whether to say anything to Tom about Michael's odd comment. Anna would have told her if she'd met Tom. The Station House didn't see nearly as much of him now, because of his job at the brewery in Canterbury. Dad was more cheerful now that Freddie was taking a real interest in following in his father's footsteps. Freddie was only twelve but whenever he could he was off on the train to the Ashford sheds, making himself useful, helping to clean engines. His clothes were the bane of Aunt Winifred's life. "Into the boiler," was the constant cry. Dad always took his side, though, and Freddie would always cheek her into a good humour.

Tom, however, seemed to think he was a cut above everyone else in the house. Mr Hargreaves, the brewery owner, had bought Fairsted Manor some years ago when the last squire died, but no one thought of Mr Hargreaves as a squire, though he would have liked them to. No one liked him much because he was big and blustery, and thought he owned the village as well as the brewery. But Tom kept on his right side and was at the manor as often as he was at home.

Jennie finally took her courage in both hands when she saw Tom that evening. "I saw Michael today," she ventured. "He said something funny."

"Be the first time. Stuck-up nob," was his reply.

"Odd, I mean. He said I was to tell you to keep away from Anna."

Tom's normally rubicund, good-looking face darkened, and Jennie continued nervously, "I didn't know you were friendly with her."

"And why should you?"

"I don't know," she stuttered. Then she found her courage again. "She's not like us, Tom. You shouldn't be seeing her on her own. Are you?"

"What if I am? Not doing anything wrong. She's only a kid. I met her once out on her bike, we had a chat and I walked her home. Anything wrong with that?"

"No, but —"

"I wouldn't encourage her, Jennie, you know that." Tom looked at her so earnestly that she believed him.

*

Three days later, Dawkins came round with a note from Anna, asking Jennie if she were free to visit her that evening. Jennie guessed why. Her parents were entertaining formally, and Anna would be stuck up in the schoolroom alone, while Michael ate downstairs. Jennie and Anna had their own routine for such occasions. Dawkins would pick her up in the dog cart, Jennie would creep in through the trade entrance to Applemere House, and Gillyflower would escort her up the back stairs to the nursery — what a stupid word for a room that contained a girl of Anna's age. Then Gillyflower would pretend she had a headache and leave them alone so that they could creep to their watching post and peer down through the wooden balusters of the old musicians' gallery on to the dining room beneath. It was almost safe, though they had nearly been caught once when Sir Roger had suddenly looked up.

It still seemed odd to Jennie that Anna had to have dinner — or supper as it was called in the nursery — up here, even though Dad had told her there was a special coming through today for Applemere, which meant it must be a very formal dinner indeed. Was it the King, Jennie had asked. No, but almost. Dad was unusually eloquent when he said that the prime minister, Mr Asquith, was coming, together with his foreign secretary, Sir Edward Grey, as well as foreign royalty. This had excited Jennie immensely: not only the two princes but yet more royalty, and this time she really could ask Anna about them, since she would spend much of the evening staring down at them.

"Will the King of Montevanya be here?" Jennie asked her eagerly.

"No, his younger brother, Uncle Georgius." Anna looked embarrassed. "He's…odd."

Lying on her tummy, legs sprawled out behind her as she peered through the rails, Jennie wondered if God felt like this looking down on His creation. He would surely approve of Applemere House and love it just as she did. She remembered the first time she had come here, fully expecting to be turned away by the dour butler who opened the front door. Instead, she had been told, "Miss Anna mentioned you might call, Miss Trent. Please come in." She felt like she had stepped into paradise.

Applemere House didn't look like paradise either inside or out, but it felt like it. Lots of comfortable wood panelling, pictures of benign ancestors staring down from the walls, not as if objecting to her presence, but greeting her, as if they still felt part of the house. Applemere had been in the Fokingham family for three hundred years and that was why it had that nice feeling about it. Each generation of Fokinghams had added bits on to the house, or knocked them down, or altered them, and then one family last century had covered the whole outside in plaster and added more beams on the outside for show, plus a turret or two, and the gables. So Victorian turrets vied with Elizabethan chimneys and there was no rhyme or reason to either Applemere's architecture or its interior.

In the centre of the house was the former grand hall, now the dining room on formal occasions. It had an enormous log fire in winter, but at other times the room was made cheerful with flowers, cushions and curtains. Applemere was a strange combination in that the house was cluttered and untidy but Sir Roger himself was neat, composed and somewhat austere, in complete contrast to Princess Marie, who was welcoming to everyone. Anna had told Jennie that her mother disliked too much formal entertaining, having had enough of it in Montevanya; she preferred a simple life, but of course there had to be quite a lot at Applemere given her rank and Sir Roger's position at court.

The French cook certainly liked entertaining, producing magnificent feasts. She and Anna often sneaked down to the kitchens, either before the feast or after it, to indulge in what was left over. It was entirely against the rules, both of Anna's family and of the butler, who commanded what was called "below stairs" — another strange term to Jennie, since the servants worked at the rear of the house on the ground floor and slept at the top.

"What's Montevanyan food like?" she asked Anna curiously.

Anna grimaced. "Terrible. Big stews and rice and things like that. Some nice things, because Aunt Zita — Max and Viktor's mother — travels a lot. She's very fond of Cannes."

Listening to Anna, even though Anna wasn't aware of it, was like listening to living geography. Jennie now knew that Cannes was in France and full of Russian princes and princesses, as well as English noblemen. It was strange that even with all that Anna seemed to prefer Applemere.

"How regal," Jennie said admiringly, looking down at the splendid silver and crockery, and the wonderful flower arrangements. How did they manage those lilies so early in the year? she wondered.

"Shhh," Anna said a few minutes later. "They're coming in."

In came Sir Roger, elegantly tailored in black, with a beautiful woman clad dramatically in a bright blue satin gown over an ivory underskirt, with Boating lace sleeves and a glittering tiara, followed by a long procession of eleven other similar couples. Though she craned forward as far as she could, Jennie failed to see more than the tiaras or flowers in the hair of some of the ladies directly below her. Finally Princess Marie entered with a very tall man with a long black beard, curly black hair and piercing black eyes.

"Uncle Georgius," whispered Anna, as her mother took her place at the top of the table.

"Are all these royal people sleeping here? What do they do with their crowns and tiaras at night?"

"Put them outside the door to be polished with the boots," Anna retorted.

Jennie giggled, and then retreated as Uncle Georgius gave a quick look upwards, stared at them with piercing black eyes for a second or two, then took his seat below them.

The princes too presented an exotic sight. No white tie and evening dress for them, although gone were the bright-coloured jackets, which Anna had told her were their national dress. This evening they wore sombre blue uniform covered in medals. How on earth did they win those? Jennie wondered.

"How glorious," she breathed to Anna. "They look like Rupert of Hentzau in *The Prisoner of Zenda.*" Aunt Winifred had forbidden her read the book, which seemed strange, but when she had stolen it away one afternoon she could find nothing shocking in it at all, and walked round for several days with Princess Flavia's noble and beautiful expression of sacrifice without anyone noticing. Some day Rudolf Rassendyl — looking just like Jack — would gallop into her life.

Jennie shut her eyes and pretended she was sitting at the table conversing charmingly with Prince Viktor and Prince Max — no, only with Max, she decided, much the more human of the two. He would kiss her hand and sing to her just as he had that morning. Everyone at the table would be murmuring, "Who is that charming girl?" Then she would have to answer, "The stationmaster's daughter at Fairsted." *Where? Who?* they would ask. And all her glory would vanish like Cinderella's. Ah, well, just for this evening at least, she could pretend.

She peered down at Prince Georgius, who now appeared to be doing a conjuring trick covering a wine glass full of water with a piece of card and, yes, he was going to turn it upside down. She watched in fascination as the piece of card seemed to hesitate, then give way, and the water promptly soaked the table. Chairs were hastily pulled back, and there were a few titters of embarrassed laughter, Princess Marie calmly organized the footmen into clearing the mess, replacing dry cloths, plates and cutlery. Sir Roger was frowning, Jennie noticed,

but doing his best to be imperturbable. Montevanyan brothers-in-law of royal birth obviously had to be tolerated.

"You can see why Uncle Georgius is not approved of," Anna hissed. "He adores conjuring — he's just not very good at it."

Jennie could see that all too well.

The face of the lady next to him was hidden, but he appeared to be talking much more animatedly to her than to Princess Marie. "Who's she?" Jennie whispered, unable to see more than the top of her head, which was one of the few to be adorned by a simple coloured band of ribbon.

"His friend, Madame Szendescu," Anna whispered. "I haven't met her yet. She's as crazy as he is, apparently, but he refuses to be parted from her, which is why he's seated next to her. Father and Mother had to let her come, though

I expect she only speaks in Montevanyan, or else she comes from somewhere like Mongolia."

"No, she's speaking English." Jennie frowned as the sound carried up. There seemed something familiar about that voice. Then the woman moved slightly to talk to her neighbour and part of her face came into view.

Jennie gasped out loud, wriggled back, and clamped her hand over her mouth in disbelief at what she'd seen. She rubbed her eyes and peered down again.

"What's the matter?" asked Anna, alarmed.

"That's my Auntie Eileen!"

*

There were exciting questions to be asked of life, Jennie thought, as she snuggled into bed later. No Aunt Eileen sleeping beside her tonight; she must be staying at Applemere. Jennie would almost have thought she'd made a mistake if it hadn't been for the fact that, on their way out of dinner, Aunt Eileen had glanced up and winked. Jennie was totally flummoxed, and sick with curiosity, but for once decided to be cautious and not ask Dad or Aunt Winifred about this strange event. It seemed there was more, much more, about Aunt Eileen than Jennie could ever have guessed; even the Silk Road to China began to seem commonplace compared with the fantasies that now raced through Jennie's mind.

The next day Aunt Eileen arrived on the train from Canterbury like a conjuring trick herself, but her satins and silks had been replaced with serviceable tweed.

"How did you do that?" Jennie asked breathlessly. How had her aunt managed to reach Canterbury — and Applemere — yesterday without being recognized?

"Years of practice, my child." Aunt Eileen peeled off her gloves in the tiny boxroom as though it were as grand as an Applemere state bedroom. "There are matters with which it is not necessary to burden one's family."

"Aunt Winifred always says duty involves telling one's family everything."

"She may well do so," Aunt Eileen rejoined. "The sooner one realizes that duty is much more acceptable when its boundaries are determined by oneself and not others, the better life becomes."

Jennie didn't understand what she meant, so she fastened on the obvious. "But what were you doing there? Anna said you were her uncle's friend."

"That is correct."

"Called Madame Szendescu?"

"Also correct. That means Madame Meek in Montevanyan. My friend's joke."

What sort of friend? Jennie wondered. And how did one set about becoming a friend of a king's brother? It occurred to her that there was still a lot about life to be sorted out, and that not all puzzles could be solved by the standards of Fairsted.

CHAPTER III

1913

"First class single to London," Jennie repeated, stamping the date on the ticket in the press. For once her mind was not on her duties as booking clerk, but on the fact that later this afternoon she'd be off duty — and so would Jack. This coincidence rarely happened, particularly on a Sunday. As she handed the ticket to the passenger, however, she had a shock.

It was Lady Fokingham. Anna's mother was here at Fairsted instead of in London with Anna, as Jennie had thought, and for a Sunday that was very strange indeed. She looked very worried, which seemed out of kilter with her elegant summery hat with its one feather, or the light-blue walking costume. She'd soon have soot flecks on that, Jennie thought wryly.

"You're very early for the train, Lady Fokingham," she said anxiously, wondering whether she should light the fire in the waiting room for her even though it was June.

"I know, Jennie. I hoped to talk to you. Are you busy?"

Her husky accent never failed to enchant Jennie. She certainly was busy — she had to fill up the forms for new ticket supplies and sort the week's collected tickets into their correct series before she went off duty — but she put that out of her mind.

"Anna's not ill, is she?"

Anna was in London for the whole season, and had been away for over a month now. From the letters Jennie received from time to time it sounded as if she was hating it just as much as she had feared. To Jennie a life of dances, operas and races sounded wonderful, but then it wasn't forced on her as it was on Anna.

"No, not ill. Could you leave your office for a moment?"

"Of course." Jennie glanced at the station clock. She could risk being away for five minutes. The small waiting room seemed to acquire an exoticism just with the very presence of Lady Fokingham.

"Anna's presentation at court is in two days' time, Jennie." Lady Fokingham did not even sit down; she seemed too agitated. "Anna's refusing to go. I believe she really means it."

"But she can't do that at this late stage." Jennie was horrified. She had never taken Anna's threats seriously, assuming that when she reached London she would come to like it. She should have known better. This was Anna and Anna had always, despite her apparent shyness, had a mind of her own, a side that even Jennie had rarely been able to penetrate.

"Please come to talk to her, Jennie. I understand how she feels, but there are some things we must do whether we wish to or not." Lady Fokingham hesitated. "We all have duties, do we not? You work here and in the house. Anna's responsibilities are different."

Jennie hadn't looked at it that way. "I could run away," she pointed out. "Anna can't."

"That's exactly why I want so much for you to come. Even if you cannot persuade her to go, you will make her happier. And that, too, is important to me. But please, *please*, try, for our sake, as well as for Anna's. My husband's position…" She trailed off, looking at Jennie in appeal.

Jennie made her mind up, but with one condition. "If I do, you must tell her *why* I'm coming."

For a moment she thought Lady Fokingham would refuse. How strange. She seemed almost nervous of her own daughter.

*

Jennie had been to London several times before. Here on her own for the first time, however, she could enjoy the bustle, the crowds and noise of a Monday morning to the full. Lady Fokingham had given her the money for a motor taxicab to their Kensington home, but Jennie was torn between this and the novelty of the Inner Circle underground train, or perhaps a motor bus. Finally the taxicab won, so that she could enjoy seeing as much of London as possible, while the cab wound its way through the streets past rows of stately homes, with glimpses of the famous parks and finally of the Royal Albert Hall.

Fokingham House was quite near the latter, and almost as imposing — at least to Jennie. She took a deep breath and marched up the steps in her Sunday-best linen skirt, feeling almost as nervous as she had been when she first went to Applemere. While she was here, she decided, she would take a ride on the top of one of the London buses, so that she could look down like a queen on her subjects below, with the wind riffling through her air. Not that queens permitted any riffling, but Jennie loved it.

"Miss Anna is in the garden, Miss Trent." A lordly footman, or at least one who would like to be thought so, conducted her through the house.

And there in the garden she could see Anna's back, which managed to convey her complete misery. Jennie rushed up to her, about to hug her, when Anna spun round and glared at her. Her heart sank. Anna was obviously taking this the wrong way. "So they've won you over too, have they?"

Jennie decided to tell the truth. "Yes. I think your parents are right. You can't suddenly refuse to go now."

"I never agreed in the first place," Anna said bitterly. "Mother has a wonderful gift for getting things to go her way. At first she said she'd invited you up so that we could enjoy the theatre performance this evening, only of course it was more than that. We were meant to be going to a presentation dance at the Ritz, but I refused. I went to *three* dances last week, and that's quite enough. So Mama said we'd all go to a theatre of my choice instead. And do you know what I chose? *The Marriage Market* at Daly's. Won't that be a happy occasion? You can try to persuade me how silly I'm being in refusing to go to the fifth Court of the season at Buckingham Palace tomorrow. Only you won't. Not ever, not *ever!*"

Taken aback by this onslaught, Jennie managed to rally. "Let's sit down, Anna. We can't discuss it standing up, and, anyway, I'm tired."

"Anything else?"

"Yes. I need your Pretty House."

Anna burst out laughing, looked rather shamefaced. "Not much of a hostess, am I? Anyway, you've already proved my point. I'm not going to fit easily into some jelly mould they've marked out for me. I'll show you where the water closet is."

"Not at the end of the garden, then," Jennie joked. Anna had always been intrigued by their Pretty House, vastly preferring it to the stately apparatus installed in Applemere House. Jennie used to point out to her that royal posteriors used Applemere, which was surely preferable to an earth closet used by peasants such as herself. Anna would have none of it, although it was true that since they had grown up the charms of the Pretty House appealed less.

When she returned, Anna put her arms round her, something she rarely did. "I love seeing you, Jennie. But I can't go to the Court tomorrow."

"Why can't you?" Jennie asked. "You're attending all the balls like an obedient daughter, so why not Buckingham Palace too?"

"It's so final," Anna answered. "Once I've done that, it's as if I've announced to the world that the lamb is ready for the slaughter, or rather the cattle market. That's all it is. We twirl around in our pretty gowns, and put on our headdresses with the plumes like peacocks, only we're peahens. After we've all tottered past the King and Queen we're penned in the market till we see someone we like enough and who likes us enough to unlock that door and let us enter another pen."

"But everyone goes through this stage in some way. Even me," Jennie said. "Village dances serve just the same purpose. Boy meets girl, girl has to meet boy somehow or other. It's just that your meeting is — well — more formal."

"I agree with that," Anna said wryly. "What makes it worse is that my father is friendly with Queen Mary, so her eye will be well and truly on me. She's inclined to think Father married beneath him."

"So your father can't be taking your reluctance well either."

"No. Do you think he'll lock me up in a tower like Rapunzel?"

"Until a handsome prince comes along to release you," Jennie added thoughtlessly.

Anna glared at her again. "Don't you dare say how nice it would be if I married Viktor. No, I *won't* go tomorrow. The minute I'm passed as available for marriage by putting those stupid plumes on my head my fate is sealed. All the royalty of Europe will be eyeing me up and down like a heifer. If they force me to go. I'll throw myself under the King's horse at Ascot, just like that poor suffragette did at Epsom last Wednesday. Papa didn't like that one bit. Nor did Mama." Anna actually laughed, while Jennie stared at her, horrified.

She decided on another approach. "But that's nonsense, Anna, and you know it. It's no use just saying no to your parents. You'll have to have an alternative plan if you flout not only your parents but the King too. What would you do?"

"I don't know." Anna stared at her. "Perhaps I'll run away or be a suffragette or be like your Aunt Eileen. She managed to escape."

Jennie had to stamp firmly on this. "Aunt Eileen isn't the niece of the King of Montevanya. She's the mistress of the King's brother." Dad and Aunt Winifred still believed Eileen was merely a lady traveller who had accidentally become caught up in the Balkan War, which ended last month. Aunt Eileen informed them she was doing hospital work at Adrianople, which the Bulgarians and Serbs had captured from Turkey. Jennie suspected she was doing rather more than that, especially as she just "happened" to be in London when the treaty was signed at the end of May.

Aunt Eileen was accepted by most of the family as a good influence on Georgius at times, so she told Jennie, but highly disliked by others for encouraging him in his eccentricities. Georgius unfortunately already had a wife who had departed from him long ago, though in theory they still lived together. She had not withstood the pressure, so Aunt Eileen explained, of having to be sawn in half at soirees.

"Do you get sawn in half?" Jennie had immediately asked her.

"I draw the line at that, and at levitation. I have no objection to disappearing in a cupboard every so often. Or assisting in ghostly illusions. Does that answer your question?"

With Aunt Eileen's assured eye on her, it did.

*

From the moment they had walked into the white vestibule of the theatre, with its lovely statues of Cupid, and then seen from the privilege of their box the cosy red walls and seating of the auditorium, Jennie had known she was going to enjoy herself — even if it wasn't the opera or ballet she would have preferred. She'd never been to a ballet, and having read in the newspapers of the exotic Russian ballet coming to Drury Lane in June, she had hoped that Anna's choice would have fallen on that. Never mind, it was going to be *wonderful* here. She knew it, especially since she was clad in one of Anna's decolletee evening gowns. She felt she was "out" herself. Suppose life were like this all the time! She fanned herself and Anna laughed. Good, so she had relaxed at least.

"There's a language of fans, Jennie. The way you're waving

that you've probably told that young man in the box opposite that you're his for ever."

"Don't tell Jack," Jennie warned her solemnly. Yesterday she'd been lying in Glebe Meadow with Jack's arms warm around her in the summer air. It seemed a long way away now, and she wished he could be here too. Nevertheless she knew she was going to enjoy it.

She did. From the moment the drop curtain rose she was caught up in the story and spectacle of this musical comedy. It was *better* than pantomime, she decided, and if all English lords were like Lord Hurlingham in this play — charming, witty, and romantic — she couldn't see why Anna complained of dullness in the dances she had to attend.

"You like this, Jennie?" Lady Fokingham asked in the interval as champagne was brought to their box.

"Oh, yes. It's how I imagine Montevanya. All songs, music and happiness."

Lady Fokingham laughed, and even Sir Roger smiled. "A little, perhaps," Lady Fokingham said. "We have our national songs, and we dance and sing there, just as you once did in England before you grew too serious and respectable. In Montevanya we still feel freer."

"You had plenty of wars in Montevanya once," said Anna. Her manner with her mother was still very stiff, Jennie noticed — and no wonder, since the issue of whether she went to tomorrow's Court was still not settled.

"Wars can happen anywhere," Sir Roger remarked quietly. "So that makes dancing all the more important."

But dancing too could be dangerous, Jennie thought, her head slightly dizzy from the glass of champagne that Anna insisted she drank. There was Hans Andersen's story of the girl with the red shoes who danced and danced and could only lose the magic shoes from her feet by death. If everyone danced to their own tunes, what would happen?

"Would you go tomorrow if you were me?" Anna asked her abruptly when they were back at Fokingham House and alone. "I've been thinking over what you said about the need for a plan. Perhaps being presented won't be so final, after all. What do you think?"

Jennie knew she must choose her words carefully. "Being presented might seem a symbol of the future to you, but it isn't — unless you want it to be. It could be only an empty gesture to please your mother and not upset your father's position at Court."

Anna mulled this over. "Stay here until it's over, and I'll do it," she said at last. "If you're here to laugh it over with when I return home, it won't be so bad."

"I'll stay," Jennie said promptly. "Anyway, I'll want to hear all about it," she added truthfully.

Despite her decision, there was friction throughout the following day at Fokingham House, with Anna tearful and resentful. Even Jennie felt exhausted when at the last moment one of the ostrich feathers refused to keep its place and bent over sideways. It looked so funny that she began to laugh. In the end Anna's complaints stopped and they had left. Anna had looked almost swamped by the white satin dress and its white brocaded train. With her fair hair, white drained her of colour, but it was mandatory to wear it. The Fokinghams had left in plenty of time to reach the palace immediately the gates were open at eight thirty — in case, Jennie suspected, Anna changed her mind yet again.

Jennie had hoped to find a quiet corner to eat by herself, but to her dismay she was escorted to the dining room where she was solemnly placed at the middle of a vast table set for one — no, for two, she suddenly realized.

Then her worst fears came true. Michael arrived unexpectedly and looked as taken aback as she did when he walked in, but to do him justice he accorded her a bow before the lizard, as she still thought of him, slithered into a chair opposite her. He was twenty now and frightfully conscious of his superior status.

"Father told me you'd talked my baby sister into seeing sense," he said in a friendly enough fashion.

"I don't think anybody talks Anna into doing anything," Jennie said ruefully. "I'd hate to think I changed her mind for her. Think of the responsibility."

He glanced at her. "So you see yourself as a shoulder for her to weep on."

Jennie suddenly realized he was waiting for her to begin eating, and quickly tackled the sole fillets on her plate, noting to her pleasure that she went instantly to the fish knife. "No. I don't do that either."

"Then what does she see in you?" He sounded genuinely curious rather than merely rude so she gave some consideration to this.

"Normality? You live a life far removed from mine."

"To us our life is normal." He seemed quite pleased when she agreed with him.

"Very well, then. A friend, an escape."

"Do you like her?"

Jennie stared at him in bewilderment. "Of course I do. She's my friend." It sounded childish, but she could not think for a moment why he should ask such a question. Uneasily she realized that he might think she was simply using Anna's friendship for her own advantage.

When all he replied was a throwaway, "Be careful, Jennie," she was puzzled. Then she forgot about it as he asked, "And how's Freddie? I haven't seen him for some time. And Jack?"

Jennie told him, and then decided to get rid of the idea that she was deliberately cultivating Anna's friendship for her own ends. "Jack's a grade two signalman now; we're still sweethearts, we always will be."

Michael laughed bitterly. "A life of rural bliss. Oh, Jennie, how I envy you."

Jennie was impatient for Anna's return. Would she be tearful and resentful or won over by the sheer excitement of the court scene? She waited in the drawing room with Michael while he played endless recordings on his gramophone. He even put on some ragtime music, and whisked her round the room in jovial mood. It was a side of Michael she hadn't seen before, and a surprisingly enjoyable one.

At last the party returned, and Anna raced through to the drawing room, tearing off her headdress as she went. There were stars in her eyes, but not for the court presentation.

"Oh, Jennie, you'll never guess what happened. When we got to the palace, there was a group of suffragettes chained to the railings, and I recognized one of them! It was May Furnell, who was presented two years ago. I didn't know she was a suffragette. The police were there, trying to remove them, but we had to stop as we entered so that Papa could hand over the card to arrange for the car to be waiting for us afterwards, and I managed to shout out to May how splendid I thought she was. She waved at me, and I felt so *envious* of her, out there, *free*. But I knew you were right. Tonight was just a formality that could hurt nobody. If May can be independent after being presented, then so can I."

Behind Anna, with a face of terrified despair, stood Lady Fokingham, who was obviously imagining her daughter turning into a militant suffragist, setting fire to buildings, or even carrying out her threat to be another Emily Davison, whose funeral would shortly take place.

Jennie longed to be back home with Jack's arms around her. There was nothing she could do for Anna now.

*

"It was wonderful, Jack!"

Back in the peace of the summer fields, Jennie tried to recreate for Jack the excitement of her visit, but already it was slipping away.

"You won't be satisfied with my old piano after Daly's," he joked.

"Of course I will," she said stoutly. "My heart's here. You know that." She knew she meant it, even though a little voice inside reminded her that one day she was going to rule the world. So what, she thought. Being in Fairsted didn't prevent that. It helped make her worldly-wise. The problems of Fairsted were the same as those of the Balkan Wars in a way. The manor tenants wanted to have their own houses and be free of Mr Hargreaves' stingy ways, just as Bulgaria wanted to be free of Turkey, Hungary of Austria and Transylvania of Hungary.

His arms tightened around her. "What do you want most, Jennie? In the whole wide world."

"I want to be here. And to work on the railway."

"Anything else?"

How stupid of her. "You, Jack." Of course that was what she wanted. She knew it now, she'd always known it really.

The great truth that had been staring her in the face, beside which all the musical comedies in the world were nothing.

"Oh, Jenny." He was hugging her, and they were rolling over in the grass together, laughing. "That be for always, will it?"

"Always. And now your brothers are earning some money, you could even become an engine driver. We could move..." She broke off, alarmed at where her thoughts were taking her. She'd said she wanted to stay *here*.

Jack did not miss this, and he sat up. "Now you've seen the bright lights of London, my old signal lanterns won't never be enough for you."

"All I want is to be with you." She rolled over towards him, pulling him down to her. His lips were on hers, and Jennie could feel his breath hot on her face. She wanted to be closer, closer, and still closer as she felt his hands moving over her and under her skirt. This time, instead of pushing them away with a laugh, she let him continue, her body tingling in anticipation. This was it, this was the great moment that everyone waited for, giving oneself to someone for ever and ever. Aunt Winifred hadn't told her much about how babies were made, but she and Anna had worked it out between them after going down a few false avenues. But it was Jack who pulled away this time.

"No, Jennie. Not till we're wed."

She didn't know whether to be disappointed or relieved. "Not till we're wed" had a wonderful, comfortable sound to it. So her future was decided. It *would* happen and, oh, she was so happy. They'd have a cottage of their own — no more Aunt Winifred. Just Jack and her. And, some day, babies. What more could she want, she thought? Come on, life, I'm ready for you.

*

In early July Aunt Eileen arrived for a visit, clad in a light wool costume, as befitted a maiden lady of mature years. Because she looked so very different from the rare glimpse of Madame Szendescu that was afforded to the villagers through the windows of the Applemere motor car, no one ever made the connection. Jennie sometimes wondered what Dad and Aunt Winifred would make of Madame Szendescu's Arabian trousers or even a fashionable harem skirt.

"What do you talk to Aunt Winifred about?" Jennie asked her when they were alone in the small room in the dark, as Aunt Eileen was buttoning her decorous flannel nightgown.

"Winifred and I converse on the world, on the appalling actions of the suffragettes and anything else that the *Daily Mail* has presented her with that day. We also talk of the old days at home."

"Do you think the suffragettes are appalling?"

"No. There are always lone female wolves such as myself, but it's the majority of women who need help, the beaten, the meek, the submissive. The vote is the first step. Your aunt and I agree on that."

"Good. She doesn't like being disagreed with."

"Are you sure you know *what* Winifred likes?"

"She tells me often enough what she *doesn't*." Jennie felt abashed. She never had thought about what Aunt Winifred *did* like. She was just Aunt Winifred who had been Disappointed at Omdurman. Over the years Jennie had come to realize that there must have been a sweetheart involved there, but half of her preferred to cling to the childish fantasy, perhaps because she did not want to tread too closely into the domain of adulthood. Aunt Eileen was quite enough to cope with.

"Poor child," was Eileen's comment when Jennie had told her about Anna's starry eyes over the suffragettes. "Be careful with her, Jennie. She needs care, and her mother can't give it to her."

Yet another person telling her to be careful. "Why not?"

"Because she's too close. Once she felt like Anna, and somewhere deep inside she still does. But she knows the world; she loves Roger and accepts what that brings. Perhaps she feels Anna should do the same."

"Does she disapprove of you then?" Jennie held her breath, in case she had gone too far.

Eileen laughed. "A little. I'd like to help over Anna, but I'm leaving tomorrow. I'm meeting Georgius in Greece."

"Greece? Why?"

"Or was it Cannes?" her aunt joked. "I'm really not sure. Curiosity, my dearest Jennie, puts an end to the cat, notwithstanding its nine lives. Shall we blow out the candle?"

*

"I'm free!" Anna flung herself on the seat in the grotto as soon as they reached it. "The season is over at last. One is now permitted to pick up one's bucket and spade, don one's straw hat, and one may then paddle. Thank goodness for holidays."

"Are you going to Italy?" Jennie asked, heart in mouth lest Anna said yes. She would see nothing of her if she went away.

"No. I just want peace and quiet." Anna tore viciously at a piece of couch grass. "Gilly and I — and you — can have such a good time together."

Jennie was hurt at the hesitation. Valiantly she told herself that it was only natural that she should cease to be so close to Anna now that she'd spent her season in

London. All the same she was conscious of her disappointment that she obviously didn't count very much in Anna's plans. But she had Jack, Jennie told herself, whom she loved. She hugged her secret to herself, waiting for an opportunity to tell Anna that they would one day be married. Anyway, it wasn't the same with Gillyflower around. Miss Gilchrist was now a sort of secretary to Lady Fokingham, an arrangement that suited everyone well — especially Anna, since Gillyflower was her ally.

"We could take the train to the seaside perhaps," Anna said eagerly.

"I do have to work," Jennie said apologetically. "I'm lucky to have my job. It's usually only men who are allowed to be booking clerks."

"You don't work every day, Sundays for instance, and there are the evenings. You don't work then."

"Of course I do." Jennie was annoyed. "It's my duty."

The fatal word was out, and Anna just grinned. Jennie managed to laugh, and all was well between them again. "I have a day off every two weeks. Jack and I — "

"So you're still seeing him?"

"Of course I am." Jennie suddenly remembered Anna's liking for Jack and wondered why she was asking.

"What's Freddie doing now? I seem to have been away for ages," Anna said rather too quickly.

"Freddie is still set on driving engines," Jennie told her. "He works as a cleaner for the Company now. He takes the workman's train to Folkestone, then up to Ashford. He's a double homer."

"What's that?"

Jennie explained about his lodging in Ashford because of the irregular hours.

"I couldn't bear that," Anna declared. "I suppose I'm a double homer too, in a way, but my real home is Applemere."

"What if…" The words lingered on Jennie's lips but she didn't want to spoil Anna's homecoming by talk of marriage. Anna didn't even notice. "And Tom, what's he doing?"

"He's living in a cottage on the manor estate. It gives us more room and he gets it very cheaply because Mr Hargreaves likes having him under his thumb for work."

"I don't see Tom being under anybody's thumb."

"He's good at pretending."

"I don't see that either."

"You're not his sister."

Anna smiled. "I have a brother too. Do you still like yours?"

"Yes." Jennie decided not to add any buts. "Do you like yours?"

"Michael's not so bad as he sometimes appears. He's doing well in the Foreign Office."

"He was quite nice to me in London, but he didn't really approve of my being there."

"Women are still a lower species to him. It's not just you. Even princesses of the realm find it hard to win the great Michael's favour. Wait till he has to get married. Once I'm off their books, they'll turn on him, you'll see."

"Who is lined up for him?"

"There's no end of choice. Of course, King George's sons have first pick, but there's all the Tsar's daughters, Feodora of Saxe-Meiningen, Victoria Louise of Prussia, and plenty of others springing up. It's a rich field. I almost feel sorry for Michael."

*

Because of work, Jennie saw little of Anna during the summer, although she would sometimes come into the railway station, usually accompanied by Michael, who would wander off in Norfolk jacket and country sporting attire to his first love, the signal box. Their day at the seaside duly took place, though their party grew. Michael decided to come, and Anna suggested Jennie brought Jack too, if he could arrange his schedule. Then Tom joined the party, and finally Freddie. An odd mixture, but everything went without a hitch. Anna thoroughly enjoyed the train journey, bringing a picnic from Applemere for them to eat on the Broadstairs beach, and she and Michael were in a happy mood. They walked up to the odd house on the hill where Dickens was supposed to have set his *Bleak House*, watched the pierrot show on the sands and even went bathing from the bathing machines. And yet Jennie found it hard to relax. It was as if she were waiting for something that never happened.

"Why didn't I enjoy it, Jack?" she asked later.

"We don't mix, that's all."

She disagreed. The one element that had not been present that day was any sense of the social division between them. So what was bothering her?

After that, Christmas seemed to creep up with great suddenness. One moment they were dipping for apples at Halloween, the next dressing the church ready for Christmas. Tom was coming home for Christmas Day. Freddie too had managed to get the day free and was coming with his sweetheart, Alice Green from the mill.

The Fokingham family was at Applemere for the holiday, but there had been no suggestion that Jennie should join them. Anna had been dividing her time between London and Kent, but with no greater appearance of enjoyment than she had in the summer. At least she hadn't fulfilled her threat to run away to be a suffragette.

"Are you still not happy in London, Anna?" Jennie asked when Anna strolled into the station one day.

"No," Anna replied simply. "Unfortunately."

"Why unfortunately? I thought you didn't want to be pestered into meeting people and getting married."

"Not to someone I don't love." She hesitated. "Jennie, that's why I've come to see you."

Jennie's heart sank. "Someone they want you to marry?"

"It's under discussion." Anna dug her hands in her pocket and stared fiercely outside. "Let's go for a walk. I feel stifled."

"I can't," Jennie pointed out. "Anyway, it's foggy outside. You'd feel even more stifled out there. I can't even see the fogman's lantern and he's only standing at the signal post. How did you get here?"

"Dawkins brought me. It took ages. He's in the pub," Anna said dismissively. "Jennie, I want you to come to Montevanya with me."

Jennie thought she must have misheard. She stared at her, flabbergasted.

"It would be for at least six weeks," Anna continued anxiously.

"But I can't. I've a job." Oh, but if she could — what an opportunity! And she had been thinking Anna no longer wanted her as a friend.

"Ask your father. *I'll* ask your father. My father could make it all right with the railway company. If you'd be willing to come, that is. It's a lot to ask."

Willing? Of course she was. She could be another Aunt Eileen; she could see the world.

"It's quite safe now the wars in the Balkans really have ended," Anna said. "In any case, Montevanya isn't involved in the fighting; it's too far north. And we would go by the Orient Express, of course, which is even safer. It stops in Budapest and Belgrade, and then goes on to Dunosova. That's the capital of Montevanya. The Varcása, the castle, is on its outskirts."

The Orient Express? Staying in a castle? Jennie felt totally lost in a dream world. Then she came down to earth with a bump. "Anna, this may be a family visit, but it's a *royal* family. I don't know to behave in court circles. I don't have the clothes — or would I eat with the servants...?" She broke off as Anna laughed.

"We can take care of all that, if only you'll come. You must. And you won't eat in the kitchens, you'll be my parents' guest."

Even more curious.

"They want to me to marry Viktor, or perhaps Max, but I won't marry either of them."

"Then tell them. They can't force you."

"The King can. Or he could put so much pressure on my parents that I have to."

"You're British, not Montevanyan; King Stephen doesn't rule you."

"This visit is to persuade me to change my mind. I told you it would happen. Michael's doing his best to persuade me, and so's Father — talking about the politics of the world and how Austro-Hungary and Germany have to be appeased, and it wouldn't do to have Montevanya tied in with either of them, or with Russia. It has to remain neutral. My family forgets I'm a person. I'm just a chess piece on their international board."

"Which piece?" asked Jennie, playing for time and thinking furiously. "Queen?"

"King, or pawn. It comes to the same thing. Jennie, I'm checkmated. I need you there if I'm going to win, so please, please come. I swear if you don't I shall really run off to be a suffragette. There's a girl I know — "

"Stop, Anna." Jennie was terrified at this vehemence. "If I go, won't your parents resent my being there?"

"No, they think it's a wonderful idea. I've already told them. They think I'll be more placid and accept my fate if you come."

Jennie felt like a puppet dancing on strings, and battled with the morals of acceptance, knowing that whatever she did Anna would still refuse to marry one of the princes. Or perhaps in the end she would. Who could tell with Anna? Therefore, optimistically, Jennie decided to do what Anna wanted. To go, puppet or not. The trip would be in March and April the following year, 1914, Anna told her.

When Jennie broke the news to Dad and Aunt Winifred, however, they only reluctantly agreed.

"If the Company will allow it," Dad added warningly. The Company had more power over Dad than His Majesty's Government.

Telling Jack was even more difficult. Jennie saw him later the same evening. It wasn't the best time to choose but he was beaming and in a good mood, so she poured out her news. "It's only for six weeks, Jack. It will be wonderful."

"I'll miss you, Jennie. I've had some good news too. I'm a Grade one now."

"That's wonderful." And she meant it. It was highly unusual at Jack's age and meant he was able to be signalman at junctions and big important stations. "Will you stay here?"

"Depends if there's an appointment nearby."

Only later, when she went to bed, did she realize what he had really meant by telling her the news about his promotion. Being a Grade 1 signalman also meant more money — they could afford to marry, when a suitable job turned up. Ashford perhaps, or Canterbury.

Which excitement should she think of first? The visit to Montevanya would be in March. Plenty of time to talk of marriage afterwards, when Jack had a suitable job.

CHAPTER IV

March 1914

Why has she never thought that travelling on a train could not be as exciting as watching it steam away into an unknown land? Jennie had been living in a dream herself ever since they had boarded the Folkestone ferry for Calais, and then in the early evening climbed aboard the Orient Express. Then her excitement had doubled, if that was possible. This was the great train that joined east and west Europe. If she travelled all the way to Constantinople in Turkey she would be staring at the mystic East itself. She felt as cosseted in the train as she had when she nearly died of scarlet fever at six years old. There were so many people just to look after her — and the Fokinghams, of course — from the imposing *chef de brigade* who was responsible for the whole organization of the train and only spoke to *very* important passengers, to the blue-coated waiters and the *conducteur* of their carriage. There was even an awe-inspiring man who stood by the *cabinet de toilette* (already she was picking up these unusual words!) to clean it after you'd left. She tried to imagine him standing outside the Pretty House when Aunt Winifred came down the path.

Jennie had clutched her new passport in Calais, and at the German border, but it seemed that the Orient Express was too grand for anyone to question their right to be aboard, for no one looked at it. The further they travelled from France the more exotic their travelling companions became, both in dress and speech, not to mention some unusual odours, some good, some very bad. They filled the corridors, dining cars, the ladies' salon and, from what she could glimpse, the gentlemen's smoking room. It was even rumoured, so Anna hissed to her, that the Turkish noblemen had their harems with them, in locked compartments in case they tried to escape. The whole world seemed aboard this train as it rushed onwards to the end of its line — but what a rush!

"This," Jennie had announced at dinner on the first night of the journey, "is the most glorious train I can imagine. Do you think I could get a job selling tickets for it in Paris?"

"Perhaps one day aeroplanes will be even more glorious," Sir Roger pointed out gravely. "You might consider selling tickets for those."

Jennie thought this over. "No. It wouldn't be the same. In a train you're part of the world outside, but up there in the sky one must be…well, like God, looking down, and not part of it. Trains for me, always."

Trains puffed, steamed and hissed their way from country to country, uniting them. "Here we come!" says the express train. "All I need from you is water," (and the fare, she mentally added practically), "and perhaps a load or two of coal, and look what I bring you: the world." Jennie had become aware that the wine she had cautiously tasted was perhaps affecting her romantic outlook just a little, but did that matter? Not a bit.

It was strange as well as exciting to be sleeping on the train, not knowing the place where she was going. Oh, how sorry she felt for Anna, who was speeding towards a fate she dreaded.

To be fair, Anna didn't look unhappy; indeed she looked rather excited. Lady Fokingham kindly said this was because Jennie was with her.

"Tell me," Lady Fokingham added anxiously, when Anna left them to visit the *cabinet de toilette*, "how do you find Anna?"

Jennie felt awkward, even though there was nothing to hide. She could only tell the truth. "She seems almost happy to be here now."

"Yes." Lady Fokingham's face clouded. "Is that not strange? Or do you think she is becoming reconciled to the idea of marrying Viktor?"

"I don't know," Jennie answered. "I wait for her to talk about it, but she says nothing."

Lady Fokingham sighed. "Perhaps it will all work out for the best. You are lucky not to have these problems, Jennie. You and Jack have a clear path ahead."

"No path is ever clear," Jennie answered at once. Once this visit was over and she was home, it would become a mere memory and would gradually seep away. She'd tell her grandchildren: "Once I met a prince." And they'd ask: "Did he fall in love with you and want to marry you?" And she would answer: "No, but I married a prince, anyway, and his name is Jack."

She decided to think about all this later. First she would enjoy the dream, then choose whether to dispel it. Reaching Vienna was the gateway to the east of Europe and the Balkans. True, Montevanya was only on the edge of the Balkans, between them and the Transylvanian Alps, but to her all seemed Ruritania. At the railway stations the country people would fill the platforms, jostling each other to reach the windows of the train to sell fresh fruit and fascinating-looking skewers of meat to the passengers. The Fokinghams would not let her buy any, however.

"They'll upset your stomach," Anna explained.

"You sound like Aunt Winifred," Jennie complained, sinking back on the cushions after Anna had dragged her away yet again from the enticing display at the windows, and, unusually, they were alone.

"I am Aunt Winifred. I'm in disguise. Like her, I have decided not to marry."

"How do you know she decided that?"

"She must have. She hasn't married. And — " Anna caught Jennie's eye — "don't tell me it was because she was disappointed."

"How do we know she hasn't turned down eighteen offers of marriage, all because she found no one to match up to her first love?"

Anna did not reply, to Jennie's surprise. Usually this kind of discussion between them would go on for ages. Anna had that look on again, Jennie saw, the one she had worn quite often recently. Content? Not quite. Happiness? No. Resignation? She thought not. It was, she decided, a kind of assurance. Anna's tenseness had left her. Like a lamb going to the slaughter?

She must have spoken out loud by mistake, because Anna looked up crossly. "No slaughter, no lamb."

"And no..." Jennie sought for the right word.

"Tantrums?" Anna enquired mildly. "No, darling Jennie, I shall don my mental white ostrich feathers, curtsey to Uncle Stephen, curtsey to Aunt Zita, curtsey to everyone — even Viktor, so he will see what a wonderful wife I would have made."

"*Would have* made?" Jennie's heart sank. There was mischief on the way.

"You don't think I'll marry him, do you?"

"I can't even guess what you'll do, Anna." She suspected Anna was kicking against the traces, just as Aunt Eileen had said Lady Fokingham had wanted to do. In the end, however, she would marry Viktor or Max and everything would settle down. Though was that right? Jennie wondered. If Anna really didn't like Viktor or Max then surely Jennie as her friend should be helping her find a way out. Impulsively she took Anna's hand. "You know I'll help, whatever you decide."

For a moment there was no response. Anna just stared at her. Then, suddenly, she threw her arms round her and hugged tight. "Stay with me, Jennie," she pleaded. "Please. Whatever happens, there's only you to understand. I won't marry Viktor. I *can't.*"

*

There weren't many motor cars in Montevanya. Too many hills, Anna explained, as calm as if her outburst yesterday had never happened. The Varcása did possess three, however: a stately Daimler landaulette, and two tourers: one Viktor's Daimler and the other Max's Rolls-Royce.

"Typical," Anna added. "One German, the other not."

Typical of what? Jennie was going to ask, but by then the Orient Express had begun to slow down for Dunosova, and she immediately forgot motor cars in the excitement of arrival. By now she was getting used to a landscape of seemingly limitless huge forests and meadows, fields with oxen-drawn wagons, and no machinery, rather as England must have looked years ago. When the Orient Express stopped for water, it gave the impression of doing so as briefly as possible, as if indignant that with all its grandeur it should have to stop in the middle of nowhere.

It had taken two days to arrive at Dunosova, and this morning the guard had awoken them in the middle of the night, or so it seemed to Jennie. By this time she had got over the embarrassment of living so closely with the august Fokinghams and her enthusiasm often seemed to make them smile.

Dunosova railway station wasn't a great deal larger than Fairsted, but very different. No clapboards, tiles and painted iron pillars here, but turrets and a small balcony, and exotic flowers growing around it, although it was only March. The carpet laid out for them, or rather for their Princess Marie, was not a plain red one like the one Dad unrolled so carefully at Applemere when the King visited. This was a patterned carpet of deep blue and red — far more romantic.

"What do I do?"

"Walk on it or at the side?" Jennie hissed to Anna.

"On it, behind me," Anna ordered.

Jennie took a deep breath. Even if she didn't know what would be expected of her, she could at least smile. So she smiled to one and all, which seemed to go down well, although the uniformed gentleman giving the formal welcome to Princess Marie looked rather surprised.

"There's the Varcása." Anna pointed.

Jennie gasped in pleasure. Now that really was straight out of *The Prisoner of Zenda*. In the distance she could just make out a white castle shimmering, it seemed, in mid-air, clinging to the side of a hill. Below it were the red roofs of the town.

"There are two ways up," Anna explained. "The track on the south side is for walking only. It used to be the custom that the royal family would always walk up to the castle after church on religious holidays while their subjects lined the path throwing flowers."

"What happened to stop it?"

"One of the peasants brought a gun, and my grandfather only escaped because the peasant was such a bad shot. The bullet killed a pigeon instead." Anna grinned. "Grandfather used to say it was his passport into the inner circle of European royalty. So many have been shot at, and some assassinated, that it's become quite a mark of distinction. Queen Victoria, Edward VII, Elizabeth of Austria, the King of Portugal…"

"What nonsense are you telling poor Jennie?" Lady Fokingham laughed. "Don't believe her, Jennie, or at least don't take it seriously. We are a happy country here in Montevanya. The man who tried to shoot my father was crazed. A Wallach. Poor fellow, he tried to shoot himself afterwards, but our doctors repaired him as good as new. We have very good doctors in Montevanya."

"What are Wallachs?" Jennie whispered, as the carriage began its bumpy journey through cobbled streets.

"Nomads from Roumania. There are a lot of native Roumanians here, just as there are Magyars and Serbs." Jennie had a closer view of the Varcása now. From this angle at the foot of the hill it still seemed half suspended in the air. White turrets soared proudly upwards and its white stone glistened. How was Jennie Trent going to live up to life in the Varcása? For a start, she must be known as Imogen. Jennie was not nearly dignified enough.

*

She'd managed it. Somehow, despite having only what seemed a few hours' sleep since she left Fairsted, Jennie had survived the curtsey to King Stephen, who was a serious version of his brother Georgius. She had even survived the curtsey to Queen Zita, despite the dragon's breath of disapproval that shot out at having to greet a commoner (very grand, was Queen Zita). Prince Viktor and Prince Max had even kissed her on the cheek — fortunately this time they waited until she had risen from her curtsey (with only a slight hitch as she trod on her train both times). She had also sat through a formal welcoming dinner, where the food was not quite so bad as Anna claimed, despite the unknown enormous fish that stared at her, glassy eyed, from her plate for daring to raise fish knife and fork to it.

The bedchamber was enormous, with rugs on the stone floor, although the heating made this surprisingly warm. She found a chamber pot under the bed (no picture of the Kaiser, she noted, which was hardly surprising) and a separate bathroom with a bath standing in the middle of the floor with large roses painted over it in blue. How strange to see roses — surely they were an English flower? Two grand water closets were nearby in the corridor, and she had a large four-poster bed all to herself, for Anna was two bedrooms away, with Gillyflower in the small room between them.

Jennie yawned, wondering what would happen if she tugged the large red-tassled bellrope to summon servants. Tomorrow, perhaps. Tired though she was, she went to the window and looked out at the moon, just as she did at Fairsted every night. Jack was out there somewhere, far away — so very, very far away. And she, a stationmaster's daughter, was standing in a Montevanyan castle, unexpectedly longing for him.

*

"So we take you to the fair, yes," Prince Viktor demanded at the informal breakfast next morning. It didn't sound like a question, and Jennie left Anna to deal with it while she tackled her *poparu* and jam. The *poparu* was a kind of porridge made with soggy bread, and the jam was a pleasant addition.

It was a holiday in Montevanya, so Viktor informed them, the feast of St Ilyia, its patron saint, who, he told them with some amusement, did his best to tight off the devils who caused wars. "Just like darling Papa," he said. This was in atonement for Ilyia having killed his parents by mistake. His other punishment was to ferry people across the River Danube and give them each a melon seed. Jennie longed to ask why.

but decided silence served her best. St Ilyia seemed a long way from Fairsted's sedate St Mary's.

"What about the Moslems?" she asked, since Anna had told her that the country was half Christian, half Moslem. "Do they celebrate the holiday too?"

"We have Moslem holidays and Christian holidays and everyone enjoys both, although only attending their own church. That way there are more holidays. It is expensive, because no work is done then, but it is a way of keeping everyone happy," Max explained.

"Otherwise," Viktor cynically pointed out, "we might have to have a real parliament."

"*We* have one," Jennie said, firing up immediately in defence of her country. "And a king. They work together."

Viktor stared at her. "Cousin George V has no power. And that is what kingship is all about."

Jennie was about to retort, but Anna kicked her under the table so she subsided.

"Today Aunt Marie commands we show you how Montevanya plays," Viktor continued. He seemed almost amused, as if he knew Anna didn't want to come. Anna found fairs daunting; she had not been brought up with the excitement and bustle of crowds.

"Is Gilly coming?" Jennie asked her when they returned to their rooms after breakfast.

"I doubt it. Mama wants you to be my chaperone, my poor Jennie. She is determined I shall get to like Viktor. I shall not, of course, and nor does he like me."

"Then he won't want to marry you."

"He will, if so commanded by the King. My uncle is not in good health and wants to see an heir for Viktor before he dies. Viktor would marry me to provide a baby calf for him, perhaps two, and then take his pleasure where he likes. My pleasure would be of no interest to him." Jennie must have looked so aghast that Anna laughed. "Don't worry," she continued, "I have a plan." She quickly changed the subject. "It would be courteous to the townsfolk if you wore national dress."

"What is English national dress?" Jennie asked, although she was wondering in alarm what this plan might be. And, it occurred to her, would she play some part in it? For the first time, she began to wonder why Anna had really invited her here. Companionship? Support? Or something else?

"Theirs, silly. Wear your dark-blue skirt and I'll find you a red Montevanyan jacket. That will do. The true female national dress involves being bundled up like a parcel of walking laundry."

Jennie enjoyed walking down the grand staircase in state, especially in the ornate embroidered red jacket and widesleeved white blouse that Anna had found for her. It gave her the regal touch, she felt, even though it was intended to be peasant wear. She rather liked this word "peasant", which seemed, from what she had heard, to be used frequently in Montevanya.

Max and Viktor were waiting for them in the entrance hall, and they too wore the ornate bright jackets of their national dress, as they had the first time Jennie had met them. This time they walked down the steep track to the foot of the Varcása hill, where the market and fair were being held, just as if they were ordinary citizens. Jennie couldn't see King George V and the stately Queen Mary mingling with these crowds. Viktor was walking ahead with Anna, and Jennie's heart went out to her. Jennie much preferred Max. With his quick eye and curly dark hair he could almost have been the daredevil Rupert of Hentzau, even though he was the quieter of the two.

"You make a beautiful peasant, Jennie," he observed.

That word again. "I am a peasant," she replied blithely, "compared with Anna and yourself."

"And you have grown into a beautiful woman, too." He ignored her comment, seemingly engaged in close study of her figure from top to foot. She didn't know whether to be amused, flattered or annoyed.

"A woman needs warmth for true beauty," he continued. "*Frumszep*, we call it. My cousin has no warmth. *Dobru*, Jennie, *netnu* Anna."

She knew what those words were. Anna had explained that the Montevanyan language was similar to that of its neighbours Serbia and Roumania, with a little Hungarian thrown in for good measure. *Dobru* meant good, approval, *nemu* meant not at all good, and extremely rudely, too. She was about to retort that he too was *nemu* — particularly in his manners, since Anna was not only his cousin but a guest in his house — but she restrained herself. They might still have laws about chopping off heads here for those who were rude to the King's son. Instead she asked, "Are you still in the army, Your Highness?"

"I am. War is never far from us."

"But Montevanya is neutral."

"We must be able to fight in order to remain so. That is how we stayed out of the Bulgarian wars — the Balkans wars, as you call them. We want nothing to do with Turkey, Austria, Serbia, Bulgaria or Roumania — we are Montevanya, and shall remain so."

Viktor must have overheard this because he turned back. "You talk foolishly, Max. You do not see the truth. Germany is the future."

Max replied sharply. "Our best interests, Viktor, lie in *not* being swallowed up into the gulping jaws of Kaiser Wilhelm, or of Emperor Franz-Josef, or of the Ottoman Sultan."

Viktor merely laughed, and Max turned to Jennie to apologize. "He often talks that way. Take no notice, Miss Jennie. Our mother is German, and Viktor fell in love with her cousin, the Kaiser, at an early age. He is his hero."

Jennie did take notice, however. The clash was a sign that all was not well in this paradise. She watched Viktor offer his arm to Anna. It looked like a snake wriggling out. "Where," she asked Max, "do you think Montevanya's best interests do lie if it needs allies?"

"You ask me?" Max laughed. "I am a younger son. I can be like Uncle Georgius, avoiding politics and amusing myself with conjuring tricks."

She was being fobbed off, and didn't mind at all. If this fair were typical of life in Montevanya, Jennie couldn't blame him for avoiding politics. It was colourful, noisy and happy, with costumes all colours of the rainbow, music from violins and lutes — no, balalaikas, she remembered — chickens, livestock, exotic jams and vegetables, conjurors, tumblers and dancers.

One particular dance with kerchiefs fascinated her in its intricacy, grace and exuberance. Max was obviously watching her closely. "You like that dance? I will ask for it at the ball tonight."

"For me?" Jennie asked with pleasure, then realized he must be joking.

Nevertheless he replied: Why not? It is a patriotic thing to do on St Ilyia's Day. Besides, Uncle Georgius would approve. He is very good at such dances. He has a good yowl."

"Like a cat?"

"Here in Montevanya cats are highly regarded. There is a Moslem legend that a cat saved Mohammed from a snake bite and is therefore blessed. We Christians have our version of the legend, too. We say that Jesus Christ created the cat to deal with the mice that overran a house where he was dining."

"I don't think our rector at Fairsted would approve of that."

"It is no more fanciful than turning water into wine at a wedding feast, and that is one of the Christian Bible's miracles."

Jennie began to look forward to the ball. Max would hardly dance with her, but she might find another partner for the country dance. "Will Madame Szendescu be there?" she asked, seizing the opportunity to solve the puzzle of Aunt Eileen's non-appearance so far.

"It depends whether my aunt or my mother wins. My mother does not approve of Madame Szendescu. My Aunt Marie does approve, as does my Uncle Georgius, although not for the same reasons."

"And your father?"

"My father approves of what my mother does. You like Madame Szendescu?"

"Yes I do. She is my aunt."

"So I have been told." Max looked as if something amused him, probably her. "We like English women in Montevanya."

"Doesn't Prince Viktor prefer German?"

He looked at her sharply though her question had been quite innocent. For a moment she had forgotten Anna. "That I do not know. For us marriage and love have to be separate."

"I'm sorry for you," she declared, looking at the dancing bear being led on a rope upright on two legs. "That bear's like Anna," she continued recklessly. "She's also being led round and forced to marry — "

"You think that?" He looked at her curiously. "For Viktor and me this is normal. You remember the song I sang to you long ago at Applemere? We can love whom we choose, but we marry whom we have to or pay the cost. I can kiss you, but I cannot marry you."

"Nobody asked you to, Your Highness," she replied crossly. "I'm going to be married to someone else soon. Someone with good manners."

"He is a lucky man, Jennie."

*

"I'm sorry we were separated," Jennie said to Anna ruefully. At the fair she had lost sight of Viktor and Anna altogether, and she and Max had walked back up to the castle (braving guns. Max teased her) alone. "I'm not much use as a chaperone."

Anna looked amused. "I don't need one. Anyway, Max left us alone on purpose. Orders from the King."

Jennie laughed at herself. And she had almost believed Prince Max had done it to be with her. She should have known better.

"Viktor doesn't want to marry me any more than I him," Anna continued. "He wants to marry a German princess, Eva of Breslau."

"Does his father know that?" Jennie asked curiously.

"No. Aunt Zita might be German, but Uncle Stephen is very anxious that neither of his sons marries a German wife, otherwise we become too closely tied with one country. Poor Viktor, I'd feel sorry for him if I didn't loathe his arrogance so much."

"But he'll he marry you if he has to?" The more Jennie thought about it, the more appalled she was.

Anna gave her secretive smile again. "Oh yes, but I doubt if it will happen."

It was almost as if Anna didn't care what happened any more. What was this plan of hers? Anna and Viktor were no match for each other, she so reserved and refined, and Viktor so military and rude. Life for royalty, Jennie decided, was extremely harsh.

*

The ball that evening sparkled and shone with colour and jewels. Flowers filled the air with their perfume and the music from the orchestra and whirling gowns of the ladies made Jennie feel drunk with the wonder of it all.

If I'm going to rule the world, she thought, looking round eagerly from where she sat with Gillyflower, I could well begin here. All of it must be gathered here. Anna, in a green charmeuse gown, was dancing with Viktor, Princess Marie was with a stately gentleman she didn't recognize, and Sir Roger with Queen Zita. At last she saw Prince Georgius, bounding down the steps like an excited puppy, and then, separately, Aunt Eileen making her graceful descent. Jennie hardly recognized her, she looked so formal. She even wore a small tiara, set off by the very low-necked blue satin gown, its slender skirt a miracle of draped and swathed colour clinging to her figure.

This, Jennie decided, was definitely an Imogen evening. She studied the dances listed on her so-far empty programme, which was written in Montevanyan, so not much help. It was very difficult to handle a fan, the programme, the train of her dress and a glass of champagne all at the same time, so she decided to jettison the programme. No one was coming to dance with her anyway. At least her insignificance meant she could just enjoy the spectacle. They were like grasshoppers whirling away, she thought. Much as she loved Anna, Princess Marie and all these wonderful people here, they were fiddling away their summer, regardless of winter, just as in the Aesop fable Aunt Winifred used to read aloud to them as an Awful Warning To Those Who Frittered Time Away.

"Is it full?" a voice asked, making her jump, and belatedly Jennie realized that Prince Max was standing there holding her discarded programme in his hand.

"It's empty," she stuttered.

He laughed. "I shall write my name for three dances. One of them the country dance. We shall make a fine show with our kerchiefs, Miss Jennie."

"I'm Imogen tonight," was all she could stupidly reply as, belatedly, she wondered if she should curtsey.

"Then I will dance two with Imogen, and the country dance with Jennie, and we shall begin now, I think. What," he asked as he led her to the floor, "have you said to Anna to make her dance so amicably with Viktor?"

"Nothing," she answered truthfully.

"Then that is strange. Aunt Marie says my cousin once threatened to become a suffragette. Viktor will not like that. Not here in Montevanya."

"Her wild days," Jennie said diplomatically. "They've passed, as you can see."

"And you, Miss Imogen, are your wild days over?"

"I don't have any," she answered as they began to dance. It was difficult to think clearly.

"Then we must give you some here."

After that, the evening became a whirl: first a dance with Prince Max, then — she thought — more champagne, and then the country dance, followed by a slower one.

It was strange being in his arms — not like being with Jack: this was far more personal. He held her closely, and though she was an adequate dancer he was better, and she felt relaxed with him. Or was that the champagne? Dancing, she hazily remembered, could be dangerous, and she was growing dizzy.

"Come outside, Miss Imogen. The air on the balcony will do you good."

That seemed a good idea, and she was led down to one end of a broad balcony overlooking the gardens where they would be unobserved from the ballroom, to give her time to recover. She was grateful for this, especially as there was a door leading back into the palace, in case she felt even worse. She looked up to thank him, and just then he came closer to her face. She felt his lips on hers, then nothing more except the darkness swallowing her up.

*

"Jennie, wake up!"

She opened her eyes painfully to find Aunt Eileen bending over her, looking crosser than Aunt Winifred. For a moment Jennie didn't remember where she was. And then it came back to her. But this was her bedroom, and it was morning. What happened to the ballroom? Her head ached slightly, and she seemed to be wearing a nightgown without having any recollection of undressing for bed.

Aunt Eileen was shaking her, and far from gently. Jennie struggled to sit up in bed to drink the coffee that her aunt was intent on forcing down her throat, "I need to talk to you. Urgently."

"What about?" Jennie asked warily.

"Last night. What did Max do to you?"

This didn't make sense. Jennie tried to remember. "I think we had supper, and danced..." She broke off for her memory went blank.

"My dear girl, can you really not remember?"

Jennie had never seen Aunt Eileen look so furious. In a trice she was fully awake. "No, but — "

"Then let me tell you part of what you've forgotten. *If* you have. I looked round for you at the ball, but you'd disappeared. The last time I'd seen you you were with Max. Trouble, Jennie, trouble. I had a word with old Kazinsku, the chief steward, and, poker-faced, he told me he'd seen Max carrying you upstairs towards your bedroom. My dear girl, have you any idea what that means? If it had been any other servant than Kazinsku, everyone in the palace would know by now. You would be out on your ear — and so, incidentally, would I. I came rushing up here to find Max calmly putting you into bed, half naked, with your gown and chemise flung on a chair. He seemed somewhat disconcerted when I found him, as well he might, especially when I told him what I thought of him. Jennie, what happened? How long were you alone with him in here? Did he molest you, did he hurt you, had you fainted?" Jennie went white at this torrent of words.

"I can't remember anything," she whispered, "I really can't. I remember having champagne, then being on the balcony with Prince Max and that was all."

Eileen looked slightly mollified. "That at least fits with what he tells me — that you fainted and he carried you up to bed simply to avoid drawing attention to you. But that, knowing Max, seemed highly unlikely to me, especially since he seemed to think part of his duty to you was to remove at least some of your clothes. However, it fits with your story."

"What did you think might have happened?" Jennie tried to sound indignant but it came out as a frightened squawk.

"That thanks to the champagne you were allowing him to have his wicked way." At least a glimpse of humour. "Did he?" Eileen added sharply.

"I don't know," Jennie wailed. "I don't remember."

"My dear child, believe me, you *would* know, one way or another. There would be blood and you'd feel sore — or have you been having fun with Jack, too?"

"Aunt Eileen!" Aghast, Jennie suddenly realized what she meant. "No. We're waiting till we're married."

Aunt Eileen relented slightly, though she still looked suspicious. "I'm sorry, Jennie. I forget what an innocent you are. It seems I might have got here in the nick of time, thank heavens."

"I suppose Max thought he was helping," Jennie said in weak defence.

"He's helped a good many other lassies in the same way, Jennie. Not so many as Viktor perhaps — "

"But Max wouldn't do that to me."

"He's a prince," Eileen retorted, "used to doing what he damned well likes, and don't forget it, Jennie. Nevertheless, you're only eighteen and whether he likes it or not you're a guest in his home. In Montevanya and many other Balkan countries that lays a few obligations on the host, which he appears to have forgotten. This is not Turkey, and neither Max nor Viktor is entitled to a harem — particularly not with my niece. I'll have a few choice words with him this morning."

Jennie struggled to gain control. "I will. It's my job not yours."

Aunt Eileen began to smile. "A chip off the block at last. Welcome to the world, my love — but don't devour it all at once."

*

Jennie knocked cautiously at Anna's door. "Are you coming down for breakfast?" she called. Please say yes, she silently begged.

"No," came a weak voice from within. "I'm not feeling well."

Too much champagne, thought Jennie crossly, though she was glad it happened to other people too. She summoned all her strength to go down to the breakfast room alone. Suppose Max were there? But to her relief, he wasn't. King Stephen was, however, and made formal enquiries as to whether she enjoyed the dance. She assured him she did, praying she could bolt her breakfast and get out of here. God failed her, for soon Max strode in as bright-eyed as when she'd last seen him.

"*Dobru napotata*, Miss Trent," he greeted her formally.

"*Dobru napotata*, Your Highness." She sounded much calmer than she felt, but her stomach was still jumping up and down despite the porridge.

"I hear Cousin Anna is not well. You must permit me to escort you round our castle gardens. There are fine displays of spring blossom."

It was a command, not a suggestion. There was nothing she could do except agree, with the benign gaze of His Majesty upon them.

"There are," Max told her when they left the castle half an hour later, "excellent follies and refuges for shelter should the sun or rain become too extreme." A pause. "Each is provided with the means of summoning instant attention from the castle."

He kept a straight face and she had to remind herself that she was here to give him a dressing down, not laugh. She had promised Aunt Eileen to put him in his place, which was going to be more difficult than she had imagined.

"We were," he continued earnestly, "caught in somewhat compromising circumstances by your aunt last evening."

"So she tells me. I must have fainted," she replied tartly.

"I imagine you might wish to thank me."

Half-naked. Aunt Eileen had said. How *dare* he mock her! "Aunt Eileen tells me I have little reason to do so."

"Madame Szendescu has a vivid imagination. She seems to have believed I was about to seduce you — or worse, that I already had."

Jennie decided to stop this in its tracks. "*Worse*? Your Highness, it's unlike you to be so modest. I imagine you would consider that to be a privilege. Furthermore, in English the word seduce implies I should at least be awake at the time."

"And weren't you?"

"You know I wasn't." Her patience snapped.

"I could have sworn you spoke of undying love for me, and how you admired my dark eyes and manly figure."

"I did not," she said steadily. "I do not like brown eyes, as it happens. Jack, to whom I'm engaged to be married, has grey eyes."

"A change is always pleasant." He caught her arm as she involuntarily drew back. Perhaps he thought she was going to hit him. "Jennie, you see this bower?" Taken off guard by his change of tone, she let him continue. "It was built two hundred years ago by one of my ancestors in honour of his love, Ingrid. She was beloved by all the people of Montevanya and she died young."

Jennie saw her opportunity. "Don't tell me. He couldn't marry her because she was a peasant."

"He did marry her, and she was the daughter of a king. They were very, very happy, so tradition says, almost the only happy marriage in my family. Most arranged marriages jog along, but they are not happy."

"I am sorry for you."

"Jennie, I give you my apologies for last night." She stepped back as he came closer, but he took hold of her and pulled her into his arms, albeit gently. "Jennie, don't struggle. You are so lovely, and I like you. I like your faithfulness to your Jack. I like your face and the way you hold yourself. Like a queen — "

"Of the railway," Jennie interrupted, to puncture this rhapsody.

"Your eyes are like the lanterns of the trains on that railway which you love so much." He drew her closer and because he seemed so sincere she did not struggle. "Your lips are as soft as the rose petals in your Kentish gardens, your breasts — "

This time she did draw back, suddenly remembering what Aunt Eileen had said. "You saw me, you undressed me. How could you?" she choked.

"Easily," he murmured. "With someone as lovely as you, with those lovely breasts like the low, soft hills of Montevanya." His hand moved over her dress to her breast, but she tore herself away.

"No!" She meant it, but he pulled her to him again.

"One kiss, Imogen, and then I will let you go. I promise. Ah, how can you blame me? You come here like the kiss of the sun after rain."

She didn't seem to have a voice now, instead there were only his lips on hers, gently soothing, exploring. She forgot where his hands were, feeling only his lips and his body against her. Then, suddenly conscious when his hands went too far, she pulled away again.

"I told Aunt Eileen I would speak to you firmly," she managed to say.

He laughed. "Then speak, Jennie."

"You behaved badly to me last night," she began.

"And would again, had I the chance."

"You won't." How could he have the cheek to do it to her again, seducing her with words this time? She had no difficulty in making her reply curt, and stalked off with as much dignity as she could muster considering the sound of his laughter followed her all the way back to the castle.

CHAPTER V

As the weeks passed, life in Várcasa seemed to pass alarmingly normal to Jennie. No longer did she half expect to be given a broom by one of the stately footmen or the silk-clad housekeeper and told to perform her "duty". Once she had overcome her awe of having people to do her bidding, it was fun, though she had a mental pact with faraway Aunt Winifred that she'd play her part in the housework without a murmur when she returned.

Prince Viktor had been reasonably polite to her, and, more importantly, so had Prince Max. He had never again referred to the evening of the ball, and when they were together remained formally friendly. Sometimes she felt his eyes on her, but she took no notice. Even on a hunting expedition to a mountain lodge, made at his suggestion, he had conducted himself impeccably, and she had enjoyed it. Perhaps this was also due to the scene being so much like her favourite book that she half expected Rupert of Hentzau to come sweeping through the trees. She'd write her own novel when she returned home, she decided.

A small cloud kept puffing across her blue skies, however, and its cause was Anna. She wasn't herself, that was clear, and Jennie had assumed that the constant company of Viktor must be the reason. Anna tended to avoid meal times and any walks or rides where they might be thrown together, though in company she seemed on perfectly good terms with him. Try as she might, Jennie was rarely alone with her either, and although she told herself that this was natural since Anna was with her family, a slight doubt remained.

Sir Roger had been called back to London. Anna told her the Home Rule Bill for Ireland had been arousing deep opposition in the country, not just from Sir Edward Carson's Unionists, but from the general public, who were deeply uneasy about Home Rule being forced on Ireland by military strength. Sir Roger himself had explained to Jennie about the divisions between the largely Protestant north of Ireland and the largely Catholic south, but to her in Montevanya it seemed a faraway issue. After all, she had asked, why didn't Ireland adopt Montevanya's solution, where the two religions lived contentedly side by side? Sir Roger said something about politics not being as easy as that, so Jennie didn't pursue it. So far as she was concerned, Montevanya had the right answer to *everything*. The episode with Max had been put into context when she remembered Dad's usual gloomy comment that there's no such thing as a perfect summer's day, except in memory. Even Montevanya could not be a paradise all the time.

Her only regret, apart from Anna's withdrawal, was that she hadn't seen Aunt Eileen again. She wanted to make things right between them, but Aunt Eileen lived with Uncle Georgius discreetly in the country, and only visited Dunosova on state occasions, such as the ball. When Max suggested he took her there for the day in his motor car, Jennie was overjoyed.

"Miss Gilchrist may accompany you for safety, if you wish," he told her gravely.

Jennie glared at him. "Thank you, but it is as *you* wish, Your Highness." Let him cope with that. No more had been said about Gillyflower coming with them, but Max told her Anna wasn't coming, since officially the Varcása did not know that the Palace Primaveru — or the Tellestin House, as he said it was popularly called — existed. Still with a straight face, he explained that the Tellestin House meant it was haunted by a jumping spirit who disordered the life within it.

"Sometimes, though," he added, "the Tellestin spirit goes hand in hand with the Vilia, who comes from outside — thought in this case to be Madame Szendescu. Sometimes the Vilias are good: sometimes their heads are wreathed with serpents."

"And which is Aunt Eileen?" Jennie enquired, busy peering to left and right at the countryside they were driving through, as the Rolls-Royce tourer left Dunosova behind them.

"*Dobru*, though a Vilia is a changeable spirit," he replied.

"Like Anna," she commented idly. His silence made her glance at him suspiciously. "Why isn't she here today?"

"She is with Viktor," he replied a little too quickly.

"She must wish to be with him very much if she gives up this chance to see Aunt Eileen's home." She knew how interested Anna was in her aunt's every move, if only because for Anna her aunt's life represented a freedom denied to her.

"She does," Max neatly capped her comment.

There was nothing she could say in reply. The road, one of the few in Montevanya, wound through lush meadows with grazing horned cattle and fields of millet, watered by tributaries of the Danube, and enclosed by hillsides whose lower slopes were terraced and cultivated with vines. The upper slopes were forested, with the barren peaks of the highest hills proudly crowning them.

Her first sight of the Palace Primaveru was disappointing: it looked just like an ordinary rectangular stone house. As they drove through the enormous iron gates, however, a line of huge jack-in-a-box saluting guards leapt out of toadstool-shaped boxes to greet them, to Jennie's delight. Odd fountains of water suddenly gushed from statues as they passed (some of them from parts of the body that Aunt Winifred would most certainly have clothed in decent calico). Then, as they approached the house itself, the dull facade was suddenly swept aside like theatre curtains, revealing the true house within. Here were the turrets and towers she'd hoped for; here were the gables, and drainpipes guarded by gargoyles; here was the house of magic. The door seemed to be halfway up the house, with no way of reaching it, and the true entrance proved to be the large window in front of them.

"How can you *live* here?" Jennie asked her aunt, entranced, when at last she could talk to her. Max had disappeared with Prince Georgius, which was tactful of him, or perhaps he just liked being with his uncle. She and her aunt were walking in the gardens, of which Jennie now had great expectations. In the house itself corridors ended in blank walls, apparently small rooms suddenly revealed themselves in their true proportions by means of sliding walls. The gardens proved even more captivating. Flowers would occasionally move to new locations, or distribute a stream of water when least expected. A grotto had a moving pageant of automata, and flower fairies hovered over spring blooms like dumbledores. Georgius might not be a good conjuror, but he could create magic.

"I don't," Eileen told her cheerfully. Today she was in Turkish trousers and tunic made of a yellow silk that shimmered like the spring itself. "Not all the year, anyway.

That's my one condition. I can travel where I like for four months provided I return for the other eight. So for normal life I come to Fairsted or London occasionally, and for the rest of my free time I go where the spirit takes me."

"And what's the penalty if you stay away longer?"

"There is none except to myself." Eileen smiled when she saw Jennie's amazed expression. "You'll understand. Some time."

"Doesn't Prince Georgius mind?"

"He knows I'll return. He calls me his jill-in-a-box." Eileen paused, then became serious. "Jennie, I have to confess that much as I wanted you to see our home, there is another reason that Max brought you."

So she had been right, Jennie thought, with sinking heart. What was wrong now?

"Sir Roger returned from London this morning, so I'm told," Eileen continued, "and since he cannot remain long, the question as to whether Anna and Viktor will marry has to be settled quickly, and their engagement announced. It will not be an easy discussion, since Anna still refuses to marry Viktor. Nevertheless, today Viktor will officially ask for her hand in the King's presence. Marie is unhappy, and Anna is ill with worry. Sir Roger, Marie, and the King and Queen all seem to believe they can make her see sense. If the doctors are right, this hardly seems the time for an engagement, but the King and Queen are adamant that it should be today." Eileen hesitated. "I should also tell you, Jennie dear, that Marie and Roger are disappointed that your presence has not made her see things more sensibly. Instead it seems to them that she is avoiding you. Would you agree?"

Jennie was appalled, hardly knowing where to begin. "What do you mean by the doctors not thinking this is a good time for an engagement?"

"They believe Anna is too weak, exhausted with worry. Certainly not —"

"Looking to the public as if she can bear the next healthy heir to the throne?" Jennie cut in furiously.

"Yes," was Eileen's simple reply.

Jennie could not speak for a moment. The hurt was too immense. So she had been invited merely to persuade Anna into the marriage, just as she had been over her presentation last year. She supposed she had half realized this, but to hear it voiced as a cold fact was a shock. Put Aunt Eileen's way, she had let the Fokinghams down, even though she had done her best to calm Anna at her most vehement. Anyway, it was ridiculous. Anna was not somebody who could be persuaded into something she didn't want to do, but no one seemed to realize this but her. Outwardly, she admitted, Anna was so compliant in many ways that no one *could* see her will of iron. Princess Marie should have known better though.

Jennie tried bravely to cover the hurt. "I did all I could," she at last answered her aunt, knowing this was inadequate but unable to defend herself further.

"So that's why Max brought me here. He's simply keeping me out of the way." Another hurt, for she had thought he really liked her. How *stupid* of her.

"Only that?"

Jennie blushed, remembering the "half naked" comment and how this must look to her aunt. "Yes, Aunt Eileen, *really*. Max was merely mocking me that night, and now he's doing his duty as host. At least Anna's straightforward about what she likes and dislikes."

"You're a good friend to her, Jennie," was all Eileen said. "And now, I must become Madame Szendescu again, and play host to my guests."

Jennie took the change of mood easily. "Do I acquire a new name as your niece? I'd like to be two people, as you are."

"You couldn't cope with being two people, Jennie," Eileen replied.

Jennie felt dampened by this comment as they went into the house — into the wrong room, of course, since there was no apparent door to the dining room, and this made Aunt Eileen laugh. "I'm afraid Georgius insists on eating in the mirror room, Jennie. I hope you won't mind."

Jennie soon found herself seated, staring straight into a version of herself twice the size in the middle, and considerably shorter. Opposite her, Max's face stared upside down from the mirror-glass table, thin and shrivelled, and in the mirror behind her like a fat giant. Aunt Eileen's reflection was like one of Arthur Rackham's fairy illustrations, and Prince Georgius at the head of the table was a veritable Old King Cole.

It was a happy luncheon, punctuated by laughter as the groaning sideboards of hot roasts and cold hams (the size of cows if Jennie looked at them in the mirror) were attacked by Georgius with carving knife and giant Fe Fi Fo Fum roars, only to reveal they were jelly creams. Clearly the footmen were used to this routine, for they stood by until he tired of this, then they stepped forward to perform the carving of the real meats.

Such was the contented atmosphere that Jennie had almost forgotten her upsetting conversation with Aunt Eileen by the time Max drove her back in the sunset through the valley. He drove slowly, almost as if he were reluctant to return to Dunosova. He said very little but she felt they were at peace with one another.

"A red sky," she observed after a while, looking at the flaming red and gold over the hills. "In England that means good weather in the rhyme, sailors' delight. Does Montevanya have a navy?"

"Of course. It sails along the Danube to show our neighbours that we can defend ourselves. It goes one way to show the Bulgarians and Roumanians, and the other to show Austro-Hungary and Serbia."

"How many ships?"

He laughed. "This is a major secret of defence. I cannot tell an Englishwoman in case Britannia's Royal Navy hears of our mighty strength."

"I work for the railway," she replied, "and I'm a stationmaster's daughter. I know about trains, not ships. Montevanya is safe from me."

"Then I tell you that Montevanya has six ships in Dunosova harbour, each with a mighty armament of two small guns to defend our country when the big battle comes."

"When will that be?" she teased him.

His mood changed again. "It may already have done so, I fear."

He was thinking of the family discussion, she guessed, watching the sun slowly sinking as the motor car began the climb to the Varcása.

*

The gates to the castle seemed to clang behind her as though emphasizing the end of a happy day. and once inside the castle Max turned to her with a formal: "Thank you for your company, Miss Imogen. You will excuse me, I must see His Majesty."

She could see he was preoccupied; they had stepped back from a day of freedom into the demands of life. She tried to laugh at herself for presuming to know what was in Max's mind, but somehow the whole castle seemed chillier.

Ridiculous, she told herself. Anyway, if Prince Max could see the King, then Jennie could see Anna. *Now.* She hurried up the staircase to their second-floor rooms. The corridor seemed lifeless and even her room lacked charm this evening. She took off her coat and paused to look in the mirror. No enchantment here now, just plain Jennie Trent. Nothing's changed, she told herself.

But it had. As she passed Gillyflower's room on the way to Anna's, the door opened and Princess Marie came out. Jennie instantly curtsied, but as she rose she realized something was deeply wrong. Princess Marie looked old to her for the first time, and was looking at Jennie as though she loathed her.

"I was going to see Anna," Jennie faltered, "to tell her of the day."

Princess Marie stared at her and Jennie thought for a moment she wouldn't even answer. "Do what you will," she said in a flat voice that Jennie hardly recognized. "You can do no harm now. Anna is taking dinner in her room. You may see her at eight o'clock and yours will be served there too. It is not convenient for you to see her now. I shall be visiting her myself."

Jennie automatically retreated to her room while she tried to make sense of these words. You can do no harm? What could that mean? There had been none of Princess Marie's normal politeness. It was almost as though she were being punished. She tried to gather her thoughts together. Cinderella's bubble had burst, that was obvious, and her suppressed fears now overwhelmed her. What harm could she have done? What was wrong with Anna? Had she some terrible disease, or was she just exhausted? Her refusal to marry Viktor, that must surely be the reason. She had been sent to her room in disgrace. She, Jennie, had been brought here to help and had failed. She saw now that she should have insisted on talking more with Anna, especially after she had pleaded for her help on the Orient Express.

She changed out of her beloved tunic-skirted green dress and put the dark-blue skirt on again, with the blouse and jacket that Anna had let her keep. It was a reminder of that first day at the fair, and made her feel better now she had a little piece

of the dream to cling on to. No need to put on her evening dress tonight, although all the best fairy stories, she reminded herself, had temporary storms.

And yet she had no idea what that storm could be. She waited impatiently until eight o'clock struck and she heard the footman trundle by with their dinner, and then walked out to go to Anna's rooms. She had never felt less hungry in her life, but at least now she would have a chance to find out what had really been happening.

She could hear voices coming from Anna's room even as she knocked. Her father? No, the language was Montevanyan. His Majesty? The question was soon answered as the door was wrenched open from inside.

It was Max, and his face changed from anger to a rage Jennie had never seen on anyone's face, let alone directed at her. "You!" he threw at her. "Are you proud of yourself? This is what comes of befriending peasants."

Shaking with anger, he pushed her aside and strode off, leaving her shocked and trembling. She wanted to go to her room to throw herself on the bed, but she knew she had to help Anna. She must be in a terrible state.

Whatever she had expected, it wasn't what she found now. Anna was sitting at the table in her salon, looking as bright and happy as Jennie had ever seen her. The world was going topsy-turvy and it was all too much. Jennie burst into tears.

"What are you crying for?" Anna asked, looking puzzled.

"They said you were ill. Everyone was shouting. Max —"

"So what if they were? You can see I'm all right, and I'm not ill."

"All this just because you're not going to marry Viktor?" Relief began to raise a surge of hope in Jennie, but it was quickly dashed as Anna burst out laughing.

"Of course not. I told you so, I told *them* so, only they wouldn't believe me."

"So why are they locking you up here?" Jennie asked in trepidation, still trembling with the shock.

"It's only what I expected."

"Did Viktor mind about your not marrying him then?" Please, Anna, don't make me wait, she silently pleaded.

"He thought it all most amusing."

"Why?" Jennie almost screeched.

"It means he can marry his German shepherd dog. Actually, I quite like Eva."

"Please tell me what's wrong, Anna." The sight of the food began to make Jennie feel sick.

"I expect it's my other news that upset them." Anna helped herself to a dish of meatballs.

"What was that?" Here it comes, she thought. At last, at last.

"I'm expecting a baby."

The jolt shot through her, then everything seemed to spin round as the meatballs acquired a terrible fascination. It was one of Anna's jokes, of course.

"A calf of Viktor's?" Jennie tried to laugh, then stopped as she realized how wrong she was. Anna wasn't joking. That was why she'd been sick that first morning, and took breakfast in her room.

"Not Viktor's." Anna smiled at her pleasantly.

"But you're not married."

"That doesn't stop the cows, does it?"

Jennie could take no more. "Tell me, Anna," she pleaded. "We've been friends for over five years; I need to know the truth. What is all this about?" Now she could understand just why Princess Marie looked so old — and why Max had been so angry.

"There's really a baby," Anna assured her.

This time the full horror of it came home to Jennie. What would happen? It was bad enough if a village girl was expecting; she had to marry the father, and though everyone pretended not to notice how speedy the wedding was, they all knew. Aunt Winifred had given Jennie lots of strict lectures, even before she understood what they meant. For those in Anna's position, however, the situation was entirely different. They weren't supposed to have *bodies* until they got married, let alone babies.

"But if it's not Viktor's child, whose is it? When is the baby coming?" Jennie heard her voice rising.

"September, the doctor said. Poor Mother, she was so surprised when I announced it to everyone. I'd ordered the doctor to tell her I was a little overstrained."

"You told them all at the family meeting today?" Jennie stared at Anna as though she had never met her before.

Surely she could have found some gentler way of breaking the news?

"It was wonderful," Anna assured her. "Just as I'd planned. They'd all made their speeches about how nice it would be if Viktor and I married, and Viktor had made his formal proposal to me. I simply said *nemu.*"

Never in a million years, in other words. Jennie's heart sank even further, if that were possible.

"Then it began in earnest," Anna continued. "Mother cried, Father roared, Viktor laughed, the King looked unhappy and the Queen hurled insults at me for being so inconsiderate to her son. So I asked them if they would want another man's baby inheriting their precious throne. Oh, Jennie, you should have seen their faces."

Jennie could imagine it all too well. Perhaps Aunt Eileen had suspected the truth, but what did that matter now? It was done and had to be dealt with. All Jennie wanted was to be back safe in the Station House as soon as possible, but she made a supreme effort.

"I'll help you if I can, Anna, but you must tell me everything."

Anna looked at her so oddly that Jennie sensed she hadn't yet heard the worst. "Is the father someone you met in London? You told me there was no one you liked, but it can't have been true."

"Darling Jennie, I told you the truth."

"Then who is the father?"

"Tom."

This time Jennie thought she really would be sick. Anna was actually giggling. The one meatball Jennie had managed to swallow came back into her throat and she could only just hold it down. "You mean my brother?"

"Of course."

"You are joking this time, aren't you?"

"No, Jennie."

With sickening clarity Jennie remembered that conversation so long ago. "Suppose I wanted to marry someone who wasn't royal — like Jack, for instance?" Well, it couldn't be Jack who had done this to Anna, but it could be Tom.

"I didn't know you knew Tom so well."

"We're great friends."

"*Friends!*" echoed Jennie in horror. "What about love? You can't mean you don't want to marry him. You'll have to."

"No, I won't. I really wouldn't like the housework." Anna saw Jennie's face. "I shouldn't joke. I know it's a shock to you. It was to my parents, too. They didn't know Tom existed, except as a brother you talked about from time to time."

"Why?" Jennie moaned. "Why the baby?"

"It was the only way I could think of to cut this Gordian knot of a marriage. I doubt if I'll marry Tom, though."

Jennie lost her temper. "I've never thought of you as stupid, Anna, but you are. A way out? You've ruined your life. What are you going to do with a baby and no husband? You can't stay at Applemere, which you love. You can't do that to your family, even if they'd let you. And what about Tom if you don't marry him? Have you thought of him? Does he love you?"

"He loves my power and position and money, so that's a start, isn't it?"

Jennie didn't laugh. It was probably all too true, knowing Tom, and moreover Anna sounded bitter now. "Tom's all talk, but he's good at heart. He will marry you though."

"Not if I don't want him to," Anna replied gently.

"What will you do then?" Jennie repeated, beginning to understand why Princess Marie had looked so desperate.

"I don't know yet." Anna frowned. "I have some money of my own, so I won't starve, even if Father throws me out into the snow, which is what he was threatening earlier on. Goodness, Home Rule for Ireland seems a simple matter compared with his daughter, judging by his reactions. I'll have to think about it, I suppose."

"Can I help?"

"I doubt it."

This was too much. "You mean you only wanted me as a friend because you liked the look of Tom?" Jennie could be blunt too.

"No. That's not it," Anna replied calmly. "I need friends. God knows how much, but I live alone inside. I always have. So does Michael, I think."

Jennie had forgotten about Michael. "Would he help you?" she asked doubtfully.

"He might be sympathetic."

"So where will you have the baby?"

"I haven't the slightest idea. But, do you know, Jennie, for the first time in my life I feel free and happy."

*

It was more than Jennie did. Her pent-up emotions raced through her as she lay awake that night. It was Tom's fault, he had planned this, she thought one moment, and the next she thought, no, it was Anna who planned it all. How long she had been secretly seeing Tom? Just this last autumn, or longer than that? Much longer, perhaps. Tom's cottage on the manor estate made sense now, but he must have known Anna's family would never allow her to marry him. Then her thoughts turned to herself. No wonder Princess Marie had looked so coldly at her. Surely she could not think that Jennie had anything to do with Anna's plans — or worse, that she had put Tom up to it?

She would soon find out. Her breakfast was brought to her room and she was informed by a very upset Gillyflower that her other meals would be taken for the rest of the day with Anna in her rooms. The whole party would be leaving at eleven o'clock next morning to take the Orient Express home. Meanwhile, His Majesty would be grateful if she did not leave the Varcása grounds, though she was of course free to walk in the gardens. What did they think she was going to do? Shout their disgrace round the marketplace? How could they be so unfair as to hold her responsible for her brother's doings? Gillyflower looked at her so reproachfully that Jennie felt as though she were indeed guilty of bringing about this fiasco.

"Of course your meals will be with me," Anna said with an attempt at humour when Jennie saw her at luncheon. "After all, my child will be your niece or nephew."

Jennie groaned. "Don't make jokes. Anna. I'm not up to it. What will happen in the train? Will we be travelling third class in disgrace together?"

"You probably would have been," Anna replied devastatingly, "but they already had return tickets."

Jennie rallied enough to throw a cushion at her. "What's going to happen next?" she asked. "Are you coming back to Applemere?"

Anna lost some of her self-possession. "They've decided, and as I can't think of anything better I've agreed. Mother and I will be leaving the Orient Express at Strasbourg and taking a train into Switzerland. The rest of you will travel on to England. So far as Applemere is concerned, I have tuberculosis. In fact, I shall spend the months away from prying eyes and after the baby is born will return pale and wan to Applemere. And then the whole business of how to marry Anna off will, they fondly imagine, begin again. Only no Viktor this time."

"You can't mean that." Jennie was horrified.

"I do mean it. That's what they would like. To wipe the whole episode from their minds, and find a discreetly respectable husband as quickly as possible."

"But what about Tom? Have you told him about the baby? *Will* you tell him?"

"No. Or if I do, it will be when I choose. Not a word to him, Jennie, or anyone." Her face went blank. She had retreated to a kingdom of her own, to which she, Jennie, had no passport.

"And that's *all!* He deserves nothing of you?"

A picture of Tom, the proud, the strong and, when he chose, the loving brother, rose up in Jennie's mind. How could Anna do this to him, or to anyone?

"He'll no doubt receive a nice sum of money from my parents to forget I ever existed. Unless I decide to marry him. I still haven't definitely made up my mind, but I think that I'd rather be free."

"Free?" echoed Jennie disbelievingly. "With a baby?"

"Didn't I say? Sorry. It will be given for adoption. It happens all the time. There used to be giggles at the coming-out dances about somebody or other being ill in Switzerland, poor thing. Perhaps that's what put the whole plan in my mind."

"You didn't have a *whole* plan," Jennie said savagely. "You do need help."

Anna looked at her in amazement. "You mean you really want to help? That you're my friend, despite this? I thought you'd never speak to me again."

"Tempting," agreed Jennie crossly. "But if I can help, I will."

"I doubt if they'll let you now, but afterwards, when the baby's gone, I shall have a plan — "

"Not another!"

Anna smiled weakly. "So if I turn up at Fairsted railway station one day with a small portmanteau, don't be surprised, will you? I could really be thrown out in the snow, you see, if I don't do exactly what they want after the Swiss trip." She looked at Jennie so hopefully that her heart melted.

"We'll find one, Anna, don't worry. I promise."

Jennie spent the afternoon in a daze. Didn't Anna care about the baby? And how could the Fokinghams be so hidebound that they would throw her out if Anna didn't obey their future wishes? Anna must be exaggerating. Then she remembered how harshly Princess Marie had spoken to her the other day. It was understandable, perhaps, since she must have known about Tom. But why condemn *her*! There must be some misunderstanding. On an impulse she decided to ask to see Princess Marie in her apartments before dinner that evening. After all, she could only refuse.

*

"What is it you wish to say, Jennie?" Princess Marie asked, not quite so coldly as before.

"You can't think I knew about this," Jennie burst out, forgetting all her resolve to remain calm.

"Can't we?" Princess Marie looked very old and tired. "It seems clear to my husband and myself that your eagerness to befriend my daughter was more due to your wishing to visit Applemere than liking for her."

"It was not and, in any case, how does that have a bearing on Anna's baby?"

Princess Marie went white, as if the very mention of it was too much to bear. "How could she have come to know this brother of yours if not through you? She accepts every suggestion you make. She has no mind of her own."

"That isn't true. What about the presentation at Court last year? She decided that herself." Jennie was furious. How could Anna's own mother so underestimate her daughter?

"By that time she was obviously in the grip of this man, which is why she refused to be presented in the first place, until you persuaded her. Oh, Jennie," her reserve broke, "I cannot believe you betrayed us so."

"I didn't — " She knew it was no use. Jennie realized that this was the only way the Fokinghams could face what was happening to them. By blaming her, they absolved themselves.

Early next morning, Jennie went into the gardens for one last look at the view down upon Dunosova and the far-off hills — the blue hills of Montevanya that she and Anna had talked of the first time they'd been together. So much for paradise, Jennie thought sadly. Paradise always had a serpent to poison it, and, for the Fokinghams and the King's family, she was it. Did the Fokinghams not see that the serpent that poisoned this paradise had come from within, not outside? It came from a belief in its own inviolability and rightness.

She turned to go, hesitating before going back into the Varcása itself. There was one other person she wanted to see before she left.

She found Prince Max alone in the garage with his beloved motor car, his back to her, and screwed up her courage to speak. That word "peasant" he had flung at her still stung and it needed blotting out.

"I would like to say goodbye, Your Highness."

She knew instantly that she'd been stupid to come. He spun round angrily. "I also, Miss Trent. And am glad to do so. Not many people fool my family, especially myself, but you have succeeded most admirably. My congratulations."

"How?" she blazed at him. "I had no idea about my brother's friendship with Anna."

"Then perhaps you should have done. In any case, it is of no consequence."

"Don't you care what happens to her?"

"I do not. She has decided her future and it is not in Montevanya. It is not often that anyone, let alone a stationmaster's daughter, can succeed so admirably in upsetting the plans of a king. Nor in fooling me."

"And I'm sure, Prince Max," she shot back at him, "that it is not often that you are so blind and foolish."

There was nothing more to say, so she curtsied — the last time she would ever do so to *anyone*, she vowed — and walked back to where the wagons would be waiting to take the party to the Orient Express. She turned her back on princes and castles for the illusions they were. The lips of a prince would not ensnare *her*, however enticing they might seem.

CHAPTER VI

Over the points at Marsham and on to their very own branch line. Through Marsham station itself, and then came the cutting and the Peasden Lane tunnel. Now Jennie could see Chapel Wood, and the rise of Stellingham Hill, before the train steamed through Applemere Halt, gathering pace as if in disdain for it. Gillyflower and Miss Partridge, Lady Fokingham's maid, would alight at Fairsted today, where the wagon would meet them. There was no order from Applemere House to stop the train at the Halt for mere servants, Jennie noted in a moment of glee, of which she was instantly ashamed. Fairsted at last came in sight, and her heart lurched. There were the chimneys of the Plough pub, the cowls of the Mount Farm oasts, and the nest of peg-tiled roofs that spelled home. It looked so peaceful, so unchanged, just as if she'd never been away.

Jennie bit her lip to keep back the tears from falling. Jiggidy-jig, jiggidy-jig, over the rails, past the telegraph poles. Clackety-clack, as the steam from the engine floated away into the skies as if to forewarn the village of her arrival. Thank goodness Sir Roger had left them at Dover. Travelling with Gillyflower and Miss Partridge had not been so bad compared with his cold presence that had cast such a pall over her.

She could see Beech Farm now, and there was Mrs Ovenden in the yard, feeding her chickens. It was a wonder they never burst, she did it so frequently. The sloe bushes were in bloom early this year; she must remember to make some more sloe gin in the autumn. It was Aunt Winifred's favourite as, Jennie suspected, her aunt had convinced herself that it wasn't real liquor if you made it yourself. Thoughts of home-made these last moments seem endless.

Giddy with excitement as the train slowed down for Fairsted, she could see Percy Wenner, the new and nervous young porter, waiting on the platform and — oh, there was Dad in his best uniform. As the train puffed to a standstill, Percy jumped in to help them with the luggage.

"You leave that to me, Miss Jennie," he ordered grandly. But there was no need, for Dad was hurrying towards her, and Jennie was quickly in his embrace.

Where was Jack? she wondered. He must be on duty at Marsham because there was no sign of him. She swallowed her disappointment. After all, she couldn't expect everything to stop just because she was coming home. Jack had work to do. She felt the relief flood over her as she saw Gillyflower and Miss Partridge walk away with only a stiff "Goodbye". She didn't care. She was home, and here was Dad.

"There, my pet, you're back. My, we've missed you, Jennie." He swung her round and hugged her again. "That Betsy in the office isn't a patch on you. Messed up all your returns and tourists, I've no doubt."

She knew her ticket arrangements would be perfect in Betsy's hands, but she was happy at the joke. "Oh, Dad, I'm back, I'm *back*, and I'm so glad. Where's Jack?"

Did she sense a hesitation as her father replied? "At the junction, of course. Been there since his promotion, he has. He'll be round later for tea. We don't see so much of him as we used to, but we will now you're home. That's if you're not too grand to talk to us folk now. None of your castles in Fairsted."

"I don't want them, Dad."

He looked at her sharply. "That why you cabled you'd be home early? Didn't take to it?"

This was her first test. She had to fib about what had happened to protect Anna. "No. Our plans had to be changed because Anna's got TB. Isn't that terrible?"

"Poor maid. Damp in that Applemere House, so they say. I'm real sorry to hear that. Well, your aunt has it all nice and snug for you at home. It'll be quite a homecoming. Tom's coming over early from the brewery, and Freddie, he managed to get his duty time changed to nights specially to be here. Jack too. Your aunt will be glad to see you, Jennie."

"You make me feel I've been away so long."

"You're back now, aren't you, Jennie girl? Come home to us at last, you have."

*

She knew she had, both in fact and in her mind. The Varcása had vanished. True, the rooms of the Station House seemed small at first — and so crowded. There were no statues and gold-painted icons here, though, just family bits and bobs, wedding photographs, studio photographs, the family Bible, the works of Dickens — her past and her present, and her future. It was wonderful. Aunt Winifred had even kissed her and did indeed seem pleased to have her home. Jennie could tell that by the tea. It wasn't every day they had ham with watercress gathered from the streamside, and prawns from the travelling Whitstable fish man. Not to mention Aunt Winifred's special trifle with custard, jelly, and cream from the farm, and her precious canned peaches.

The table seemed to fill the whole room by itself, but somehow they all managed to squeeze round it, when at last teatime arrived. She nerved herself to face Tom, wondering how she could do so now she knew how he'd behaved, but when he strolled in he was just his usual boisterous self, looking so smart and happy in his lounge suit, and it was suddenly easy.

"Where's your crown, eh?" he joked.

"Swapped it for a couple of bottles of Montevanyan beer."

"So why are you home early then?"

A casual question, but she forced herself to be on guard. "Anna isn't well. The doctors say she should have a few months to recuperate in Switzerland. They think she's got TB."

"Poor kid," was all he said, but Jennie was aware he was watching her sharply.

Freddie looked so grown up now that it was hard to think of him as not yet eighteen. His round, cheerful face was just the same as he demanded every detail about the Orient Express.

"You won't be driving that yet," she laughed.

"I'll be on the footplate through the Simplon one day. You'll see." Eight years ago the Orient Express Company had opened another route eastwards when the Simplon tunnel through the Alps in Switzerland had been opened.

No Jack yet, although it was past five o'clock. Jennie tried to ignore this as she chattered on about the wonders of Montevanya and the castle. She did quite well, even though she had to keep back so much. She couldn't talk about Anna lest what she said didn't tie in with a tubercular condition. She did not want to talk about Prince Max, and worst of all was not being able to talk about

Aunt Eileen. She had been so much part of her visit that it was more difficult than ever to remember that no one here knew of Aunt Eileen's other existence. How was she going to remember not to reveal all these things by mistake, Jennie worried anxiously, when she had been used to sharing everything with her family? It might become easier as time passed, she supposed, but tonight it was hard, as the pain of the truth sucked at her from within.

At last Jack arrived. She saw him walking up the path, still in his cap and uniform. He was so proud of it, especially now it was complete with the new trade union emblem as well as the company badge. She sometimes wondered if the company knew how hard all its staff worked for it. She rushed out to meet him and his face lit up as he caught her in his arms and hugged her.

"Here's my princess back then."

"And glad of it, Jack. So glad. Have you missed me?" An idiotic question, but it bridged the gap. She knew that when they were alone he'd show her how much he'd missed her, and she him.

"You know I have, Jennie," was all he said.

When she went to bed that night, she relived the evening in her mind. She was home and it was glorious — and yet it didn't seem quite the same as usual. She'd felt not so much amongst them as with them, watching them from the outside. She was tired, she supposed, and what she had experienced in Montevanya had temporarily set her apart. She had sensed that something wasn't quite right, even when she walked down the lane with Jack as he returned home. She went over this in her mind, but could not give any substance to her fear. His kiss had been as tender as ever, his arms as warm. Finally she realized that it must stem from the gulf caused by her need to keep so much back about her visit. Tomorrow she would be back in the booking office and she would be one of them again, as if Montevanya had never happened.

If only that were true! Out there in the dark was Montevanya, a part of the world she had singularly failed to rule. Perhaps she wasn't meant to rule in a castle, she thought. Her world might be different. She was too tired to think about this now, but someday she would. Tomorrow everything would be all right.

*

Marsham, where Jack was working, was four miles away, and Jennie decided to take the train there after she had finished work the next day. Jack wouldn't be free for another three hours, and it would be dark by that time, which made bicycling no fun. As she walked along the platform, she could see him in the junction signal box, his earnest-looking face with its mop of fair hair sticking out from under his cap, intent on his beloved levers. There was something intimate about a signal box, high above the ground beneath, removed from it, yet responsible for everything that happened on the track.

"There's nothing wrong, is there, Jack?" she asked after they had been talking for a few minutes. He seemed tense, probably because he couldn't relax as he was on duty. Nevertheless something made her ask.

"Nothing, Jennie, now you're here."

"I thought you might have changed since you'd been promoted?"

"What about you changing after gadding around in castles?"

"There's a lot to tell you, Jack." And a lot she couldn't.

"I'll have a Sunday off week after next, if I do nights to make up."

She sighed. "I thought your union was going to do something about your hours."

Ever since the big strike of 1911, when the railwaymen had won recognition for a union from the railway companies, there had been talk about fighting for a forty-eight-hour week, but here they still were, twelve hours a day, no day off unless you worked the two nights instead. Dad put his faith in the company — everyone did — but in Jennie's view the company didn't play fair. Long hours led to accidents and many was the signalman who'd made a mistake simply through tiredness, or been mown down by a train in the pitch dark or fog. The strike might have ended, but nothing much had happened since to make their jobs safer.

"If I ran the union I'd get things moving," she declared.

"You?" Jack squeezed her hand. "Not a woman's job, that."

"Why not?" she asked indignantly, remembering Anna's impassioned talk about the suffrage movement and votes for women.

"Women don't run offices, that's all. They're better at other things."

"Babies?" she retorted.

"That's it, and loving and tending. Keeping us fellows in order."

"Then why can't I keep a trade union in order? It's only a lot of men together." Jennie was triumphant at the argument being so handed to her on a plate.

Jack obviously didn't see it that way. "It's different, annit?"

She wanted to ask why but stopped, as Jack was looking put out. Instead, to cover the awkward silence, she asked:

"Have you seen any other jobs vacant that you'd like? Away from here."

"Not yet." He hesitated. "You don't mean *far* away, do you? I thought of Ashford, like your Freddie."

"Of course," she said, confused. Just what *did* she mean? she wondered. It was she who'd said she never wanted to leave the Fairsted area. Ashford had seemed just about tolerable, but now she had sudden doubts.

"I thought perhaps with all this Orient Express and Montevanya, you might be wanting to try your wings."

She flushed. "No, I'm not. I'm glad to be here. I really am." And yet she didn't think he believed her, and was conscious that somewhere deep inside her was that feeling that part of her was still watching from the outside. Even watching Jack. And perhaps he felt it, too, for he still looked anxious, glancing at her as though he didn't quite recognize her. She opened her mouth to say something reassuring, but as she did so the Folkestone bell rang, and the moment was gone.

*

How difficult life was, Jennie thought as she handed over yet another cheap-day return to Canterbury. Why couldn't she put into exact words everything that was in her mind? There seemed to be a wall between her and Jack. There was she, with all her love on one side of it, and Jack with all his love for her on the other. Why couldn't she just leap over it? Easy answer to that: she could, and she would, when she saw him next.

Happier now, she smiled up at her next customer then realized, heart sinking, that it was Tom. He must have come on the six o'clock from Canterbury and be on his way home.

"What can I do for you, sir?" she enquired warily. Usually he didn't bother to seek her out like this.

"Thought you might like to walk back for tea with me."

Tom being so interested in her company? No doubt at all now. He wanted to know more about Anna. She'd refuse, was her instant thought, but then decided to grasp the nettle as soon as Betsy arrived to take over.

"So you liked this Montevanya, did you?" Tom said casually as they left the station to walk down the lane to the manor.

"Very much."

"I'm thinking of going to France myself. Been invited by a fellow to go with him to Calais."

"That's good," she replied, waiting for his real reason for seeking her company to be apparent. She didn't have to wait very long.

"So when will Anna be back?" Tom hardly bothered to make it sound casual now.

"When she's well again. Some months, I would think."

"Only I met her on the train one day before all you toffs went off on the Orient Express and she asked me for some advice on motor cars. She wants one of her own, and there's a good little Lagonda 11.1 HP for sale in Tylers of Canterbury."

Jennie nearly said, "I'll let her know," but stopped herself. Tom would immediately demand Anna's address — which she didn't know, but this would appear very odd to Tom. Oh, how difficult!

"Thought she was going to marry her cousin," Tom fortunately continued, as he opened the door to his cottage.

"She refused." That much she could say, since it was more or less publicly known. She glanced at him and saw an odd smile on his lips which seemed to be saying, "She prefers me then." If only you knew, she thought.

Tom's cottage was one of several built for estate workers, and was attractive, redbrick and tiled, and, thanks to Bessie Sladen, the girl who came in daily to clean and cook for him, was well kept and clean. Bessie was sixteen now, and were it not for the fact that her father was a formidable fighter and built like an ox, Jennie suspected her virtue might have had little chance against Tom. She was a good worker, however, and Tom would always steer clear of harming his own interests.

"What about you, Jennie?" he continued after she'd greeted Bessie and sat down in his parlour. "Going to marry your Jackie, are you?"

"My business." She wasn't a younger sister anymore; she wasn't going to be bullied.

"Reckon he must be worried you'll think yourself too good for him now."

"Then he'll find out he's wrong." She clung to her temper with difficulty.

"Perhaps he's not."

"That's for me to say," she whipped back. "Not you."

"Keep your temper, little sister. Just trying to look after you."

"It'll be the first time."

"You'd be surprised. It's what brothers do when necessary. I'll wager you that snooty Mr Michael looks after Anna." He paused. "Next time I see him I'll tell him about that car."

"You make it sound as though he pops into the Plough every evening."

"He's done so often enough. Still likes playing with trains, does Mr Michael, for all his posh London ways. He still reckons Anna will marry Prince Viktor."

"She isn't going to," Jennie snapped. Tom was very pleased with himself for some reason. Moreover, she'd forgotten about Michael and her heart sank. He must surely know all about Jennie's disgrace. His father would have gone straight to him in London to relay the story. Heaven help Tom if Michael knew he was the father of Anna's baby — and as for her, she would just keep out of his way. Michael had always disliked Tom and now she too had joined the untouchables.

*

Spring had never seemed more beautiful than this year. Weather seemed to take a perverse delight in being at its best when Jennie was not, and at its worst when she was. This was definitely a "worst" time, not only for herself, but it seemed for England too. Everything was wonderful on the surface, but underneath it seemed to be festering. The birds were singing at their sweetest, the grass and the trees burst out their fresh greenery, the King and Queen had had a wonderful state visit to Paris at the end of April. Yet Ireland remained in a state of turmoil and civil war looked likely. There was talk of strikes here, too, and the suffragettes were more militant than ever, battling at the Palace gates, and burning churches.

Meanwhile, life in Fairsted jogged on as if on some endless path to an eternal nowhere. They all seemed like the sheep in the fields, munching away at their daily grass while the world passed them by, Jennie thought, half relieved, half anxious. She heard nothing from Anna and was at last beginning to relax. Applemere House was a closed chapter until September at least, and Montevanya was merely part of a far-off dream from which she had woken up.

And then, one day in early June, Michael came.

She hardly recognized him at first, since she hadn't seen him for nearly a year. If he had visited Applemere, no news of it had reached her. He was waiting for her outside the station one day after work, and asked her to go back to Applemere House with him for dinner.

"Aunt Winifred — " She was wary, taken aback by the unexpectedness of the invitation.

"Knows all about it." He smiled at her. Once again he was doing his best to please, but she couldn't believe in it. Once she was in Applemere the recriminations would begin. Worse, he might interrogate her about Tom.

She took hold of herself. She did not have to go. "I know I'm not welcome at Applemere," she replied stiffly, "and I prefer not to go, even with you, Michael."

"Ah, but I have a letter from Anna for you," he told her, "which is why I'd like to talk to you. Nothing else. She wants to tell you about her plans for this autumn."

She wasn't convinced, and Michael saw it.

"Jennie, please come. We could talk here or in the Plough or go for a woodland stroll, but I imagine that might cause rather more comment than your coming to Applemere." Reluctantly she agreed. She had promised Anna her help and had to see the letter. Nevertheless, Michael must have more in mind, or he would simply have handed over the letter to her. It felt odd to be whisked off once more in a motor car to Applemere, and it would not go unobserved in the village. Tom would hear about this from Bessie by tomorrow morning. Michael held the car door open for her. "My father is not at home, and Miss

Gilchrist and Miss Partridge are out for the evening, so there'll be no black looks from anyone."

So little had changed in the house, except in her, Jennie realized, when she stepped inside. When she saw Anna's old waterproof hanging in the cupboard it brought back memories so vivid she had to force herself to stifle them. All her love of the house crystallized so clearly that she could hardly bear to think she was to be a stranger to it for ever. It seemed to wrap itself around her senses, as it had always done, so that she was once again, briefly, part of its ancient charm.

"If you feel you require a chaperone," he said mockingly as he closed the dining-room door, "feel free to pull the bellrope to summon the servants."

She laughed as he had intended. She had never felt fear of

him — not physically at any rate. He was no Prince Max, despite his classical features and dark hair.

"Not necessary," she replied. "And I won't tell Jack or Tom or anyone about this," she added as he looked rather taken aback. She might as well be direct.

"Ah. We'll come back to that gentleman," he murmured. A cold supper was laid out — a feast by Station House standards — and they took their places opposite each other, just as they had a year ago.

"Why are you doing this?" she asked, still wary. After all, he might be a traitor to Anna, fishing to find out what her secret plans were, in order to tell his father. "Your parents would hardly approve."

"You don't trust me, Jennie. I don't blame you. Read Anna's letter though. It might reassure you."

He pushed it across the table to her and she eagerly opened it. It was quite short, not the rambling impulsive letters she remembered from the past.

Dearest Jennie,

I hate it. It's a gaol here. All mountains, sterility, neat green fields, obedient cows and cheese. And *doctors*. You can trust Michael by the way. I want you to know that I do have a plan now, and that late September and October, if the *thing* is on time, will be when I'll need you. Remember you promised. Don't let me down. Please.

All my love, Anna.

Jennie looked up at Michael with a frown. "I don't understand. Why does she need me if you're willing to help her? And this tells me little more about her plans than I knew already. You must think as your parents do, that I had some part in my brother's friendship with Anna, so am I here so that you can test me?"

"I'm not sure about the word friendship in relation to that brother of yours," he replied drily. "Knowing him, I tend to believe that you were in the dark too. My sister and I are two of a kind. We choose our own paths and don't require pushing by our parents. Will you still help her?"

"I promised I would, and I will, but it's not easy, since she insists on keeping her blessed plan secret. Do you know what it is?"

"No. Does that brother of yours know about the baby?" he shot at her. "Or Jack?"

"If they do, it wasn't from me." She was shaken by the unexpectedness of the assault.

"Good." Michael smiled, looking genuinely relieved. "Anna is a good chess player, as you know. She's good at plotting, so I doubt if she's told Tom herself. She wants a clear path ahead."

Jennie had been thinking this through. "I'll have to tell Jack sometime, when we marry."

"Ah yes, I understand. When will that be?"

"When he gets the job he wants and we can have a house of our own."

"I wish you well, Jennie." He looked troubled, indeed I do."

Jennie heard no more from Anna after that one short note. Loyalty battled with annoyance. It seemed typical of the Fokinghams that they took loyalty for granted without seeing the need to earn it or display gratitude. Rather like the Company, which grandly assumed the total dedication of its workers. One day…One day what? she wondered. One day she'd be married to Jack. Her path ahead was clear.

*

Summer promised to be even more glorious than early spring. Despite the eruptions of discontent in England, Ascot and the London season were sunnier than ever. The newspapers had recorded that the royalty of every nation in the world seemed to be at Ascot, including King Stephen and Queen Zita of Montevanya. There was no mention of Lady Fokingham, who was clearly too busy looking after Anna, if only to ensure she didn't run away. The funniest thing, at which Jennie wished she could laugh with Anna, was the presentation of girls at the Court of June 4th, when one of the girls suddenly stopped in the line walking past King George and Queen Mary and began to plead the suffragette cause. Her mother was said to have fainted with shock, and the King was outraged, though why he was quite so extreme, Jenny failed to see.

She occasionally saw Michael, who sometimes called with

some snippet or two of information about Anna, and it did not go unnoticed. Jack saw them together and was clearly uneasy. "You be careful with that Mr Fokingham," he would say worriedly.

"There's no need to be jealous, sweetheart." Jennie was rather flattered. "He just had some news of Anna for me." The times that Jennie managed to be alone with Jack were often spoiled by her feeling quarrelsome and cross. She couldn't understand why, and was delighted when at long last Aunt Eileen came for a brief visit. Jennie managed to talk to her alone only briefly, for her aunt was proudly allotted the "spare" bedroom, formerly Tom's. Jennie was on tenterhooks until Eileen stole in to see her late that night. Her aunt said nothing about Anna or the Fokinghams' treatment of both her and Jennie, and she was too proud to press her. Instead, Eileen seemed preoccupied with politics.

"It is not good in Montevanya, Jennie. There is constant fear that the Balkan Wars could begin again, and this time involve Montevanya. If only Archduke Ferdinand could succeed in bringing more liberty into his uncle's empire, it would be easier, but old Franz-Joseph is too old to change. Like Europe itself. Sabres are rattling, Jennie. I feel it, and so does Georgius. Viktor's happy, though. He marries his beloved Eva next week, and Zita has actually invited me to the wedding. Imagine that. That proves there's trouble in the air, if she has to descend to courting my favour."

Her aunt's visit was a welcome interlude, for when Jack next had a Sunday off, he was very silent again. Jennie put it down to tiredness, since he'd worked all the previous night in order to spend most of the day with her. She tried chatting about everything — anything — but nothing worked, and the day was dancing by without their usual loving togetherness. In desperation she mentioned her birthday in a few weeks' time, and that animated him.

"You'll be nineteen, Jennie," he said eagerly. "Lots of girls are wed by nineteen. Why don't we?"

Startled, she replied, "Marry?"

"It's time, Jennie."

Her stomach turned over at having to decide something so important so quickly. She had put the idea of marriage to one side, somehow thinking that nothing would happen before September, because of her secret promise to Anna. She belatedly became aware that Jack was still talking.

"...Ashford, Jennie, and I've got it. We can live there."

"Where? What?" she asked, bewildered. "I'm sorry, Jack. I don't understand."

"A deputy chief signalman at Ashford. What do you think of that?"

"That's marvellous, Jack." So it was — for him. But for her? What would she do?

"And a little house with it, right by the railway. We can get married."

She couldn't get her thoughts in order. Control of her life seemed to be slipping through her fingers. "Yes, we could," she tried. "Later in the year perhaps." She must *think*.

"Why not now? Why not August? No point waiting."

"But I can't!" she cried immediately. "That's not possible."

All the happiness went from his face. "Don't you want to, Jennie?"

"Of course I do." She threw her arms round him, appalled at this gap that had opened up. "It's just sudden, that's all."

"September, then. Give you time to get used to the idea of having me around all the time."

"Later," she blurted out. "November, December, perhaps." September and October were Anna's months, the ones she promised. And besides, autumn really did seem too soon.

"So you don't want to." His face went very white.

"I do, Jack, but not so soon. I have to help Anna, and then I'll be free." But was that all? Really?

"She has a family to help her. The Fokinghams. Remember them? Those days are past, Jennie. We have to get away from them. Help ourselves instead."

"But I made her a promise." Jennie knew she had to tell Jack at least some of the truth. "She wants to leave her parents' home when she's better and needs my help. Let's get married in December, or next year. We'll save up to furnish the house. That will be fun…" Her voice trailed off as she saw the hurt on his face.

He seemed to pull himself together, and sounded more cheerful. "Yes, you're right. Let's do it that way."

Deep inside she realized that her relief was due to the postponement, not just because of her promise to Anna. Jack had been right, and so had Michael and Tom. Those few short weeks in Montevanya had changed something in her. It wasn't that she sighed for the Varcása and the life of the Fokinghams. It was more complicated than that. What it was, she didn't quite know, but she guessed that Aunt Eileen had once felt the same, too, and still did. Something in her was Madame Szendescu's niece as well as Aunt Eileen's.

CHAPTER VII

By late June the summer looked as if it would be a hot one. The flies were already dancing around in triumph, Jennie's uniform stuck to her in the stuffy booking office, bluebottles buzzed excitedly, and everyone appeared cooler than she felt. Everything Jennie tried to do seemed twice as difficult to achieve. She'd run out of weekend tickets, the series numbers wouldn't add up, and the goods department was causing problems, especially the S and S — the station to station baggage. The carrier who collected and delivered passengers' luggage seemed determined to give as little help as possible to the loading and unloading. He pointed out it was no matter to him if the company employed a lady booking clerk; she could still haul with the rest of them if she fancied she was as good as a man. Sometimes Jennie saw sense in the suffragette movement.

There still seemed rumblings of discord everywhere. In London, politicians argued on about Ireland and Home Rule. Here at Fairsted, Aunt Winifred bewailed the fact that though the family numbers grew smaller, the work grew harder. The meadows where Jennie walked with Jack were no escape. Though she and Jack did their best, their problem lay between them like an impassable wall. Soon Jack would be leaving Marsham Junction to take up his Ashford job.

"Nice little house," he would venture every so often, stealing a look at her, and then they would fall silent.

There had been no word from Anna, and Jennie had no reason to pass Applemere House, but every so often she would glance across the fields to see its tall chimneys and gables through the tops of the summer-green trees. She did see Michael again, however, when he appeared in the booking office on a Sunday morning. It was a warm day, and Jennie was trying to keep cool by waving a fan, feeling remarkably stupid as she did so — which Michael noticed.

"You look as if you're at a ball at the Varcása," He grinned. His eyes were sharp, as if he were summing up how she would react to this reference. Well, she wouldn't give him that pleasure.

"Not much of a ballgown." She glanced ruefully at her heavy serge skirt, jacket and hat, which she was forced to wear by company regulations, come sun, come snow, for otherwise the company might seize the opportunity to get rid of her. She knew she let their side down as a mere woman presuming to be a booking clerk, even at such a small station as Fairsted.

"Returning to work on a Sunday?" she joked to Michael. "My, the Foreign Office is working you hard."

She no longer felt in awe of the Fokinghams. If they could so much misjudge her — and indeed Anna — then there was no need to. Michael seemed to like being twitted anyway.

"It's this Sarajevo business. Have you heard about it?" he asked.

Jennie had. She would never confess it, but her eye was always caught by anything to do with the Balkans or Montevanya in the newspapers. She knew that Sarajevo was in Bosnia, which was part of the Austro-Hungarian Empire but longed for its independence. There had been a brief paragraph about it in her father's *Sunday Chronicle* this morning. The Emperor's heir, Archduke Franz Ferdinand, had been assassinated by a young Serb while on a visit to the town.

She'd remembered Sir Roger explaining to her that Balkan politics were extremely complicated and that the political boundaries brought about by successive wars in recent years paid scant attention to the races of the people living within them. Just as Montevanya had both Magyar and Slav inhabitants, so Serbs, Croats, Slovenes and other Slavs were split up amongst Albania, Montenegro, Serbia, Bulgaria, Roumania and Bosnia. There was a large Serbian population in the latter, which was now divided from its kin in Serbia, and in the constant switching of boundaries, the problem could only get worse.

"That doesn't affect Britain, does it?" she asked Michael. "We watch the good old Dual Kingdom like a hawk, especially since Emperor Franz-Josef is so chummy with Kaiser Wilhelm, who can't wait to let off a few guns to throw his weight around. Even he isn't so batty as to get involved in Balkan problems, though. So everyone's just waiting to see how Austria reacts to the assassination. If she declares instant war on Serbia on the pretext that it encouraged the assassination, it means trouble. Especially for me. It's my area, you see."

Typical Michael, she thought, to make the grand statement. "Will it affect Montevanya?" she asked in mock grave tones.

"Nothing affects Montevanya — not even you, Jennie," he replied in revenge.

It served her right, she supposed. "First-class single then?"

"No. I bought a return when I came down on Friday." He paused. "I hear you're off to live in Ashford."

More revenge on his part. "Not yet," she answered evenly. "Jack's going first."

"Some time in July, isn't it?"

"Yes." She didn't want to think about that. "Did he tell you?"

"I called in at the junction box." He grinned self-consciously. "It must be the Hornby train set Father gave me years ago. I always plead with Jack to let me pull a lever or two, but you know Jack, conscientious to the last."

"So why go to the signal box?" she asked tartly.

"The atmosphere, Jennie darling. We're all kids at heart, and want to feel in control of those monsters steaming along beneath us. No wonder Jack loves it. I suppose it's why I like being in the Foreign Office. I pull a lever, the semaphore goes down, and the Emperor of Austro-Hungary decides to overlook the assassination of his heir."

"Is that likely?"

"No." He awarded her a charming smile. Charm was part of his job, she supposed, but perhaps he meant it too. He seemed to like talking to her, and as he was her only lifeline to Anna she had no objection. Anna and Jack — she felt like a punchbag between the two of them, although she knew that was unfair. It was in herself, not in them, that her dilemma lay. Once she got Anna's problem out of the way, she could put everything from her mind but her love for Jack. Then everything would come right — wouldn't it?

*

"I saw Michael Fokingham this morning," Jennie commented, since Jack seemed very silent. Their hours together in the evening after Jack finished at eight o'clock were precious, especially since they could not rely on many more until Jack had settled into his new job.

"What did he want then?"

"Not even a ticket. Just passing through. He was going back to his office because of some trouble in the Balkans."

"Wanted your advice on policy, did he?"

She looked at him in shock. Jack was never sarcastic, so what was upsetting him? She supplied the answer for herself. "What's so wrong in Michael talking to me?" she demanded. "Not jealous, are you?" The idea was so silly it was hardly worth asking.

"It's always those dang Fokinghams," he muttered.

"You know that's not so. I just ask him for news of Anna." There had been none in fact. "Is it the new job that's worrying you?"

"Don't be so daffy. It's you."

He was right. There was no point in ignoring it. "It won't be long, Jack," she said softly. "I'll come to help you get the house ready," she added desperately, seeing his stony face. "I could take the train over nearly every day for an hour or so. I'd like that. Would you?"

"No. I want you with me all the time, Jennie."

"Soon. Not long to wait, I promise."

*

When she reached home that evening she was glad to find Freddie there. Dad and Aunt Winifred were out at the evening gathering that followed church, but Freddie was sitting reading the paper by the window. He was double homing occasionally now, since he had already been promoted to a Black Ink Fireman, which meant he was qualified to act as fireman on shunting and shed work. He was rising rapidly for his age.

"What's going on at Ashford?" she asked. "What it's like there?"

"Crackerjack. You should see those new express engines from Germany in the sheds here. They're beautiful machines, even if they are German. And so different, Jennie. Not seen anything like it, never I haven't. Only black and yellow lining out the engines, not like in Mr Wainwright's time." He had been the famous superintendent of locomotives for the SECR, and had retired last year. "No polished copper and brass on the dome and chimneys. It's a whole new world. Wonder if I'll ever drive one…"

"You will Freddie. You will." She was sure of that, even though she knew it could take up to twenty years for him to be promoted to driver. Freddie was good; it wouldn't take that long, Dad said. "Will Jack like it there, do you think?"

"Sure to. Not like Fairsted. There's hundreds of us all talking about trains all day. Different in the signal box, of course. Lonely, but we all get together at nights, those who sleep over. It's a world of its own. Social clubs, everything you could want."

"What would I do there?" The thought suddenly struck her.

"You might get in the booking office." Freddie looked doubtful, though, and she knew this was unlikely at such a prestigious railway station as Ashford. "But all the wives seem to know each other." Freddie seemed to be avoiding her eye.

"Would I like them?"

"They're a good bunch, but you're different," he said awkwardly.

"Because of Montevanya?" she asked crossly. "I wish I'd never been there, Freddie. Everyone seems to think I'm different and I'm not. Even Jack can't see — " She broke off.

Freddie looked embarrassed. "Perhaps he can, Jennie. And anyway, you've always been different. Our own little Mrs Fawcett, Aunt Win calls you sometimes, when you're in one of your hoity-toity moods."

"Not Mrs Pankhurst at least," Jennie said wryly. Mrs Fawcett believed in peaceful methods, Mrs Pankhurst in militancy. "I don't go around burning churches." She tried to come to grips with the fact that easy-going Freddie must think she was moody. Then she came back to the heart of the problem. "Do you think I'm *too* different from Jack?"

"Jack's an odd one," Freddie muttered. "Everyone likes him, but he's one on his own."

"Ambitious, you mean. Like Tom?"

"Not like Tom. Knows what he do want, does Jack, and gets on with it. Tom only thinks he knows. Jack loves you, Jennie. No matter…"

"What?" she asked sharply when he stopped.

"How he appears sometimes," Freddie said, but somehow that wasn't how Jennie thought he had intended to finish his sentence. "Are you going to marry him?"

"Yes, but not for a few months." She tried to sound casual, as though her mind wasn't still churning with indecision. "We're planning November or December." It sounded so unreal when put into words.

She should have known better than to hope Freddie wouldn't pick up on her doubt. "With all this Irish business, you never know what's going to happen. I reckon Jack's still hoping you'll marry him right away."

*

Jennie forced herself to cycle over to Marsham signal box after work. It was Jack's last day, and it would be a difficult meeting, however happy she tried to make it for them both. Tomorrow, Sunday, when they usually met, he would be going to Ashford to move in to his new home. She caught herself. Not *his*; she should be thinking *theirs*.

Ever since her talk with Freddie, she had been worrying about her future in Ashford. Much as she loved trains, she would no longer be able to delude herself that she would be able to travel away for ever and a day, like Aunt Eileen — or even just for a day.

She found Jack busy polishing the brass surrounds of his instruments, unaware of her arrival, and then he grinned self-consciously as though ashamed of what he was doing.

"Have to leave my old girl spick and span, don't I? Can't have the new chap thinking I'm a sloppy worker."

There was no fear of that with Jack. All signalmen were tidy and proud of "their" box, but Jack was in a class of his own. Glass shone and brass gleamed; lamps were expertly trimmed.

She was relieved to find him so cheerful. "Dad's asking all the drivers to give you a whistle as they pass. Have they?"

"The whole lot of them," Jack assured her. "You'd think I was leaving the railway, not just moving on."

"Michael says — " She broke off as Jack suddenly turned on her, his mood changing abruptly.

"Isn't there anything you can talk about except those flaming Fokinghams?"

"I'm sorry, Jack," she faltered. "I thought you liked Michael, because he's so interested in the railway."

"Perhaps I do, but that doesn't mean they can rule our lives. You're still thinking about that Anna, aren't you?

What about me?" Jack had never spoken to her like this. It was her fault, but that didn't make it any easier. "What are you going to do for me?" he repeated desperately. "Forget the Fokinghams. I tell you, Jennie, I wish Applemere House could be burned to the ground, I do, I'm that sick of it. Sick of the Fokinghams, and what they've done to us. They think they're still lords of the manor and all that, ruling all our lives. Well, they aren't and they don't."

"Anna was my friend — " she began indignantly.

"*Was*. You said *was*" Jack pounced. "The truth of it is, Jennie, you think you're too grand to come to Ashford with me and be a signalman's wife, isn't that it?"

"No," she protested, horrified that he could think so. "All my life there's been no one but you, Jack."

"But now you don't want to marry me. All very fine having me as a sweetheart, but when it comes to marriage you've got other ideas. See yourself as Queen of Montevanya, do you?" he jeered.

She lost her temper. "Forget Montevanya, will you? It changed nothing about you and me. You think you should rule the roost and we should get married when you like, but that's just men all over. Don't I have a say?"

"You have a say all right, Jennie. You can say no, or you can say yes." Jack spoke more calmly now, but that didn't make things better.

"Or what?" she retorted. "Who said you could set the rules?" This is stupid, she thought frantically; why wouldn't the words come out right? "I've as much say as you about what we do."

"It's what you're *not* saying that's important. And that's that you don't really want to marry me. You want to be free so that you can carry on with your swishy friends."

"It's not true," she hurled at him, all the while thinking *was it true*? "I just don't know what I want. I need to think."

"You've had all but nineteen years to think, you have. We've known each other since we was babes. If you don't know now, you never will. You think I want to go to Ashford alone, knowing you might or might not follow me? Make your mind up, Jennie. Which is it to be?" Jack was red in the face, almost crying with anger. But then so was she.

"I won't," she shouted. "You're out of your mind. It's something we both need to think about when you're established there and not worrying about the new job too."

"Then it's no." Jack did calm down then, and gave her an odd smile. "I understand, Jennie. It's all right. I love you and you don't love me. Not enough, anyway."

"That's not true. I need — "

"*You* need." He stared out at the railway line beneath the box. "You know I love this line. Ashford will never be the same. But it's not your fault. It's the fault of those Fokinghams."

"I'll come to Ashford with you tomorrow," she said eagerly. "We could discuss it quietly then."

"Course we could," he said. "Course we could. See you tomorrow then."

She gave him a wave as she rode off on her bicycle. For all her relief that the quarrel was over, she felt shaken and sick. What was she going to do? What did she *want* to do?

*

The air was heavy and oppressive the next morning as she sweated in the ticket office, hoping against hope that everything would come right this afternoon. She'd expected Jack to pop up and tell her what train he'd be on, but there was no sign of him. The clock ticked on, people came in, complained about the weather, asked for their cheap-day tickets to the seaside, then left on the down trains for Folkestone or Hythe.

The twelve sixteen down had not long left when Jennie began to feel faint with heat, and put her hand to her head in a vain effort to stop the room spinning round. And then it began, noise distanced by dizziness rose and fell like a tide, washing over her, bells ringing, voices, the sound of people running. She could hear her father's voice calling out, and the signal box bells ringing.

Jennie forced herself on to the platform as Percy dashed past her into the lane towards the village.

"What's wrong?" she managed to call out. Something was wrong. Porters should not leave the station while on duty.

"Accident at Applemere Halt. Doctor..." he called back to her but the air took the rest away.

A train accident? It must be. Dear God, no. But the train didn't stop at Applemere Halt. The words *accident, doctor*, kept repeating themselves inside her head, as she saw her father peddling on his bicycle along the footpath to the Halt.

She ran to the gate to call after him. "What is it?"

He briefly dismounted. "Don't you come, Jennie," she heard him say, his words half lost in the heat haze as he remounted and cycled on.

Don't come, don't come, don't come...But people seemed to be gathering. She felt sick now as well as dizzy, propping herself against the wall. She could hear the sound of Dr Prince's motor car starting in the distance, and noise, more noise, and people running after her father along the footpath. She found herself running too. Had the train been derailed? Were passengers dead? Her feet felt leaden, as if in a dream. Each step seemed to slow her down rather than propel her forward. She was late, but what for? Had someone fallen from the train? What was she doing here? she thought hazily. She should be in the booking office, yet here she was running along in the sun to Applemere Halt, as dizzy as she had felt that day so long ago when she, Jack, Tom and Freddie had gone to the Halt together and first met the Fokinghams.

As she drew nearer she could see the twelve sixteen train stationary beyond the platform. There were people gathered on both sides, and the sickness inside her welled up. There was nothing she could do, and yet she knew she had to be here. Then Dad came running towards her, white-faced. "Go back, Jennie," he cried. "No place for you here."

No place for her? "What's happened? What's wrong?" She clung to him to stop herself falling.

"It's a man dead, my pet," he said gently.

And then she knew. She knew what had happened at Applemere Halt as clearly as if he'd spelled it out. "It's Jack, isn't it?" The words seemed to have a terrible inevitability. But they were just words. Beyond was a great numbness.

"Yes, my love. It was an accident. Now home you go to your aunt. I'll get someone to come with you."

The words didn't seem real, but they were. An accident. Dad had said.

"Go home, my love, go home."

Someone came with her, she never remembered who, she just remembered falling through the door of the Station House into Aunt Win's arms and the sight of another fly caught in that jam-jar trap, before she felt her senses reeling.

*

When Jennie woke up, the evening sun was gentle on the window, and Aunt Win was sitting by her bed. The yawning pit in her stomach opened up again as she remembered.

"He's dead," she repeated, to make herself believe it.

"An accident, pet." Aunt Win smoothed her hair over and felt her flushed forehead.

Why did everyone keep using that word? It wasn't true, she knew that. "Jack killed himself, didn't he?"

"No one can say that for sure, Jennie. Now be quiet, and rest. I'll bring you some hot milk."

"He killed himself," she repeated with dull certainty. "What else could he have been doing at Applemere Halt?"

This time Aunt Winifred did not deny it, and Jennie noticed with detached surprise that there were tears in her eyes. Tears for Jack, for her, and perhaps a world in which this could happen. She suddenly felt quite calm.

"What should I do?" she asked dully. "Go to see Mrs Corby?"

"No, darling. Think of yourself first. Stay here and rest. There'll be time enough tomorrow."

This puzzled Jennie. Tomorrow? Now was the time Mrs Corby needed her. And why think of herself? She had done too much of that. She should have thought more of Jack. Then she realized what Aunt Win was trying to tell her.

"Everyone blames me, don't they? Even Mrs Corby. They think — Oh Aunt Win, we had a quarrel yesterday. Everyone thinks it my fault, for not wanting to marry him right away and go to Ashford. And it *is.*"

"People say anything at such times, Jennie. You know that. It's the shock, and it will die down. It's nobody's *fault.*"

Aunt Win might be right, but Jennie could not accept it. "It was my fault, it was," she repeated. Then great gasping sobs seemed to come from nowhere, and she was aware only of Aunt Win's arms around her, and the smell of the lavender water she always wore. Aunt Win had never hugged her like that before, and Jennie felt safe again. Aunt Win loved her after all and despite everything. She clung to this amazing thought to prevent her falling into the abyss below.

"He must have thought I didn't want to marry him at all."

"Jennie, no one knows what was in poor Jack's mind. He was disturbed."

The balance of his mind was disturbed. That was what they always said, otherwise suicide was a punishable crime, the only crime Jack would have committed in his life. She felt very sick and then she *was* sick, while Aunt Win held the basin for her.

"A nice hot drink for you, my girl," she said sternly. "And then we'll get some food inside that stomach of yours."

After Aunt Win had made her drink some water, and then some hot soup, she felt calmer. "Where's Dad?"

"He was with the police and now he's to do a report for the company. He's been out seeing people, too."

Seeing people? Jennie never wanted to see anyone again apart from Aunt Win and Dad. How could she bear to live on knowing she was responsible for Jack's death?

Aunt Win took her hand, and held it between hers. "Now, Jennie, I'm going to tell you a story, and then perhaps you won't blame yourself so much, and you'll see that each of us is responsible for our own life." She cleared her throat, and Jennie waited. Normally this preceded a lecture on duty, but not tonight.

"Years ago, when I was young," Aunt Win began awkwardly, "I had a sweetheart who looked rather like Jack." Looking at Aunt Win's dull hair and lined face this was hard to believe, even though Jennie had seen a photo of her when she was young. "Your mother had married your father," Aunt Win continued, "and I wanted nothing more than to marry my Alfred. Oh, he was so handsome — he was a soldier, a drummer, and off he went to war, so eager to take the Queen's shilling. When he'd earned some money and came back we'd be wed, he said, and he'd leave the army in due course, or become an officer, so we would be grand folks. I believed him, and I waited here, so happy. But he never came back."

"Omdurman," Jennie murmured.

"Yes." Aunt Win looked surprised. "I can never hear that word without thinking of my Alfred. You see, I blamed myself for his death. We had a quarrel before he left; I was a vain little thing, I didn't want him to go. He hadn't told me he'd enlisted, he sprang it on me, thinking I'd be so proud. I was, later, but then I was scared in case I lost him, and instead of telling him so, I was cross with him, all hoity-toity, saying he preferred the army to me. But there it was, and off he went. And when he never came back, I thought it was my fault because he'd gone just to make money so we could afford a home together.

"I was wrong. I've realized that Alfred chose to go, something in him made him *need* to be a soldier. And then he was killed with not even a grave I could visit to tell him I was sorry. Yet it wasn't my fault any more than it's yours that Jack has died. He faced the fact that you don't really want to marry him and decided he didn't want to live on. He took that responsibility, as we all have to."

"But I did want to marry him." She stopped. *Had* she?

"Oh, Jennie. If you'd wanted to marry him, you'd have done it by now. Don't you know yourself yet?"

Jennie remembered Jack saying something like that to her. *The trouble with you, Jennie, is that you see nobody and nothing.* That included herself. Was that true? The wound opened up again. "Do you still think sometimes that you were responsible for Alfred's death?"

"Of course I do. Just occasionally. I look at his photograph, Jennie, and think we could have been married and it's all my fault. But, you know, then I think of something else. I think of me living alone in a small house with children, with a husband away, perhaps for years. I wouldn't have wanted that."

"But then you threw everything away to look after us." Aunt Win flushed. "You make me so cross sometimes, Jennie. You know that's not true. Throw away? Nonsense. I got what I wanted. A family to look after and to be with always, to provide food for and to share my life with. I wouldn't have got that with Alfred, no matter how much I loved him."

"Oh, Aunt Win." This time the tears burst out not just for Jack but for the dear aunt she never knew she had.

*

Jennie knew she had to face the walk down the lane to see Mrs Corby, knowing that the eyes of the village would be on her. The sun seemed to beat down relentlessly, and the newspapers were full of the August bank holiday ahead. Only if one turned to the inside pages was there talk of the Irish crisis and ultimatums to Serbia, side by side with the holiday news.

Today was Jack's funeral. It was to be a men-only funeral, Mrs Corby had told her when Jennie had visited her. It was Jack's brothers who had decided on this, and Jennie believed that she was the reason. They didn't want her there and she nursed the hurt inside herself. No one wanted her, except Mrs Corby.

Jennie had asked whether she might sit with her during the funeral and she had not only agreed but been pleased. "Not your fault, my dear," she'd said. "If a lad and a maid aren't meant for each other, not even the good Lord can make it right." Jennie wasn't convinced, but grateful. Aunt Win was staunchly at her side again, wearing her funeral clothes. She had been there throughout these last terrible days, including during the inquest. No one dared criticise Jennie in Aunt Win's presence. She and Jennie had prepared the sandwiches and cake at the Station House for the gathering afterwards in the Corbys' cottage. All the while she buttered and cut bread, Jennie tried to connect this growing pile with Jack, but failed. Jack was somewhere else; he was in the meadows and in her arms, not in these sandwiches.

Tom and Freddie were going to the funeral with Dad — and so was Michael, who had come down from London specially, Aunt Win told her. For all his dislike of the Fokinghams, Jennie thought that would have pleased Jack.

As twelve o'clock approached, Jennie glanced at Mrs Corby, who was standing by the window, head bowed. She seemed to guess what Jennie was going to ask, for she simply said: "You play that piano, girl, just for Jack."

She slipped on to the familiar stool, trying hard not to think about hundreds of Sunday evenings she had spent here listening to Jack himself playing. She began to play "All Things Bright and Beautiful", since that was one of Jack's favourites, but Mrs Corby stopped her. "No, Jennie girl, he don't like that no more, he didn't. There's that bit in it, see, about a poor man at the rich man's gate. He wasn't going to wait at no one's gate, he said."

Jennie shivered, remembering Jack's outburst against the Fokinghams. And yet Michael was at this moment walking after the coffin in Jack's funeral procession. So Jack had been wrong. The Fokinghams did have hearts after all.

*

Afterwards she walked home with Aunt Win up the lane to the Station House. It seemed so unfair for the flowers still to be blooming without Jack to enjoy them, especially as this, she belatedly remembered, was her birthday. It meant nothing to her now.

"What will you do now, Jennie?" Aunt Win asked gently. "Have you thought?"

"I don't know." She was alone. Not even Aunt Win could help her now. How could she stay here in Fairsted without Jack — and yet where and why should she go? Away from here the great gulf and tearing agony that Jack's death had brought might be assuaged, yet how could she leave Aunt Win and Dad, her rocks?

Neither Dad nor Michael had appeared at the funeral gathering after the burial and when they reached the Station House she discovered why. Dad was in his telegraph office with Len Bennett, his telegraph operator and general assistant station master, and when he came into the garden where she and Aunt Win were sitting under the cherry tree, he told her that Michael had been summoned back to London by telegram.

"Daresay you didn't see the newspaper this morning, Jennie," he said, sitting down in the deckchair. When she shook her head, he continued, ""Europe Drifting to Disaster", that's what the *Daily Mail* reckons. Didn't take much notice myself, you know what newspapers are. But Mr Michael's telegram was calling him back because the Stock Exchange closed this morning. That's serious, that is."

Stock Exchange? Jennie found it hard to take in, and what did it matter anyway? "Because of Ireland?"

"No. Telegram said that Russia had ordered full mobilization of its forces. That's bad, he said."

"I thought the worry was about Austro-Hungary going to war with Serbia, not Russia?" Aunt Win said, puzzled.

"That's it, Win. Austro-Hungary's at last declared war on Serbia, and Russia wants to support Serbia as always, but the chief reason, so Mr Michael says, is that if Austro-Hungary goes to war it might stop Russia's trade routes through to the Aegean Sea, through the Bosphorus and Dardanelles. So Russia wants to frighten Austro-Hungary into believing she'd go to war too. She wouldn't, of course, so he says. Danger comes if Germany believes it."

"It sounds to me, George," Aunt Win said gravely, "that someone ought to wring their necks and get them to sit round a table together."

"With a nice cup of tea." Jennie managed a trembly laugh. How could they talk of politics on a day like this? All that mattered was Jack.

"Mr Michael thinks it will blow over. He's got this theory, you see, that's it's all to do with railways," her father replied.

"That young man would," Aunt Win said crossly. "And don't you go encouraging him, George. Railways indeed."

"You think about it, Win. What with this mobilization talk, they've got to get the men to the places where they'll need to be to fight. They need railways for that, and it takes time to organize specials, especially troop trains. You can't just wave a wand and say: go here today, and there tomorrow. There's supplies to be thought of, too. So Russia couldn't *really* be sending troops to attack Austro-Hungary — she's just hoping to scare them. And as for Germany, Mr Michael says, the Kaiser would have to take on France, too, if they went to war, because France is Russia's ally. Which way are they going to send the men first? It's an awful lot of trains would be needed. They got the tracks all right, they've been laying them for years, but it's trains it all comes down to."

"Aren't we France's ally, George?" Win asked quietly. "If you're wrong about the railways, what about us?"

"Don't be daft, Winnie. We won't get drawn in."

"So why has the Stock Exchange closed then?"

*

Jennie woke up next morning feeling, if anything, worse than she had the night before. This was Saturday and a normal working day. She had to drag herself to the booking office; she couldn't expect Betsy to carry on doing her job. At breakfast she looked at the newspapers and was relieved to see that Michael might be right. Germany had formally requested the Tsar to cancel the mobilization order. So Germany didn't want to go to war. That was good.

Or was it? At first the numbers of people who came into the booking office and were talking of nothing but war in Europe dazed her. She could not cope with the sickness still within her, the demands of her job and all this talk of war. Eventually, however, she began to welcome it. At least people were speaking to her again, even those who had cut her dead earlier in the week. Gradually she realized she was getting caught up in the strange atmosphere that was everywhere, and that it was taking her mind off Jack.

At dinnertime, Aunt Win popped in to suggest they both went to the seaside on Monday, even if Dad couldn't come with them. Monday was usually his free day, but on bank holidays he was often too busy to go. He'd see, he promised. Jennie leapt at the idea of being in the sea air and away from Fairsted, where every little thing reminded her of Jack. It was a straw to cling to.

By Sunday, the matter was decided. Dad would most certainly not be coming with them. Telegraphs and telephone calls were coming through thick and fast about "specials" running through Fairsted, and they weren't for the usual seaside trips. Jennie pored over the newspapers and discovered the worst had happened. Germany had mobilized and declared war on Russia — railways or not, as Aunt Win pointed out. Consequently France had mobilized its troops yesterday afternoon.

"Only sabre rattling again," Dad said comfortingly. "They want Germany to know they'd have to fight them, too, and they won't want to do that."

"Because of the railways," Aunt Win and Jennie chorused.

But it was no longer a joking matter. Dad and Len were in the telegraph office well before breakfast, busy with the telegrams, and Percy had already made three trips to deliver them. The government had ordered mobilization of the Royal Navy. Even if this were only to remind Germany that England, with her command of the seas, was watching the situation, it was not good news. Furthermore, it became sickeningly real when Bill Ovenden, farmer George's brother, came in with his distraught wife and with his kitbag over his shoulder to leave for his depot, and he was followed by a dozen others. Dad said foreign nationals were hastily returning, too, and the London stations were overflowing with them.

"You go," Dad told them on Monday, and Jennie was grateful though worried about leaving Dad to cope more or less alone.

"I don't like to leave you, George," Win said.

"Think you can stop the war if you stay, Win?" Dad joked.

"Someone has to," she replied grimly.

Once at Folkestone, Jennie took great gulps of sea air and felt some strength returning. All round them on the beach, rumours were capping rumours about what was happening in the outside world. Nevertheless here children paddled, there was a Punch and Judy show, and sandcastles were being erected, just as normal. As the day wore on, they listened to talk of "stocking up" larders, then came a rumour that the British Army mobilization was imminent, and that ports and trains on the continent were overwhelmed by troops and those on holiday trying to get back home. Beside her, Aunt Win unpacked the sandwiches; it was a family day, but one Jennie could have been sharing with Jack. A sharp pang of agony pierced her.

When they returned home, not only had many of the rumours proved true, they had worsened. Germany had invaded Belgium, whose neutrality was guaranteed.

"It looks as if you were wrong, George," Win observed. "You still think everyone's sabre rattling? The only one who isn't on the march is Austro-Hungary, it seems to me, and that won't be long coming."

The next day, while the country waited to know whether war would be declared or not, Jennie returned to the ticket office. *Something* had to remain the same. In a few days her life had changed completely. Jack had gone and war was probably coming. What now of her resolve to rule the world? Empire could be pitted against empire: the Russian, the German, Austro-Hungarian, and probably the Ottoman and British, too. Whoever won this war, if anyone, would decide who ruled the world, and it wasn't going to be a nineteen-year-old girl. Even so, there must be something she could do. Something to atone for Jack's death.

CHAPTER VIII

Only a few short weeks ago, Jennie and Aunt Win had been sitting on Folkestone beach. Now everywhere was transformed by war. Many young men were rushing to answer Lord Kitchener's plea to volunteer for the forces, and Fairsted was suddenly a village of women, children and old men.

Freddie had tried to enlist, but had reluctantly been persuaded that he was doing a more valuable job in helping to keep the railways running. He had been bursting with pride when one day she saw him on the footplate as fireman of a special from Canterbury, and since then he'd risen to even dizzier heights as an engine driver, albeit only for shunting and in the sheds, since drivers were in short supply.

On the morning after war was declared, Jennie's father had come in from the telegraph office to announce: "No company any more, Jennie. It's the military. They've taken over the railways, and the managers are now colonels. Government property, we are."

Jennie had a vision of Mr Asquith, the prime minister, on the footplate of the Kent Flyer, with Lord Kitchener, the minister of war, shovelling coal as fireman, and even in her personal misery found this faintly funny. Dad saw nothing funny, however. He was half suspicious, half excited at the sudden importance of the Fairsted line.

Life certainly changed for their loop line. The bulk of the British Expeditionary Force to France had left from

Southampton, since the new Dover Marine harbour was not yet fully ready, and could not take so many troops at one time. Nevertheless, the line was chaotically busy with troops travelling in both directions, and endless goods trains. Civilian traffic was all but halted and those trains that ran spent more time in sidings than on the track. Heavy goods were being taken to Richborough port, but every effort was being made to finish the new Dover harbour quickly so that ambulance trains could be brought in there to meet the ships. That sounded ominous to Jennie. Special arrangements for the wounded? That meant they were expecting a lot.

So many labourers had left the village that the women were out in force to take in the harvest. The Corby brothers had both volunteered, which tore Jennie's heart out for their mother. They said it was in tribute to Jack, but the result was that their mother was alone, and so Jennie had spent many evenings with her.

The manor had been requisitioned as a hospital, including all the cottages on the estate. Tom, to his disgust, had had to move back temporarily into the Station House. No one dared ask him if he were going to volunteer, but it seemed clear he had no intention of doing so. He had confessed to Jennie that a woman in Canterbury had given him a white feather.

"They don't understand," he complained fiercely. "I'm a brewer, the men have got to have beer to drink, and I'm better at that job than waving a bayonet around." Jennie saw his point, but in these feverish times, when the whole nation was aflame with patriotism, Tom stood no chance of being understood, other than by those who loved him.

Anna's name was never mentioned. Sometimes Jennie wondered what was happening to her, but with the present horrors of war, coupled with her own guilt and grief over Jack, Anna was one problem she was forced to lay aside. Anna at least had her mother with her, and a brother and father perfectly placed to see to their safety.

It seemed to Jennie that war had brought her an opportunity to atone for her own selfishness. At first she had been bewildered about which way to turn. Then Freddie had provided the perfect answer. He told her that the Folkestone booking clerks had vanished, one because he was a military reservist and the other because he was the son of a German bandsman. The German band had delighted the crowds in Folkestone for many years, but now they were the enemy. The son had been called up in Germany, and the whole family had gone.

So here she was in Folkestone. Dad and Aunt Win had seemed almost as relieved as she was that she'd made up her mind.

"But what will you do at Fairsted?" she worried. "Betsy can't manage alone."

"No," Dad agreed. "Your Aunt Win's going to have a go at it."

Aunt Win? Jennie laughed at first, but then realized it was the perfect answer. Why not?

"You'll find it busy at Folkestone, what with the military and the war goods traffic," Dad had warned her. "And there's a lot of folk coming over from Belgium and France, they reckon, as well as our own poor souls returning as fast as the steamers will carry them."

Dad was right. She had now spent three weeks in Folkestone, first in the ticket office at the Central Station, and then, when her ability to stammer a few words in French was recognized, at the port directing the thousands of refugees who had fled before the advancing Germans, either to the hastily set up receiving centres in the town, or on to trains to similar centres in London. Then she had been moved to helping organize the centres, after lending a hand in her spare time to join Joey Marsden, the son of the housekeeper at her lodgings, in house-to-house collections. Word must have reached the owner of the house — Lady Pelham-Curtis, who was on the Belgian Relief Committee. Jennie liked Lady Pelham-Curtis, but had mixed feelings about Joey, who was a mischief-maker but fortunately seemed to like her.

Thousands of refugees arrived daily, hungry, thirsty and tired, stumbling off the boats and steamers in weakened condition, and the challenge of dealing with them became familiar. Early one morning in mid-September she was watching the disembarking passengers for signs of future trouble from the few who seemed to think they deserved a first-class trip to London to lodge in Buckingham Palace. As usual the steamer was packed, with standing room only. The well-dressed mingled with the shoeless peasants who seemed to have come straight from the fields. Few had possessions of any kind, and the old, the young, nursing mothers, wizened workers from the land, and shabby professionals jostled side by side to the point where the boat must have been dangerously overloaded. This had clearly been an exceptionally bad crossing, and she noticed one poor woman being half carried off the boat by a stalwart man. She was wearing what had once been an expensive coat, and suddenly Jennie felt a strange sense of familiarity. Then the woman raised her face.

It was Lady Fokingham.

With a cry of horror at her appearance, Jennie found herself running towards her, throwing her arms round her, half to support her, half in grief to see her in such a state.

Lady Fokingham didn't seem to know who Jennie was at first, but at last there was recognition in her face.

"Jennie?" she asked tentatively, as though looking at an apparition. Then she clung to her as though she would never let go, tears rolling uncontrollably down her face.

"Anna? Is she with you?" Jennie asked immediately. Could Anna possibly be somewhere in this heaving mass of dispossessed humanity?

Lady Fokingham shook her head, and Jennie didn't waste time with more questions, but instead led her to the receiving centre at St Michael's Hall, leaving her to one of the helpers, while she hurried back to her job. As soon as she was free, she returned to her, her mind racing with all the terrible alternatives.

"Jennie…" Lady Fokingham tried to say more, but her whole body began to shake again.

"Is Anna dead?" Jennie asked quietly, fearing the answer.

"No. No. I'll tell you. My husband — "

"I'll put a telephone call through to him if you give me the number, then we'll get you back to Applemere House." Before the war this would have been the easiest of tasks, but now who knew when the next train to Fairsted might run? Refugee trains ran to London via Ashford, not Fairsted or Elham to Canterbury. Jennie decided to telephone both Applemere House and her father — they could sort it out.

Applemere House had not yet been requisitioned, and this had caused murmurings in the village. Something seemed to be happening there, however, although no one knew quite what. There were still specials that mysteriously stopped at the Halt, with passengers who were promptly whisked away by horse and carriage or motor car.

"Will you be strong enough to travel alone to Fairsted?" she asked gently.

"I think so." Lady Fokingham hesitated. "Jennie, I'm so sorry, we misjudged you. I've wanted to say that — "

"Don't, please." Jennie could not bear it. She needed to live *now*, not in the past. "Just tell me about Anna. Where is she?"

"I don't know."

What on earth did she mean? Jennie stared at her in amazement, and Lady Fokingham tried to speak again. "She had twins, a boy and a girl. We found a home for them almost immediately, and because of the war we knew we should get home as best we could and as soon as we could. She recovered well, didn't seem to miss the babies, and we planned to come home by the Simplon Orient Express. Then at the last moment I found out it was no longer running because of the fighting around Paris, so I arranged for us to travel from Geneva to Marseille and take a boat to England. And then it happened."

"What did?" Jennie gently probed as Lady Fokingham's voice faltered.

"Anna simply vanished the day we were leaving, and so I missed the trains and connections we had planned. No one had seen her. It took days to find out that she had taken a train to Italy during the night. Apparently she was alone, with hardly any luggage. What could I do? I had no idea where she might be. Then the news of the war seemed so bad, I knew I should leave for my husband's sake. I managed to take various trains through France, anything that took me north-west, avoiding Paris, and eventually I reached Calais. Perhaps," she added hopefully, "Anna is already home."

"Perhaps," Jennie agreed comfortably, although it didn't seem likely to her. Whatever Anna's original plan had been, she had chosen a different path and neither her parents nor Jennie were included.

*

With the fall of Antwerp on October 10th, after a two-day siege, the Belgian coast fell into German hands and the last of the heavily laden boats came in to Folkestone. After that the Relief Committee turned to organizing the welfare of the

Belgians still in Folkestone, though in fact this was almost organizing itself since the institutions of the town took their own generous measures. Bobby's department store had donated seven of its staff houses in Sandgate Road for war work, first for refugees and now for mysterious British civilians who arrived from London. Lady Pelham-Curtis was highly amused.

"Spies sent to catch spies," she snorted. "Where better than Folkestone? Where better to communicate with their fellows in Holland and elsewhere?" With Belgium fallen, Holland was of vital importance, for it was taking no part in the war.

As the pressure diminished, Jennie felt oddly dissatisfied. Where next? Once working in Folkestone booking office would have been the pinnacle of her dreams, but now she was restless. There must be something else worthwhile that she could do.

With the worst over, she was allowed a precious two days off to travel back to Fairsted, and her heart leapt as she saw Aunt Win at the gate taking passengers' tickets. It seemed quite natural to see her there, as Jennie demurely displayed her travel warrant. Aunt Win gave a stifled scream, and then as the last passenger came through, gave her a hug, whispering, "I've some eggs for tea."

"The hens aren't at war yet then?" Jennie laughed.

"You'd think so, the stingy way Mrs Ovenden sells the eggs."

"Perhaps she's saving them to hurl at the Germans if they invade."

"No talk like that here, my girl," Aunt Win declared severely. "They're not going to. Our brave soldiers will see to that."

Perhaps they would, Jennie thought, but the numbers of ambulance trains that she knew had been meeting the steamers from France were increasingly disturbing.

*

Lady Fokingham still did not look well when Jennie went to see her the next morning. It was warm for an October day, and Lady Fokingham was sitting in the gardens. Applemere looked tidier than it used to, with some of the family touches Jennie had loved, such as the garden boots by the door, now banished.

"Has Michael joined the forces?" she asked Lady Fokingham. She couldn't ask about Anna immediately.

"No, the Foreign Office wants to keep him — liaison with the army and so forth. Oddly enough, he's working in Folkestone for a week or two. Just as well, there's hardly room here now."

No room? Jennie blinked. Applemere was huge. It must have twenty bedrooms at least. "Is it going to be a hospital?" she asked as innocently as she could.

"No, so far as the village is concerned, Applemere remains our home, but in fact the government needs it for special purposes. Don't ask me what, you know what the government's like." Lady Fokingham managed a brilliant smile but Jennie knew what it meant. Don't ask any more questions. And Michael in Folkestone? Could that have anything to do with those mysterious civilians arriving in Sandgate Road?

"Have you any news of Anna?" she asked anxiously.

Lady Fokingham's face clouded. "Not a word. She could even be in Montevanya. It would make sense — Italy, then by boat across to Greece."

That didn't sound like Anna to Jennie, but she didn't say so. The word Montevanya had sparked off another concern. The newspapers were full of stories about every country *except* Montevanya. Austro-Hungary had at last invaded Serbia on August 12th, and terrible atrocities had taken place, although the Serbian forces were still holding their own. The newspapers had been pleading for help for Serbia, and the Red Cross and other medical units were already out there, including the wife of the former British ambassador there, Sir Ralph Paget, who had launched the Serbian Relief Fund in London. All Serbia, nothing about Montevanya.

"Is there any news of Aunt Eileen?" Jennie pressed her. Surely Lady Fokingham of all people would have heard. "All I know is that she left Fairsted in June to return to Montevanya for Viktor's wedding."

"Jennie dear, that's one of the reasons I wanted to see you. Roumania is still neutral, and while that is the case, Montevanya can remain so too. Eileen did return for the wedding, but when Austro-Hungary invaded Serbia in August she went there to offer her services to one of the Red Cross units. When she heard that Leila Paget — Sir Ralph's wife — was coming out to Serbia herself, she decided to switch to her unit. I haven't heard since."

Immediately Jennie's anxiety over her aunt sparked a wild idea in her mind. Why shouldn't she go to join Eileen in Serbia? She could be more useful there than here, and even though she had no nursing training there must be other jobs she could do. She could be a driver perhaps. She had learned to drive in Folkestone, though the word learning hardly applied to her rudimentary training. She had done quite well — even if the volunteer teaching her had looked rather white as she climbed down from the motor car. There must be administrative jobs too, she reasoned.

"I admit I'm worried about Eileen, Jennie. I'd expected to hear from her. In her position she could be in danger."

"But no one would harm her, surely — not even the Austro-Hungarians, because of Prince Georgius." Jennie's alarm increased.

Lady Fokingham replied carefully. "She could be a diplomatic pawn, Jennie. There is a difficult situation in Montevanya. My brother and Max lean towards supporting the Allied powers in principle, as does Roumania, but Viktor is all for throwing his lot in with Germany and the Central Powers. At the moment Viktor can do nothing, but if Austro-Hungary takes Serbia, or Roumania capitulates, Montevanya could be overrun and my brother deposed, if not worse. Viktor would seize the throne as a puppet king. We still talk here of the war being over by Christmas, but I fear it might be a different matter in the Balkans. Old scores have still to be settled in Montevanya, for all its pleasant appearance before the war, and my family is in the midst of it. Suppose, Jennie, if it were your family, if battle raged round the Station House and you could do nothing to help. That's how I feel."

Jennie understood. She would be in just as much turmoil as Lady Fokingham obviously was, but she had to ask her gently: "Can you tell me more about who adopted Anna's babies?"

"We were fortunate enough — I think it made Anna a little happier — to find someone who would take both children."

"Who was it?" So Anna had suffered, Jennie realized. It was hardly surprising that her blasé attitude could not have withstood the emotional tug of the actual birth.

"The hospital would not allow us to know. It seemed better that way."

"For you perhaps, but for Tom, perhaps not," Jennie pointed out, trying to keep calm in her frustration. "Did she ever tell him about the twins?"

Lady Fokingham spread her hands hopelessly. "Think, Jennie. What good would that have done? And besides, suppose Anna was lying about Tom? Suppose she merely wanted to shock us by telling us Tom was the father? Even if he is, would he want the burden of bringing up two twin children alone? Anna has shown no signs of wanting to marry him. On the contrary. I fear that Anna used him for her own ends, as, in a smaller way, she used you."

The sore in Jennie's heart opened up again, and Lady Fokingham must have sensed it for she quickly added: "That doesn't mean she does not like you, Jennie. She likes you very much, but sometimes we use those we love for our own purposes, don't we?"

Did she? Jennie only knew that for her a line had been drawn under her life so far. Above it was Applemere. Below was the unknown — except that she now knew for certain where her path lay.

*

"You're very young." The woman looked at her severely over the top of her pince-nez. She made it sound a crime, as perhaps it was. The enquiries office at the Serbian Relief Fund in London's Queensgate was a busy place, and Jennie had been left in no doubt that they were overwhelmed with offers of help. Just *her* luck to get the one volunteer who looked as if she was the stickiest of the four in the room.

"I've been working in positions of responsibility for four years," Jennie replied firmly. If she didn't get past this first interview, she would never pass the committee itself.

"That, unfortunately, does not give you experience of *life.*"

Jennie wanted to laugh and cry all together. Life? This elegantly clad ancient totem pole looked unlikely ever to have

ventured into her own kitchen, let alone the battlefields of Serbia.

"Surely none of us gains experience until we begin, Mrs Hawker."

"You are still a young *gal*, my dear."

"Who has just spent several weeks organizing the Belgian refugees."

"Most praiseworthy," Mrs Hawker allowed graciously. "Unfortunately, the committee has to have rules and, while age itself might not *necessarily* be a barrier, you would need VAD nursing experience first."

Typical, Jennie fumed. If women offered government departments their skills where they were most needed they were told to go home and keep quiet. Fortunately all the women of vision were out there in the field already, as were people like Aunt Eileen or Lady Paget herself, but that left the volunteers, good and bad, in charge here.

"But," Jennie fought back, "if I can organize in Folkestone, I can organize anywhere in the world, and I didn't need VAD training for that job." The Voluntary Aid Detachments had been formed to provide extra nursing services for the thousands of expected war casualties.

"My dear Miss Trent, let me assure you VAD qualifications *are* necessary." The unspoken words were: *we are inundated with enthusiastic young girls who would be more hindrance than help.*

"I can drive," Jennie replied. "And cook. And organize."

"Perhaps, but you are too *young* for this particular unit."

Round and round the maypole. "Doesn't that mean I have more energy?"

"Perhaps, but it also means you might be — " Mrs Hawker coughed delicately — "in danger. I understand you would be operating very close to the Serbian army."

"Balkan countries have rules, too, particularly about guests in their country, and I assure you my virtue would be in no danger." Her temper was in real danger of slipping now.

It was a mistake, and she received a snappy reply. "I suggest you acquire VAD experience in a military hospital, Miss Trent, and come back to us in a year's time."

"By then my virtue would certainly be in no danger, for the war will be over."

"It follows," Mrs Hawker whipped back, "that there is little need to continue this conversation."

Jennie apologized, and the woman accepted it stiffly. But the damage was done. It was her first battle, and she had lost it.

*

Fokingham House, where Jennie had arranged to stay, bore little resemblance to the house she had once known. The house still maintained some rooms for the family, but the remainder was filled with Belgian refugees — under the surprisingly martinet eye of Gillyflower. Gone was the subservient governess of former years; Miss Gilchrist had come into her own in a position of authority.

The Belgian families — one to a room — were terrified of the lady, and with good reason, Jennie discovered. She arrived to find an altercation between two of the Belgian families, which Miss Gilchrist was umpiring with grim determination.

"fa *suffit*," she said to quell them as Jennie entered. "Quiet!" Her voice would have done justice to a sergeant-major at a spit and polish parade. "*Vous, monsieur. Parlez?*"

And Monsieur did. Meekly this time. The quarrel seemed to be over towels, and who had or had not requisitioned the one remaining large towel available for their use, but ended abruptly when Gillyflower pointed out that in exchange the two smaller towels should go to the other family. And. as a coup de grace, she added that both parties had been guilty of forgetting to close their green holland blinds for blackout restrictions.

"*Voulez-vous Germans ici? Les Zeppelins vont immediatement.*" That shut them up. The dreaded Zeppelin airships were a threat for the capital, expected to shower bombs down upon them, but so far nothing had happened. Even if it did, however, Jennie put her money on Gillyflower to ensure that Fokingham House survived.

"How nice to see you again, Imogen," Gillyflower greeted her warmly.

Considering the way they had parted only months ago, this seemed unlikely to Jennie. But this was wartime, and all was different. War was a fog, it was said, and one of the few nicer aspects was that old quarrels might be lost in it.

"Not for very long, I'm afraid." Jennie pulled a face. "I was sent off with a flea in my ear today. I'm too young, and I have no nursing experience, which apparently is essential for a driver or cook out there."

"Tck!" Gillyflower gave an exclamation of disgust. "It's all the same nowadays. You have to fight even to offer help. You go on fighting, Imogen dear. It's just the same with the food situation. I telephoned the butcher today, requiring a somewhat larger order, of course, and was denied it. It's for Belgian refugees, I told him with great indignation. My regulars come first, was his rude reply. The nerve of the man! I told him he should be at the front, and he told me if he was I wouldn't get any meat at all. So I told him that if Lord Kitchener, *whom I had met*, heard how he was denying food to refugees from gallant little Belgium he wouldn't *want* him at the front — and furthermore all his regular customers would be hearing about his attitude to those less fortunate than ourselves. I received my meat. A nice stew for you this evening, Imogen." A sideways glance. "Not Montevanyan."

A joke? From Gillyflower? "A pity. I was so looking forward to millet dumplings and stodge." Jennie laughed.

"Go back to this fund of yours, Jennie, that's my advice. Tell them you won't take no for an answer, or Lady Fokingham will hear of it."

Jennie was duly grateful, but Lady Fokingham would *not* hear of it. She would do this on her own.

*

Mrs Hawker heaved a sigh. "I have already refused ten ladies this morning and to you, Miss Trent, the answer is still no."

"Then I will come back every day until it is yes," Jennie said calmly.

Mrs Hawker was a match for her. "By all means, come back every day, Miss Trent," she snapped. "And each time you come, I will tell you as politely as I can that the answer is no."

"What *is* going on?" The door from the next office opened and a woman entered, clad in a familiar old-fashioned long

raincoat, and Jennie almost cheered with surprise and relief. Aunt Eileen had once more miraculously appeared in her life.

"A mere administrative matter, Mrs Dellon," Mrs Hawker greeted her.

"Oh, Jennie. In trouble again?" There was welcome warmth and love in her aunt's voice.

"I thought you were in Serbia, Eileen." Somehow the "aunt" had been lost for good.

"I was. And now I'm here," Eileen said briskly. "Jennie is my niece, Mrs Hawker, and I quite understand she must have been giving you trouble."

How unfair. Jennie suddenly wondered how this new persona, "Mrs Dellon", had come about. "I volunteered to help but Mrs Hawker believes I should have nursing experience first. I want to go to Serbia — "

"Why?" Eileen cut in coolly.

"To find you." Even Mrs Hawker found that funny, and, still seething with the injustice of it all, Jennie was forced to see the funny side too.

"And now?" Eileen enquired.

"I still want to go. I want to help. I can do lots of things, anything that's needed except nursing."

"But I agree with Mrs Hawker. You need VAD experience."

*

Jennie was fuming with frustration as Eileen accompanied her back to Fokingham House. Her aunt had stabbed her in the back. "Why did you take Mrs Hawker's side?" she demanded.

"You're too young. You do need training in nursing, because you have to know what the medical side is all about. Most importantly, though, you haven't asked me what *I* was doing in Serbia."

Jennie was aghast. "I'm sorry, I just forgot — "

Eileen brushed this aside. "That's understandable, but if you were genuinely interested in helping Serbia you would have pestered me with questions about it, and you have not. So I ask again, *why* do you want to go there?"

Her aunt's intelligent, weather-beaten face demanded she answer, and wretchedly Jennie sought to do so. Could she honestly claim it was because of Serbia's plight?

"A general need to help," she ventured.

"Without knowing what's it's like and being able to weigh up whether you're suitable or not? Mrs Hawker may be a battle-axe, but she is right. You're too young and inexperienced to judge whether you could help or merely be in the way." Jennie was silent as Eileen continued more gently. "I know about your tragedy. I can't help wondering whether it is not so much Serbia you want to help as Fairsted you want to avoid."

Misery flooded over her. "I went to Folkestone to escape Fairsted," she replied, "but that was the right thing to do

— and I made a success of it. Why should Serbia be different? How did you get there?"

"I have friends there from the old war days. So as soon as the Austro-Hungarians invaded in August, I went to see what I could do. I set up a hospital unit for the Serbian Red Cross at Kragujevatz, as Dr Soltau has done for the Scottish Women's Hospital, and Lady Paget in Skopje."

"Are you trained as a nurse?" Jennie was puzzled. Eileen's story made sense, and yet she had a feeling this was a carefully worded selection of the truth.

"Experience trained me in the earlier wars." Eileen smiled sweetly. "And experience also taught me that the leader of a unit has to know every side of it, not just leave it to others. One is respected for it, and, believe me, you *need* it, too."

"Why did you leave?"

"I was some way from the front, and arrangements for transport of the wounded were primitive to say the least. So at the battle at the Jader in August, I took two ambulances with doctors and equipment to form a flying unit at the front line at the River Drina, but then I was not so fortunate. Some of the unit was captured, including me. I worked under the name of Madame Dellon, but they discovered who I really was. I was interned while they gloated over what to do with me."

"Eileen! You've been in prison?" Now she was even more certain there was more to Eileen's story than she was telling.

"Not to put too fine a point on it, yes. Not an experience I would care to repeat, so it seemed sensible to escape. I made my way across the border and eventually back here. It was not easy without money, but in war people are kind as well as savage. It brings out extremes not dreamed of in peacetime."

Jennie wondered what on earth Aunt Win would make of all this, and, uneasily, what she, Jennie, would have made of it. Could she have coped? The first doubts crept into her mind. "Where are you going now, Eileen?"

"Montevanya — somehow. Georgius needs me and, I suspect, so does Stephen. I gather young Viktor is making martial noises."

"But how can you get back there?"

"It should be possible at present, from Salonika on the northern Greek Aegean coast, to Serbia and then up to Serbia's north-eastern boundary with Montevanya. While Bulgaria remains quiet, there is no danger on the Serbian eastern border. I gather the Austrians are making headway again on the other borders, though it looks worse this time. The Serbian army is retreating. Even Kragujevatz is under threat." Eileen suddenly switched tack. "Do you think you could face an active war front, Jennie?"

"Yes." She was sure of it.

"And could you stomach seeing limbs torn off, gaping wounds, bombs, bullets, the smell of gangrene, the constant battle for hygiene, the grieving widows and the constant demand for more essential supplies to help, which rarely come? Could you live side by side with soldiers, sharing their lives at the front line, their latrines, their jokes, the filthy stuff they smoke?"

"I could try," Jennie said valiantly, "and once I've tried, I *can*."

Eileen nodded slowly. "Very well. Get your VAD nursing experience here, which means not smoothing the brows and holding the hands of the wounded, but scrubbing floors, removing their urine and excrement pans, and standing by while gory operations take place. Help unload the ambulance trains at Charing Cross. Get acquainted with the smell of decay and death."

Jennie held her course. "And then?" she asked steadily.

"See what the situation is, and I'll use what influence I have to help. There might soon be no free Serbia to help any more, and you must be ready to help *anywhere*. Is that agreed?"

CHAPTER IX

Nineteen was not viewed as too young in the military hospital under Dr Louisa Garrett-Anderson in Endell Street, to which Jennie had been posted as a probationer by the VAD department. Indeed she was actually welcomed. She was not the most competent of probationers, but she did her best from the time she was awoken at six thirty until she fell exhausted into bed at ten thirty. Eileen's predictions came true: there was no smoothing of brows and rarely time for a friendly word, but there was a lot of sweeping floors, emptying buckets and treating suppurating wounds.

Jennie gritted her teeth and watched for her opportunity. Finally, in February, it came: she heard that the Serbian Relief Fund was financing another unit for Serbia under Mrs Muriel St Clair Stobart. This time she prepared for battle more cunningly than last autumn, by approaching Mrs Stobart direct. Thanks to Eileen, she knew the right cards to play and the stars seemed to be with her. She was successful, as the typhus epidemic now raging in Serbia meant there was a great need for extra helpers. A delay in arranging transport fortunately gave her time to leave Endell Street less abruptly than she had feared, and also to bid farewell to her family — without mentioning Eileen.

Tom was home for goodbye tea, but not Freddie. Tom was living in Canterbury now, so she appreciated his coming, despite her disappointment over Freddie, especially since she'd missed his eighteenth birthday in

September. "How is he?" she asked Tom while they waited for Dad and Win to join them. "Still shunting and shedding," Tom said dismissively. "Rather him than me. Devoted to the old railways is Freddie. Alice — remember her? — got tired of the competition, and she's walking out with Fred Brewster now."

"And you, Tom?" she asked awkwardly. Anna was still casting a long shadow between them.

"Thinking of getting married to Mary Patcher. Wanted to talk to you about it."

This seemed too good to be true. Jennie raked her memory. "Isn't she John Patcher's daughter? Your brewery's rival?" she asked guardedly.

"In a way." He caught her eye. "Got to look out for myself. Can't let anything stay in the way of true love."

"Provided it is true love," she said bluntly. "Is it?"

"You know me." Tom seemed unusually frank, which was mysterious. And then all was explained. "Thought I'd ask if there's any news of Anna before I tie the knot. I went to Applemere when her snooty ladyship was there, just to ask about her. She said they'd no idea where she is. Seems odd to me. Taken to Switzerland with tuberculosis and then her parents don't know where she is."

"It's true, so far as I know, Tom." Jennie was thinking desperately. She could not break that final promise, even though Tom must really have loved Anna if he had taken the trouble to find out about her. Jennie felt ashamed of her misjudgement of him.

"It takes a fair time to cure tuberculosis, and patients aren't up to running around thinking up ways to disappear." Tom was watching her carefully.

"Anna's a law unto herself. You know that."

"Do I? Well there's a thing, sister. I didn't know I *did* know Anna that well. I only called in on Applemere as a chum. You're the one who's thick with her."

Or used to be, Jennie thought sadly. She had pondered whether to visit Applemere or not before she left. The Fokinghams were in London, but Michael might be there and *might* be glad to see her. Once there she had felt her usual rush of affection for the house. She had remembered its gardens and the pool breaking into life in the spring. The wild daffodils would be in flower, and the violets and primroses by the woodland path.

A servant she did not know had opened the door. Michael was not there, and so she had walked away, disappointed. Irrationally, she felt rejected yet again. Applemere was closed, spring or no spring.

Now she struggled to think of Applemere from Tom's point of view. "Why don't you talk to Michael?" she suggested, defeated.

"Michael?" Tom seemed amused. "Think he'd pass the time of day with me? He thinks we're all slugs under his feet — even you, Jennie. *Especially* you. You be careful. You see all those Fokinghams as saints. Well, good luck to you. They've treated you like they treat me — like dirt. Judases, all of them."

*

The steamer from Liverpool was far different from stepping on board the Orient Express, and Jennie's khaki uniform and sturdy boots (essential for Serbia) were a poor substitute for her Sunday best that she'd worn on the luxury train. Was that only a year ago? It seemed hardly possible. Determined as she was to enjoy her first sea voyage, she missed much of it, laid low by seasickness, and was grateful when the party joined the train at

Salonika for the two-day journey past mountains and huge rivers, and through spectacular gorges.

By the time they reached Kragujewatz, their party of forty-five doctors and staff was a united one, and Jennie was aware that she had much to learn — even if she could drive. She consoled herself that every organization needed a "let me do that for you" person around. The whole unit was tented, high above the town, which, despite the cold and damp at nights, was far better, Mrs Stobart explained, than infected buildings. The typhus epidemic was still raging and, although Kragujewatz was the headquarters for the military, the front was luckily relatively quiet. Typhus was a greater enemy than even Austro-Hungary, and one that came by stealth.

Their tents were arranged in a sort of three-sided oblong; the administration and medical tents along the shorter top side, staff tents on one long arm and those of the patients facing them on the other. Even at Endell Street, Jennie had never worked so hard, nor been so tired, although here it was far more rewarding. She indeed helped in all departments, as well as driving military patients in the rickety ambulance over the rough roads (if that's what they could be called) or taking messages or requests to military HQ. Kragujewatz was set in the midst of rolling hills, whose greenery, together with the blossom in the fruit orchards, made it hard to believe that the battlefront was close to them.

There was an unexpected bonus for her when Eileen arrived mysteriously one day after visiting her former unit, which was now part of Lady Paget's unit at Skopje. The epidemic was particularly bad there.

"Country people are dying in their thousands," she told Jennie soberly, "but the staff are completely selfless.

There's one orderly whom the Serbs call Dr Dobro-Dobro, who was indefatigable, not only in caring for the sick, but ensuring their families didn't starve to death. A remarkable man."

Dr Dobro-Dobro — Dr Good-Good was what that meant. Jennie knew that *dobro* didn't just mean good, but, like its counterpart *dobru* in the Montevanyan language it signified strong approval. She had a vision of a saintly grey-haired man with a halo round his head. She was to hear his name so often from Eileen's lips that she grew heartily sick of it. This saint had won his spurs; she still had to do so. She knew it wouldn't be long before the test came. Last December the Austrians had actually taken the Serbian capital, Belgrade, in the north of the country, before they were repulsed, and that couldn't last.

One spring evening there was an extra-large group of visitors to the camp when King Peter's son, Crown Prince Alexander, the new Regent of Serbia, came with attaches of seemingly every nation in the world. Certainly Jennie didn't recognize most of the languages being spoken. The kitchen was hard pressed to cope but turned up trumps. Stew, of course, but a delicious one that had more than a touch of local wines or spirits in it.

The convalescent patients, eager to impress, decided to put on an entertainment for the royal visit. Not to be outdone, Jennie decided in honour of the King's presence to don a skirt once more. She had become used to wearing breeches, and tried not to think of Aunt Win's shocked expression if she'd seen them. Jennie was sharing a tent with Eileen now, just as they had shared a room at the Station House, as Eileen had remarked.

"In a way," Jennie conceded wryly. Their eyes had met. Nothing was like the Station House, tucked away from the world, a rock to cling to when the future seemed so uncertain.

The good feast meant the mood for entertainment was right, and its audience sat in the warm open air, while the patients organized themselves. Jennie watched Eileen deep in conversation with the Crown Prince, wondering what they were talking about. Considering she was a mere foreign relief worker, he seemed uncommonly interested in what her aunt was saying.

Jennie quickly realized why Eileen had looked amused when she said she was looking forward to the entertainment. This seemed to consist solely of ordeal by gusla. This instrument, whose melancholy sounds she had often heard in the camp, looked like the Montevanyan version of the balalaika, but it did not sound like it. It only had one string, and was plucked with a bow. It sounded like a cat yowling, though after plenty of wine it had its own charm, she supposed. One patient after another sang or played lengthy plaintive melodies, which had many of the Serbs in tears.

Then someone else stepped forward who didn't look Serbian to Jennie, although he was dressed in khaki, but the Serbs didn't seem to mind his requisitioning a gusla. He proved to be adept at it, and his voice was low, musical and seductive, and he was applauded vigorously.

"*Dobro, dobro,*" came the shout.

Eileen craned her head to look more closely. "It *is* Dr Dobro-Dobro!" she exclaimed with delight, and Jennie peered curiously at this saint.

"Does applause make him Dr Dobro-Dobro-Dobro?" she asked mutinously, wine making her head swim.

Eileen looked at her reproachfully. "He's a good man," she said quietly.

The saint was not grey haired, and wore no visible halo. He was quite tall, young, thin and dark haired. He did have lovely blue eyes, Jennie conceded, just right for singing mournful songs of the homeland. Eileen had told her that he was English, or perhaps Welsh, and Jennie wondered what had brought him here.

Then she forgot him as the *kolo* dance began. A ritual, but tonight more exuberant than ever. Men only, of course. The gusla began to play, two men began to dance with linked arms, and then more and more men joined them, each linked to the others — including the saint, she noticed. This evening, as a great honour, the women were eventually beckoned to join in. She and Eileen were swept into the slow but exhilarating shuffle, and sounds of *dobra, dobro* echoed through her dreams that night.

*

As spring passed into summer, the typhus epidemic raged on and, to their great alarm, Mrs Stobart caught typhoid fever. She recovered, but several of the nurses were less lucky, and their funerals were hard to bear. How easily it could have been her, Jennie thought soberly, and how terrible for them and their families. With such poverty and sickness in the countryside, Mrs Stobart set up roadside dispensaries in country areas to relieve their suffering, one of which, at a village called Rakova about twenty-five miles away, Eileen was deputed to organize. Jennie was promptly allotted the ox cart to drive since the six new ambulances sent from England had been held up in Salonika through red tape.

Driving oxen was not her favourite job, but it seemed worth it, for the next day at dawn crowds were already assembling at the tented roadside dispensary. Disease, broken limbs, sores were all attended to and now Jennie blessed those months at Endell Street, for she too could take part in some of the minor procedures.

With the autumn of 1915 came the bad news that the dispensaries would have to close, however. There were rumours of mass troops assembling on the Danube, and the Serbian army was mobilizing once more for all-out war. Events escalated quickly and the next weeks were only a blur for Jennie, from the first moment that Eileen told her she was to run another flying hospital unit for the Schumadia division at the eastern front, where the Bulgarians were massing their troops on their border with Serbia. An extra driver was needed, and Jennie immediately volunteered.

The First Serbian English Field Hospital (Front), as the unit was designated, boarded a train (oxen, carts and ambulances included) early one morning for Pirot in the east. Though the camp they set up a day later was much like she was used to, the sight of the massed army in the valley was a reminder that this peace would not last long. Soon Bulgaria would attack; that was obvious. And yet Jennie felt quite calm. This is what she had come for. If the Corby brothers could volunteer to face the enemy on the Western Front, then she could do the same here. If Jack had lived, he too would probably be at the front. She was here in his place, that was all.

"I have good news," the colonel had said to Eileen. The English and French troops were now landing in Salonika and would be coming to help immediately. The danger was that otherwise the Serbian army could be caught in a trap of three fronts all closing in from different directions: Germany from the west, Austria from the north and Bulgarians here in the east.

"Let us hope he's not disappointed over the British," Eileen commented soberly. "It's our only hope."

Jennie shivered. It was an ominous forecast as news reached them that fighting had broken out on all fronts. The orders for the division changed daily. They were withdrawn from the Bulgarian front and sent to the north. The nearer the train steamed, the clearer the sounds of distant gunfire could be heard. No one had seen the British and French forces despite the flags in all the towns to greet them. The division's slow railway journey north then stopped well south of Belgrade, as the Serbian army retreated under the onslaught from the Central Powers. As their unit set up roadside tented hospitals, civilian refugees were streaming along the road and the noise of battle grew ever nearer. Red Cross ambulances from the front ferried the wounded to their camp, where they were immediately tended by the medical helpers, some their own, others from evacuating units further north. Jennie ran a continuous ferrying service herself, evacuating as many wounded as possible by ambulance to Palanka hospital south of where they had camped.

Those too seriously wounded to travel stayed in the tents for what help they could give them, and the dead, of which there were many, lay outside the tents for burial. Driving was a nightmare, for the roads were knee deep in mud, and ambulances jolted and stuck continually.

By the time Jennie returned from Palanka on her last ambulance trip it was about eleven at night. Orderlies were digging graves for the dead, and nurses were working flat out in the tents with the doctors. There would be no more trips tonight but at dawn it would begin again. Eileen was nowhere to be seen, and Jennie forced herself into a tent to see what help she could give there. She fetched and carried, too busy even to care about her nausea.

And then she saw a patient lying on a stretcher awaiting attention, pale and still. *It was Jack*, she thought instantly. Her heart pounded until she realized it wasn't him, although the features and the light-coloured hair were painfully similar. It was all too much, and she ran out, taking in huge gulps of air. Not Jack. It wasn't Jack. Of course it wasn't. He lay in Fairsted, and she was here, in the middle of a nightmare.

"What's wrong?" A male orderly in the tattered remains of a medical jacket seized her none too gently by the arm. "You're needed inside. Don't just gaze at the stars. Come and help, for God's sake."

She recognized him because of those steady blue eyes. It was Dr Dobro-Dobro. The saint. Well, she wasn't a saint. She *couldn't* go back in there and look at Jack's face again — not anybody's face.

"I can't...I can't," was all she could stammer.

He looked at her with contempt. Then dig a grave to bury them. Serbian soldiers like to be buried by the roadside so that passers-by don't forget them. But you forget them before they're even dead. Proud of yourself?"

"I can't do it," she repeated dully. Blood, limbs, wounds all swam before her face, followed by Jack's reproachful face.

Dr Dobro-Dobro just went back inside and left her. She was sick, very sick, then with a great effort she forced herself back into another tent, not the one where "Jack" lay. Later that evening she saw his body with the others, waiting for burial.

For her the cock had crowed twice. She had failed Jack, and she had failed here.

CHAPTER X

"What will you do?" Jenny asked Eileen quietly. No word had been said, although for three weeks now they had been steadily retreating south with the enemy on their heels and to left and right while the Serbian army fought desperate rear-guard actions. Eileen had been prevented by the suddenness of the attack from returning to Montevanya across its short border with Serbia.

Eileen shrugged. "The war has changed. There are no rules now. These armies shoot refugees, men, women and children — anyone and anything that moves. They're trying to wipe out Serbia for good by driving out or killing its people and destroying the towns and the land itself." Her face wrinkled in sadness in the light of the camp fire, necessary now that it was well into November. "There's a wonderful saying in Montevanya. "Ask Allah, for He is the boss." So I did, and He replied that if I tried to reach the Danube I would die one way or the other. There are other ways to reach Montevanya, He pointed out. If I could reach the Black Sea and then the Bosporus..."

"Past Gallipoli and Turkey?" Jennie interrupted, appalled. Everyone knew of the disastrous campaign being fought at Gallipoli in order to keep the Bosporus open. What chance did one lone woman stand? Quite a bit, if that woman was Eileen.

"With Roumania neutral it would be dangerous, but possible," Eileen continued.

"But we don't yet know where we are going."

"I can guess. There is only one hope for us — to slip down to Monastir and on to Salonika through the narrow corridor between the Bulgarians advancing from the east and the Germans from the west and north. But we move so slowly."

Jennie hardly needed telling. Slow progress was all that was possible, with driving the cars and ox carts on roads several feet deep in mud. Add to that the sheer length of a convoy with 200,000 military, including the wounded, let alone the civilian refugees, baggage carts, wagons and animals. It required just one ox to decide to lie down across these narrow paths between mountain ranges to hold up the whole column.

Camping was sometimes in towns, more often by the roadside, sleeping in the cars and eating round their own camp fires. Jennie had, to her pleasure, proved amazingly good at the chore of lighting and tending these for the cooks — thank you, Aunt Win. With the smell of food — of a sort — in the air, even retreat seemed possible, surrounded by the vibrant colours of the hills and countryside and with the stars above. They'd seen so much, they seemed to offer a protection far above the routine daily problems. Nevertheless, tomorrow at first light it would begin again: the trek to the next official stopping place, arranged by the military, to provide — in theory — shelter and supplies. Thousands and thousands would have preceded them when their unit arrived, however, and even though they were officially part of the army and had priority as a hospital, theory and practice were different things.

If only the British forces would arrive. No one spoke any more about this. The Serbs bore their disappointment stoically and with dignity. "They have been prevented by the Bulgarians," they would say, yet they still clung to this one hope of saving Serbia, even though the enemy was so close on their heels.

"Do you think we are heading for Monastir, Eileen?" No one *knew* where they were going; the division just followed the convoy. Monastir was the Serbian town on the border with Greece, and was where the British troops were thought to be.

"There'll have to be a decision when we reach Pristina," Eileen replied briskly. "Either we travel to the south to Monastir, which means the Serbian army can rally or, if that road is blocked by Bulgarians, we go westwards, over the mountains into Montenegro and the sea. But that means Serbia will be destroyed, and who knows if and when the army and refugees can ever return."

Eileen seemed so matter-of-fact that Jennie stayed silent. The rage and frustration inside her that such terrible things could happen remained unspoken. This was the world she had confidently wanted to rule on her twelfth birthday — and look at it.

All the while the rear-guard fighting continued to protect the column, the unit was still operational. No sooner were their tents set up than the Red Cross wagons would appear from the battlefield with the wounded, to be treated as best they could and carried onwards.

Jennie battled on, pinning her thoughts on reaching Pristina, as though reaching that goal alone marked some kind of achievement. As time passed there was less talk of the British coming, which meant there was little chance that the road to Monastir would be open. There had been talk amongst the soldiers that to the British Serbia was always seen as the aggressor and not a victim as Belgium was; they did not see the Serbians, as Jennie now did, as home-loving, poetic, gentle folk who only turned into formidable soldiers when their homes were threatened. War changed people, she realized. It revealed frailties and it built strengths. Even hers. Jennie had tried hard to put that incident with Dr Dobro-Dobro at Palanka from her mind, but his words still stung keenly.

Applemere lingered on in Jennie's fractured dreams. The house had stood there for hundreds of years, set in its quiet gardens and silent pools. It was not conventionally beautiful or impressive. And yet she loved it, as did Eileen. Here shivering in the November frosts, she remembered the sun streaming in through the morning-room windows, the dining room with its ancient battered furniture, and the wooden panelling that had been lovingly carved into life by unknown hands. She remembered the newel posts with the carved shepherd surmounting them, and the door with the carved knights chasing each other on horseback up and down its length. She clung to the thought that, even in this mayhem, Applemere was slumbering on peacefully.

"*Ide!*" *she* shouted at her ox. Terry was her favourite ox since he had a character all his own, lumbering only for exactly an hour then stopping, wherever he was, until goaded onwards. She had managed to strike up a rapport with him — or so it seemed — so that he knew exactly when she *really* meant it was time to move, and she always ensured she got Terry to drive. That's how he got his name, from the Serbian for hurry up, "terrai".

"*Ide!*" she shouted again at poor Terry. "Get going." And the ox did.

At last they approached Pristina, but there were still no orders as to which way the unit should go. When they did receive them, they were two days behind the rest of the column and the sounds of gunfire from behind were deafeningly close.

"We're taking the western route," Eileen told her glumly. "Over the mountains to Montenegro."

Terry and Jennie formed a steady companionship as they concentrated on the boulders and mud that constituted the way forward. She seldom saw Eileen until the evening as they plodded onwards, constantly stopped by rivers, mud and ploughed fields. And they had not yet even reached the dreaded high mountain tracks. Jennie fancied she saw reproach in Terry's eyes as she forced him onwards, and informed him that she understood but there was nothing she could do. At the next major stop, Petch, orders came that the carts had to be cut in two and most baggage dumped and burned. Only the forward half of the cart would stand any chance of getting over the mountains.

"*Nema, nema,*" came the reply when Jennie passed this order on to Serbian soldiers.

"*Ja, ja,*" she insisted firmly. The Serbian answer to everything was "not a chance", just like the Montevanyan *nemu*, but one had to insist. It was rather like ordering Freddie down from the footplate when he was younger.

Ahead lay the Montenegrin mountains, and over the other side was freedom — but how far away? And what kind of freedom?

The track was only two feet wide at best, and the higher they went was not visible at all; they followed only the tracks where people and animals had passed before them. Upwards they climbed, through rivers, through snow, over ice, over rocks, in silence. At least there was supper for them; for the animals there was little, for there was no hay available. Even when there was a village or town nearby to which they could make a detour, there were no supplies to be had. At night there were fires at least to provide warmth and comfort, but in the day death was starkly with them. Oxen and horses, women, children and men lay dead by the roadside. The column stopped for nothing. One took one's own chances. Through it all, Terry plodded on. At night there was no thinking in terms of man and woman, only of removing one's boots and lying down. And still the mountains stretched out before them, an endless fight with snow, rocks and ice.

One morning, when Jennie thought she could go no further, she glanced ahead to see before her appalled eyes Eileen's pony slipping off the side of the mountain, throwing Eileen off. Almost in slow motion she watched aghast as it slithered down. The column could not halt, but Jennie thrust Terry's reins into a soldier's hands, so that she could slide down to where she could see Eileen lying face-down in the snow.

"*Ide*," Jennie cried fatuously, to herself as much as to Eileen, slipping, hurting herself on the rocks, buried in snow, and aware of the chasm beneath. At last she reached her aunt, dreading what she would find, and was relieved when Eileen opened her eyes and managed to get to her feet. Eileen's ankle was sprained, but somehow they scrambled up to rejoin the column passing by them like the souls of the dead. Terry was far ahead, and it was nightfall before Jennie found him again, and was amazed at her relief. He was her good-luck talisman. Once at the night camp, willing hands took care of Eileen.

"After what you've done for me, Jennie," Eileen said, "you can look Mrs Hawker in the face."

Not only Mrs Hawker, but Dr Dobro-Dobro, Jennie thought. It was a small contribution towards restoring her faith in herself.

At the Station House they would be preparing for Christmas, wondering where she and Eileen were. Far better that they did not know. It would be a darker Christmas than last year in Fairsted, for the war was still raging on the Western Front. Aunt Win would still be making the Christmas pudding, though.

Tonight the tinned beef tasted just as good to Jennie as the goose, and the tea like the finest nectar. At least she was alive, and so was Eileen.

Terry grew weaker by the day, a mere skeleton compared to what he had been. The small communities they passed had no hay or food to spare and even if they had, they would not part with it. Jennie watched him anxiously, urging him on, whispering in his ear, and he seemed to rally. But then one day he just keeled over beside her. Bending down at his side, still holding the reins, she knew he was dead. Hundreds of thousands of people and animals had died, but she had expected Terry to go on for ever. Even now she couldn't believe it, but soldiers behind her simply pushed him to the edge of the path to clear the way, tore the bags from the dead body, put them in her arms and swept her on.

As she stumbled onwards, the first tears she had shed since they began this trek shook her body. Ridiculous, she thought, to weep for Terry as she had not done for herself or for Eileen, or for the nurses and soldiers she had seen die. The whole senseless war seemed to be summed up in the plight of one animal.

She was on the point of despair. The next slip and she surely would not have the strength or will to fight any longer. And then it happened.

"What is it? she asked her neighbour wearily. A whisper reached her, a soft shushing sound that she could make no sense of, until at last she was at the top of the last incline, and there before them was the plain. In the far distance were more mountains, but still came that shushing sound of voices. Fingers pointed to a gap in the distant mountains where the sun shone. Then she realized what the shushing was.

"*Scutari!*" Their destination. From the port of Medina, only two days' journey from there, there would be a steamer to Brindisi in Italy. And then home, blessed home. All of Montenegro to cross first, but there in the distance was Scutari. There was hope.

It was December 16th, and they had been in the mountains for over three weeks. Now, with renewed energy, they descended into the town they could see in the valley. The welcome was surly because, as usual, it was overflowing with army personnel. With no cars or tents to sleep in now, they were forced to share a large barn with what seemed like half the army.

Mrs Stobart's firmness achieved the women a section at the far end. Jennie wondered briefly how Aunt Win would have reacted to this, but was too tired even to smile at her answer as she nipped outside the barn for the usual non-existent sanitary arrangements, before the longed-for sleep.

As she came back into the barn, however, she felt her arm seized by a soldier in tattered uniform. Indignantly she threw it off as she came face to face with him. She couldn't see much, for his face was covered by his army cap and lengthy beard. But the dark eyes seemed familiar.

"Jennie. Miss Imogen…"

It was a long time since she had heard that voice, and her senses reeled. *Here*? This grim-faced soldier in the remains of a khaki uniform was looking as startled as she was.

"Prince Max?" she half choked.

"No prince here. No kingdom save a barn, Miss Jennie."

"We'll get there," she replied automatically, repeating the phrase that had become a litany throughout the long hard days and nights. *"Terrai,"* she managed to add brightly. Onwards. Hurry up.

"Where, Jennie. To Montevanya?" There was a bitter note in his voice.

"Eileen wants to return there through Roumania, if she can reach the Black Sea."

"Madame Szendescu is here?" he asked incredulously. "Of course. She would be. But you, Jennie Trent. What of you? Come, sit down with me."

She found herself sitting on the ground, aware her clothes were stiff with mud, unchanged for weeks, and no doubt smelling — but then everyone did. Her back was comfortably resting against the wood of the barn, with the latrines area to their right and the mountains of Montenegro to their left. Above them were the stars and the moon in the dusky sky, and she could see Max's face. Not the face of the self-confident, proud prince she had once known, but a new Max, disillusioned, tired, exhausted by the trek. But more than that, there was a hopelessness about him that surprised her. So she began to talk about how she came to be there, about Eileen and the refugees and the work in Kragujewatz.

"Now tell me about you," she said quietly, and she felt him take her hand. This was no dance in a large castle ballroom, but it gave her a comfortable feeling of unity for this brief moment in the middle of war.

"I was in Kragujewatz with the Crown Prince when the Germans attacked. There were urgent political decisions to be made about my country."

"Viktor?" she guessed.

"Yes." His hand tightened on hers. "My father wanted Serbia to ally with us in case Viktor's following became too strong. But the war came first, and now the British do not." He said it matter-of-factly but it was clear how deep the wound was. "The Serbian army fights alone. I received instructions from my father to reach the British to plead with them to come to Serbia's aid. They say they do not have enough forces to break through the Bulgar lines, but I was to point out that if Serbia could not save itself, then Montevanya could fall to the enemy, too, and Roumania would follow suit. The whole of eastern Europe would belong to the Central Powers. So I travelled with the King's party."

"King Peter is here? But he is an old man." Jennie was horror-stricken.

"Not in this barn." Max managed a smile. "He has come over the mountains carried on a litter borne by bullocks and now by men. Crown Prince Alexander was with him, and with them travelled the casket with the remains of Stefan Prvovencani, the first King of Serbia, seven hundred years ago. If this sacred relic is safe, the army believes that Serbia will rise again, and not submit to defeat. Their homeland will be re-won."

"And what of Montevanya now?" Jennie imagined the peasants she had seen there in the same state as these poor Serbian refugees.

"It might already be too late. I don't know. I only knew I must reach the Allies, but if I took the road to Monastir and could not get through, it would have been too late to return to this escape route, as the Germans and Austrians are so closely behind us. I could not risk being captured. My father needs me. And that is how, Miss Imogen, I am here with you — once more in the night." Another squeeze of her hand. "Now tell me of that sweetheart of yours. Are you married? Does he weep for you at home, or on the Eastern Front — is that why you are here?"

She had tried to keep it back but it did not seem so important to do so now. "Jack died," she said calmly, "before the war began. It was my fault. He died because I could not make up my mind to marry him and he thought I did not want to."

"And did you?"

"I suppose not. And that, Max, is what I am doing here."

"Thank you," he said quietly.

"For what?" she asked surprised.

"For the Max. The time for princes is past."

"Between us?"

"In every way. War makes us all equal. There must be leaders, and whether they are generals or kings or prime ministers seems not to matter now. Viktor and I thought ourselves so grand in our officers' uniforms, and that is what I wore when I came to the Crown Prince, but I was ashamed, for by then I could see what war really meant. I changed it for the khaki of the Serbian army. The Regent approved, and so did the King. Now, Jennie, again tell me of you. You are a nurse?" She shook her head. "I do everything. I'm a general VAD orderly. I drive the cars when there are cars; I drive the oxen when there are oxen; I make fires and I cook when there are none of these. I hold bandages and do what I can."

"Why here, Jennie? Why not in France?"

With the stars above, with danger before and behind them, perhaps she saw at last why she was here. "Because of Montevanya."

"Explain, please."

"Montevanya was a happy place, so it seemed to me. It seemed to have balanced politics and religion. I thought if I was helping Serbia I might be helping to keep your country safe and to help my own as well."

He let her hand go and put his arm round her. "Happy? When we were so unkind to you, little Jennie?"

"That was a mistake."

"Was it? We made fun of you, Viktor and I. We thought of you as just a little English peasant girl pretending to be a grand lady. You remember that night of the ball, Jennie?"

It seemed far away. "Of course."

"Your aunt was right," he continued soberly. "Had she not come in, I would have taken you as you lay there, looking so beautiful."

She managed to laugh. "You wouldn't touch me with a bargepole now. Look at me, covered in smelly mud, unwashed and no change of clothes for weeks."

"You are wrong. You are truly beautiful now, Jennie. It shines out of your eyes. You are the princess now, and I and Viktor the peasants. Viktor with his stupid dreams of being part of the Kaiser's mighty empire; I with my failed mission. The soldier with the impeccable jacket who has not yet won his right to wear the soil and stain of battle, only to retreat."

"You will, Max." She would think later of what he had said; now she only felt a great tiredness.

"I would like to kiss you, Jennie, as I kissed you once before, for I doubt if we'll meet again. Only this time it is for you, and not in jest." He drew her towards him and she smelled the rough tang of his uniform, then his lips were on hers. The touch of a human being, the touch of their lips, and she returned his kiss as though the future of the world depended on their loving touch.

"Your cheek is wet, Jennie. Are you crying for what is gone?"

She did not know, but after she returned to her allotted space in the loft, it was some time before she fell asleep.

*

It took several more days before they reached Scutari. By now it was nearly Christmas, and they had learned that the whole of Serbia was now under the control of the Central Powers.

"And Montevanya?" she asked Eileen anxiously.

"Still neutral, though goodness knows how much longer it can hold out."

"Where will you go now?" That was the burning question Jennie had been longing to ask. She and the other staff were going back to Britain for convalescence, but the army was travelling on French ships to Corfu to regroup and convalesce, and then to join the British and French forces at Salonika.

"Max and I will take our chances together to reach Montevanya. I am of more use there than drinking tea at Claridges, don't you agree?"

She missed her aunt sorely after she had gone. During the journey home by boat and train, and surrounded by her friends in the same condition, Jennie thought nothing of her tattered clothes until she saw the stares when they stopped at railway stations in Italy. In Rome it was particularly noticeable. These well-dressed ladies had no idea what war was. Jennie was even still wearing her breeches underneath a long tunic, and worn clothes were the unit's badge of service.

Nevertheless, Jennie was conscious of one pair of eyes gazing intently at her on Rome station. She smiled to herself and was about to mount the train after her friends when something made her look round. A whisk of movement, and the woman had turned her back and was running up the stairs to the exit.

It was Anna.

Jennie was certain of it. She leaped from the train and rushed after her, but by the time she reached the top of the stairs there was no one in sight. Anna — if indeed it was her — had vanished.

CHAPTER XI

Jennie's first tea at home began so easily. It seemed as if she had never left, with just Dad, Aunt Win and herself, sitting round the familiar table eating scones and salmon-paste sandwiches.

"Just look at the state of you," Aunt Win had said fondly, tears streaming down her face, before Jennie was allowed even to have a cup of tea. "You get those clothes off you — and straight into the ragbag with them. Mind you, you're as skinny as a rake; any decent clothes will fall off you now."

"I can't ragbag these. Official uniform," she had managed to laugh, half choking with emotion at the reunion. She felt like a child again. The old bath had been tugged out, and Dad forbidden to enter the kitchen until she was scrubbed *really* clean.

If only they realized that privacy was a state of mind, not layers of clothes. The Serbian retreat had taught her that. The body was the mind's servant, but, like any servants, could rebel if asked to do too much. Luxuriating in the old tub she could see the scars that the ordeal had left on her; the scrapes and cuts had healed quickly in the cold, but left their marks, and there were other less definable signs in the face that stared back at her from the mirror. Max had called her beautiful — was this body of hers beautiful? She'd expected to share it with Jack, but many mountains had been crossed since then. Jack had been dead for nearly two years, and that wound had also healed, even if its scar, as those of the retreat, still remained.

"Where have you been, Jennie, or can't you tell us?" Dad asked as he passed her favourite cup to her — the bone china one with the daffodils on it, which had belonged to his grandmother. He looked older now, she thought, and Aunt Win too. Or was it just that now she had the eyes to see them?

"I was on the retreat." She looked from one to the other, but saw no sign of comprehension. "Serbia," she added. Still nothing. "The Serbian army had to trek over the mountains to escape the Austrians and Germans, together with the half the population — "

"I hope you wrapped up well," Win said immediately. "It can get very cold up high."

"It did," Jennie said solemnly. "The snow was two or three feet deep most of the time, and the ice was very dangerous. But the camp fires were nice — and eating our dinner round it." That sounded wrong, but where were the words to bridge this gap?

"Eating in the snow?" Aunt Win was trying hard to grapple with this cosy picture.

"Yes." What to say next? "The army — it was a great tragedy — is going to Corfu, an island off the coast of Greece, to recover."

"Sounds a bit warmer there," Dad contributed.

"Yes." Jennie struggled on. "And then the troops will probably go to Salonika, where the British and French are."

"Our lads will see them through," Dad said approvingly. Jennie fought against both tears and an inane desire to giggle, and her father must have picked this up for he added quietly: "Had a hard time, did you, pet?"

She felt her lip wobbling. What could she say?

"Tell us, Jennie," Aunt Win urged. "We'll understand."

How to convey the sheer nightmare of constant death and the battle for life so often lost, the horrific wounds made by man and the gruesome carcasses betrayed by nature? All that came from her trembling lips was: "My ox died."

There was a silence, which finally Dad broke. He cleared his throat. "See the price of bread's gone up again, Win." Jennie's tears won then, and she was shaken with heavy sobs until Aunt Win took her firmly up to bed. "And that's where you stay, my girl, till you're rested. I'll bring you some nice hot broth later, and then you can get a good night's sleep." She did, but not until she had looked through her window on to the world outside. She had wanted to rule it. But not now. Fairsted was world enough for her.

*

It was like looking at the village through the wrong end of a telescope. She was there, but removed from it. There was a new air of business about it. Fairsted was no idyllic paradise, and had known trouble, but that had always been contained within itself. "This is what I am," it had seemed to say, "and this is how I shall stay." No longer.

Women were now tending crops and animals, serving in shops, and those men who were strolling around were in uniform, convalescents at the manor hospital. The Plough no longer opened all day, but only at dinnertime and in the evening, then shut early. Everyone complained at the weak beer.

Everyone complained about everything, in fact, and yet there was a cheerfulness about it, as they though almost relished the struggle.

The railway, too, had changed. Fairsted station, she had quickly discovered, was no longer a backwater, just a branch of a country branch line — the Twig, as Tom sneeringly used to call it.

"What are all these trains?" she had asked, bewildered at breakfast on her first morning back. After the initial heavy use of the line after the outbreak of war the traffic had more or less returned to normal.

"We're a main line now," Aunt Win said, whisking around in her uniform to clear the table before hurrying to her booking office post. "Most of them don't stop here, but the signals — " She stopped short.

"It's all right, Aunt Win," Jennie said gently. "It's a long time ago. What's this about a main line?"

Win looked relieved, and glanced at Dad, who coughed to presage an important announcement. "Big accident last month," he told her gravely. "Half the cliff came down at Folkestone Warren while a train was passing. No one killed, which was a mercy, but the train was swept away with the chalk. The track's gone too, and no sign of it being repaired. A tragedy it was."

The dead waiting for burial at the side of the road; the dead tossed to the side of the pathway, the haggard starving faces of men and beasts...

"So the line from Dover to Folkestone is closed, and all the trains have to come round the long way. Goods, troops, ambulance, the lot," Dad continued.

"Your father's working too hard with only Percy to help, and he'll be going soon if they call him up," Win commented. "Only one man in the signal box. Betsy and I lend a hand to your father, but it's hard work. That's what war brings."

Old women trudging over high mountains in the ice and snow, their menfolk dead, their children scattered, their homes destroyed...

"And keep your windows blacked out," Jennie heard Aunt Win say. "We try to keep them pulled on the trains but it's hard work; a Zep will get one one day, you mark my words."

"The Zeppelins came, then?" Jennie asked. When she had left last April they were a bogey yet to materialize. Everyone knew what they would look like though: cigar-shaped silver monsters that came by night, airships supplied with bombs to drop where they chose.

"Oh, they came," Dad told her. "Bombed half of London, right in the middle of theatreland, in the autumn. The Lyceum and the Gaiety got it."

Kolo dancing, the gusla, men singing of their homeland, Anna at Daly's...

She began to feel faint and to sway. Aunt Win must have stopped her table-clearing for suddenly she was supporting her and clicking in disapproval. "You shouldn't have told her about the accident, George. It's all too much for her. It's the shock. She won't have seen anything like those Zeps out there."

Aeroplanes bombing armies and villages alike, tented hospitals rushing their wounded away, destroying the land...

Jennie made a huge effort. Before her she saw the two of the three faces she loved best and realized the fault was in her, not them. What this war was doing to them was just as important, just as traumatic, as what she had seen in Serbia. While she was here she must live by the rules of what she saw here. She must share Fairsted life and put everything else aside.

"I'll help you on the station while I'm here," she offered.

"While you're here?" Aunt Win's face fell. "You're not off again?"

"I don't know." Jennie was appalled. That sentence had slipped out naturally, she hadn't even thought what she would do next, so what did those words imply?

"Everything's changed," Win lamented. "We had a card from Eileen, though."

"In Montevanya?" Jennie asked joyously, without thinking.

"What would she be doing there?" Win looked startled, as well she might.

Jennie could have kicked herself. "It's still neutral, so she might have made her way there."

"I wouldn't know about that. Her postcard was a lovely one of Athens. The Parthenon, it was. She's studying Greek ruins, she said, and doing her bit for the war effort with a spot of nursing in local hospitals."

"Can I see it?" Jennie asked, and Aunt Win fished it out from behind the clock on the mantelpiece. Win hadn't looked at the card hard enough. The postcard might be of Greece but the stamp was for five *bani* — it was from Roumania. So she, and presumably Max, had managed to smuggle themselves through the Bosporus, and must be home by now. Jennie felt like cheering, but all she could do was hug her aunt and say time and time again: "I'm so glad, I'm so glad…"

*

On the kind of bright, crisp day that January could occasionally produce if it wished, Jennie walked through the fields to visit Applemere. She had heard little about it, but now no one enquired about anything. Each person got on with his or her own war business.

The bare branches of the trees were hard against the clear sky, and the house was visible as she approached, not screened as in summer. Above the high walls she could see the gables sprouting, and the chimneys, and affection made her hurry her step.

Michael opened the door; he was uniformed, and she took a moment to recognize him. He too looked older, and seemed to have the same difficulty recognizing her.

"Good heavens. Jennie! I didn't know you were back."

"How did you know where I was?"

He grinned. "Through Eileen." He took her through to the library, and she was aware of the rumble of voices as she passed the dining room. The assortment of homburg hats and uniform caps and sticks outside in the old coat rack was a suggestive one, but she decided it would not be politic to comment on them. Once in the familiar library, with its comforting mix of impressive bound volumes side by side with dilapidated novels, she went immediately to the windows that overlooked the gardens.

"Not much to look at now," he said. "The gardeners have all joined up, except for the halt and the lame and, though they do their best, it's hardly Joseph Banks' standard, is it?" Applemere had always been proud of its several roses and a cranberry bush said to have been given to them by the great botanist. Another pause. "You came out over the mountains, didn't you? Well done, Jennie."

He went on to mention Folkestone and Lady Pelham-Curtis, so he was obviously well entrenched there.

"And Joey?" she asked, since she couldn't question him too closely about work. Despite her mixed feelings about the housekeeper's son, she thought she should enquire after him.

"Useful to us," he replied rather too quickly, and she guessed that Joey's mischief-making could be a mixed blessing.

"I came here to tell Lady Fokingham that I met Max — though I expect you know he's safe anyway."

His face lit up, and she recounted her conversation with him, or rather *some* of it. Then she plunged into her main reason for coming. "I caught a glimpse of someone at Rome station — I thought it was Anna, but I couldn't be certain." His face changed, and he thought for a moment. "Jennie, don't tell my mother. Anna clearly has no intention of coming back here, and it might give her false hopes."

"Doesn't she have a right to know after all that happened?"

"No one has rights where Anna is concerned, only her."

"Do you really have no idea what happened to her, Michael?"

"I can guess — again only if you don't chat about it with Mama. My hunch is that she's with her children."

This astounded her. "But they were adopted."

He shrugged. "It's only my guess, Jennie dear. And it's not to be passed on to that charming brother of yours."

*

"Three cheers for Freddie!"

A bottle of homemade rhubarb wine from Dad's precious pre-war supply toasted his imminent departure in April. Now that general conscription had been brought in, he had been posted to the military Railway Operating Division to go to France. Earlier in the war only platelayers, carpenters, telegraphists and blacksmiths had been required to help construct track and railheads to serve the front lines, since the French ability to look after the

British as well as their own troops was heavily overstretched. Now in the spring of 1916 there was a demand for the higher grade inspectors, signalmen and, glory be, for engine drivers and shunters.

"We're proud of you, Freddie," Dad said, shaking his head in wonder. "Fancy driving trains over there. Different gauge, isn't it? Troop trains will you be driving, or goods?"

"Don't know. Provided I'm driving a train, that's enough for me. And then when the war's over, I'll be put on the expresses, you'll see. That's if we're not all electrified by then. Take all the fun out of it, that will."

"And the dirt," Aunt Win pointed out.

"Why don't you come over, Dad?" Freddie joked. "They want stationmasters in France too."

"And who's to look after Fairsted?" Dad replied with dignity. "Expect me to leave it to Jennie, do you? No, I'll stick to what I know."

Jennie was thrilled that Freddie had at last got what he had always wanted. No longer a shunter and sidings man, he would be a real driver. Because of the shortage of experienced men, he'd explained, they were taking the next grades down and giving them short, intensive training for France.

"Suppose those Germans bomb the lines?" Aunt Win said anxiously.

"Suppose a Zeppelin drops one on the Station House?"

"Don't say things like that, Freddie, even in jest," Dad rebuked him. "It's hard enough having all that explosive stuff coming through here. If the Germans find out, the Fairsted loop would be for it, is my guess."

"The Kaiser would swagger over here personally waving his sword, would he?"

"Not funny, Freddie."

"It is, Dad," Jennie pointed out. "If we don't laugh, we're only playing the Germans' game."

At that point Tom strolled in. He had fleshed out, Jennie saw, and looked every inch the businessman. He had married during Jennie's absence, and Freddie had said to her, unkindly for him, that they married so quick either because Mary was in the pudding club or because Tom wanted to get out of being called up when conscription came in, since married men would be called up after the unmarried ones.

"Where's Mary?" Aunt Win asked.

"Didn't want to make the journey."

The pudding club theory hadn't been quite accurate. Mary was going to have a baby in August, another few months yet, but Aunt Win tut-tutted and said of course, she couldn't travel in her condition.

"I hear you're off to play trains at the front, Freddie," Tom remarked carelessly. "Worked out nicely for you, hasn't it? Get what you want and be a hero too."

"Yes." Freddie didn't seem to notice the sneer. Or did he? Jennie wondered. "What will you do, Tom? Wait to be called up or volunteer now?"

"Neither. Now Mary's expecting, the war will be over before I'd be called up," he said complacently.

"I wouldn't count on that," Dad said. "There's more and more wagons coming through. Looks like a big offensive on the way."

"There he goes again," Tom sighed. "Back to the railways. Don't you ever think of anything else, Dad?"

"No," Dad said simply. "Why should I? The railways are enough for me and enough for any man. Freddie understands that, don't you, lad?"

Freddie grinned. "Reckon I do. And Jennie, too."

There was a knock at the door and Aunt Win leaped up. "That'll be Mrs Corby calling to pay her respects to you, Freddie." But it wasn't.

"Well, look who's here," Tom jeered as Aunt Win ushered Michael Fokingham in. "The lad from the big house in his big boots."

"Tom!" Jennie cried, appalled.

Michael's face didn't change. The contrast between his uniform and Tom's lounge suit and waistcoat was all too plain to see. "I just came to wish you well, Freddie."

"Thanks, Mr Michael." Freddie flushed with pleasure.

"Mr Michael," Tom jeered. "Those days are over."

"No, they are not," Jennie retorted furiously. "And he's Lieutenant Fokingham to you."

"Worked your way up through the ranks, did you?" Tom enquired.

"I worked," Michael replied. "And *I'm* in uniform."

Tom rose from his seat, seeming to tower over Michael for all they were much the same height. For a moment Jennie thought he was going to punch him, but instead Tom asked quietly: "And what about your sister, eh? Tuberculosis, my foot. You were keeping her away from me, weren't you? And now it seems you've mislaid her. Could it be that she wanted to marry me?"

"Tom, sit down!" Aunt Win ordered sharply. She looked completely bewildered, as well she might.

Tom took no notice, but forcibly pushed Michael outside through sheer bulk. Jennie rushed after them, telling Freddie, as he showed signs of following suit: "You explain to Dad and Aunt Win." This would be a shock to them.

"You're safe now," Tom was yelling at Michael outside on the path. "I'm safely shackled, so Anna's safe from my pawing peasant hands — "

"Thank God for that at least," Michael shot back at him.

Tom's fist came out before Jennie could haul him off and Michael staggered back from the blow, losing his balance and falling on to the gravel accompanied by Tom's raucous laughter.

Jennie rushed to help Michael up, but he pushed her aside as he scrambled to his feet, red in the face. "Haven't you caused enough damage to my family, you buffoon?" he hurled at Tom. "Seducing my sister — raping her, for all we know. Taking advantage of her."

Tom was suddenly white-faced. "What the blazes do you mean? *Raping* her?" And then he stared hard at Michael. "I've been a bloody fool. She didn't have tuberculosis," he said slowly. "But it wasn't just that you were keeping her from me. She was expecting, wasn't she? That's why she went to Switzerland."

"You think the Fokinghams would have wanted a child of yours in our family?" Michael's controlled white heat was more terrifying than Tom's bluster.

All the punch went out of Tom. "My kid. Why the hell didn't I realize? Where is she, Fokingham? Tell me. And where's my kid?"

"I've no idea. She ran away, so my parents don't know either. It's no use bullying them. The child was born dead anyway."

Jennie froze. Surely that wasn't true. There would be no reason for Lady Fokingham not to have told her if so. Now Michael was making it worse and she wouldn't have it. She *wouldn't*. "The twins were adopted, Tom."

He turned on her without gratitude. "So you knew, too, Jennie. Of course you did. Everyone but me, the father. And twins. Oh, dear God." It came out as an explosion of anger, not of pleading.

"Father? You, the man who forced himself on her. On *my* sister?" Michael hurled at him. "You're damned lucky we don't have you charged."

"You can't, otherwise you would," Tom answered matter-of-factly.

"We'll manage somehow if you bother us again." The threat was obvious. They would bring pressure to bear on the police.

Tom stared at him, then astounded Jennie by beginning to laugh. "I shouldn't if I were you," he said. "I really wouldn't do that, Fokingham."

Michael seemed about to retort then thought better of it, flushed and abruptly strode away.

Tom didn't comment. Then he put his hands over his face. "You bloody well knew," was all he could say.

"I was sworn to secrecy, Tom," she tried to explain. "It was as bad for me, and I truly don't know where she is. And I don't know where the babies are. I was kept out of her confidence too, despite my promise to her, and that's why I didn't marry Jack."

He glanced at her then. "I don't follow."

"Anna made me promise I'd be here when she returned in the autumn of 1914 to help her with her new life. So I told Jack I couldn't marry him till later that autumn, and that's why he killed himself." The other reason she could not speak of. It was hard enough to admit it even to herself. "It was my fault he died. I've tried to make up for it since, by doing what I could for the war."

Tom was still staring at her, and then he said flatly, 'I didn't seduce Anna, Jennie. I know you must believe I did. She sought me out, and made her wishes quite plain."

"She was so young then, Tom, so inexperienced in life. You knew that and yet you took advantage."

"I don't expect you to believe me. Inexperienced, she might have been, but she knew what she wanted, no doubt about it. I loved her, Jennie. I really did. I'd never have hurt her, never. And this — finding out she was having my kid, and she never even bothered to write. Twins, you tell me. Suppose, just suppose, she threw herself at me just so that I could put her up the spout, not love me at all. Is that possible?"

He looked at her so pleadingly that Jennie was torn apart, longing to say no. But how could she when she understood as little of Anna as Tom did? All she could say was: "I don't know, Tom. I don't know."

He shrugged and returned to the Station House, where he proceeded to be the life and soul of the party.

*

The postcards from Freddie were eagerly discussed as the summer wore on. To beat the censor they had invented their own code to find out what he was doing. It turned out he was driving one of the special ambulance trains between the front and the base hospitals at Boulogne. Dad had been describing the ambulance trains to her, and seeing Freddie's latest postcard, a Bairnsfather cartoon of the war at the front, the questions inside herself had begun to form into an answer as to where she should go next.

Hard though she worked at Fairsted station, she felt she was merely marking time here. The experience she had gained in Serbia could surely be put to better use. But what? Railways were part of her life, but the ambulance trains required nursing staff, not general hands. But she had thought that of the Serbian Relief Fund units, and in practice there had been as much need for general willing hands and drivers as for nursing staff. Excitement, then conviction grew. She would offer her services to the Railway Operating Division for working overseas.

At first there was talk of her working for the Assistant Military Forwarding Officer in Boulogne, recording and despatching the kits of the wounded or dead officers. She was on the point of accepting this job when she thought better of it. If there was a need for such organizers in Boulogne, then there must surely be a need for someone to be on the ambulance trains to take care of details, particularly a French-speaking person who could liaise with local railway stations. So that was what she would do, if she could. She argued her case successfully, and to her delight was appointed to one of the permanent ambulance trains. At last she could actively contribute once more. The weeks passed, however, and it was the end of August before she could leave for France, and before she did so there came some chilling news.

"I see Roumania's seen sense. She's gone and declared war on Austro-Hungary," Dad remarked one day.

"What about Montevanya?" Jennie seized the newspaper from Dad, to his annoyance.

"Nothing much. Only that they're giving free passage to Roumanian troops to march through into Transylvania on the attack."

"But that means they'll be drawn into the war." Jennie was horrified. "Roumania is sure to be beaten."

"What's the matter, Jennie?" Aunt Win asked impatiently. "Eat your breakfast. Just because you went to Montevanya once, it doesn't mean you own the place."

"But Eileen's there."

A dead silence. "Repeat that, Jennie, if you would," Win said firmly.

"Aunt Eileen's in Montevanya," she said miserably. How could she have been so stupid? It was too late now. She would have to tell the truth, but in such dangerous times was the secret so important? Win was Eileen's sister after all. "Eileen lives in Montevanya much of the time," she confessed.

"Doing what?"

"She has a house outside the capital city."

"Doing what?" Aunt Win asked again.

"Eileen was in Serbia with me. I couldn't tell you, you'd have worried so much. When we reached the Adriatic, she left to try to get back to Montevanya." Perhaps that would be enough. But no.

"Why her enthusiasm for Montevanya?"

Jennie could see her aunt was deeply hurt. "She has a friend there she was worried about."

"And who is this friend?"

"Prince Georgius. Lady Fokingham's brother."

"Does she cohabit with this friend? Is she married to him?"

"No. He loves her. Aunt Win."

A deep silence, and then: "Oh, the silly girl. Why didn't she tell us?"

CHAPTER XII

"That way miss!"

The burly sergeant pointed as Jennie looked round in bewilderment at the seeming chaos of Boulogne. Each one of these scurrying large ants had a job to do. So did she. if she only knew where.

The sergeant exasperatedly rushed her across rails in a way that would send Dad into a fit of apoplexy. Up they went along narrow platforms, in between carriages, in search of Ambulance Train No. 31. She felt as though she were Alice in *Through the Looking-Glass*, where everything was topsy-turvy and no one was quite sure, especially her, what they were doing.

Perhaps this apparent chaos was actually organized. "Ask for *train sanitaire trente et un"* Freddie had said, which was the French name for ambulance trains. It seemed so simple at the time. It was by remote but happy chance that she had been posted to Freddie's train, especially since most of the trains didn't have permanent drivers allotted to them. Freddie, it seemed, was an exception. Standard gauge track had just been laid in the Somme area so that British trains could get nearer to the front, where there had been bitter fighting since the beginning of July. Freddie was the expert on where all the snags on the new track were, including the sidings, in which, she gathered, the ambulance trains often spent much time in order to let the trains with higher priority get through. That had sounded strange to her, until he'd explained that not only troop trains had priority, but also their ammunition. The more well-equipped soldiers there were, the fewer the casualties, for the fighting would be over sooner.

"There you are, love. 'Ome from 'ome," the sergeant said in relief and was gone in a flash.

Ambulance Train No. 31 didn't look like anyone's home to Jennie when she clambered aboard with her permitted one piece of luggage. The coach she entered was a pharmacy with a narrow corridor linking it to the next coach, which proved to be an empty ward with cots folded up against the walls. Eventually she reached a room full of VADs and baggage, and a tall young woman in her mid-twenties with golden hair tied back bore down upon her.

"Are you the new Roddy?" she demanded. Then, without waiting while Jennie worked out this must be her shorthand for Railway Operating Division staff, she continued, "Count these comforts in, would you?" A list was thrust into her hand, and the VAD laughed. "Oh, and welcome aboard Applemere Halt."

"*Where?*" Even more puzzling.

"It's what Freddie calls this train. Goodness knows what the Applemere means, but the Halt we can understand. More halting than going on this train." She took Jennie's bag from her. "I'm Paula Simmons, VAD staff officer. I'll dump this on your patch. Come back here when you've finished, by which time I'll have cleared a space for you."

Jennie braced herself as she obediently set off. It was easy enough to see where the stores were being loaded, from the flock of hopeful Tommies hanging around in case a few cigarettes fell out of a box. This wasn't her first encounter with the military, and she knew the way to cope was to be as brisk and loud as anyone else. Tongue in cheek, therefore, each time they yelled, "Twenty boxes fags," she'd shout back: "Five, ten, fifteen, twenty, *yes!"* Sometimes stores came for which she had no paperwork; sometimes she had the paperwork but no stores. There seemed to be everything from drugs and pharmacy equipment to balaclavas knitted by zealous ladies' circles for the winter and, once it was piled aboard, someone must miraculously have whisked it away from the doorways. Goodness knew where to.

Jennie soon discovered. When she at last reached the women's staff coach again, her six-foot allotted space was still entirely covered with boxes. "All aboard?" Paula asked brightly. "I'll tell Freddie we're ready to go."

"Where to?" Jennie asked.

"High-speed empty run to the CCS — casualty clearing station — on the Somme front again — don't know where yet. It was Guillemont last time. By the way, high speed here means ten miles an hour if we're really lucky."

"Ten? What's slow?" Jennie wondered how Dad would react to this.

"Don't ask. Have a cup of tea and I'll show you round our steam palace. All the women VADs sleep in this coach. You'll be with us since you're the first female Roddy we've had. It was a man last time. Maybe we'll get more sense out of you." Paula was grinning, and Jennie relaxed. Perhaps this wouldn't be too horrific. At least she had this "empty" journey to become accustomed to train life before they took on board the battlefield casualties.

"You're Freddie's sister, aren't you?" Paula continued. "You'll be the only woman on this train who hasn't got a yen for him. We all think he's wonderful. The Prince of Wales wouldn't stand a chance if Freddie were in the room."

Freddie a ladykiller? Jennie laughed at the idea. "I'd better not get in the way of his flirtations then."

"Oh no. Mr Touch-Me-Not is Freddie. Treats us all the same, and yet I swear he's no poof. Does he have a girl at home? Lucky her if so."

Jennie had often wondered about that. Since Alice, Freddie had kept his private life to himself, and she was used to thinking of Tom as the handsome one, not Freddie. And what did Paula mean by poof?

"Prepare yourself for the grand tour," Paula announced.

It was grand from one point of view, with everything thought of, even an operating table. There were nine coaches of cots for the lying-down patients. The cots unfolded, Paula explained, into three tiers. There had to be two kitchens, each with a Soyer stove, since they would sometimes be cooking for up to 500 at a time. There was room for seventy-six sitting patients in coaches equipped with two long comfortable bench seats, an infectious diseases brake coach, and another for stores. There were two coaches for staff in the middle of the train, then the pharmacy coach, and another for the doctors.

"It's like a hotel compared with Serbia," Jennie commented.

"You wait. Once we've loaded up, it won't seem so. There's heavy fighting at High Wood, and my guess is that's where we're off to again."

The Somme offensive had been raging since the beginning of July, and the troop trains through Fairsted en route to Folkestone or Dover told their own stories of how it was going. The new offensive had seemed to offer hope for an end to the war, but that was becoming increasingly unlikely as the weeks passed.

This had been obvious from the tour round the train, it usually takes two to three hours to load a full train with stretcher cases for the cots, let alone the sitting-up cases. We have to ensure that the numbers, names, wound reports, diet sheets and so on are all tickety-boo before we give the signal to Freddie." Paula hesitated. "Do you think you can cope by yourself the first time if I do the diet sheets?"

"I was in Serbia doing much the same job," Jennie replied, half amused, half saddened to see the look of doubt still remain on Paula's face. To those here and in England, Serbia must seem like the other side of the world and hardly real, even though the wounds and grief she had seen must be every bit as bad as anything she would see here.

The train clanked and jolted its slow way onwards, often going into sidings for interminable waits, as Freddie had warned her, and when darkness fell they were told that they would be in this siding at least until midnight. Freddie joined the assembled staff, male and female, at dinner — by Serbian standards this was a feast, but hardly so compared with Fairsted.

When he appeared, Freddie seemed a different person compared with the brother she knew at home. His bright-blue eyes shone out of a matured face, even though he was only just twenty.

"Welcome to the Applemere Halt, sis." He gave her a hug and several pairs of eyes gazed enviously at her. Clearly being Freddie's sister was going to give her status here.

After dinner he took her up to see the engine, partly, she suspected, as an excuse to leave his adoring harem and return to his beloved footplate.

"Not like the old Wainwright Cs, is she?" he said ruefully. "Fancy being my fireman, do you?"

"Haven't you got one?" She was astounded. How could he possibly cope alone?

"Off and on. I've a Number Two, but he's not fully trained. Does quite well, but not up to company standards," he replied seriously.

"Of course not," Jennie agreed solemnly. Then she broached the question she'd been longing to ask. "Why call her the Applemere Halt, Freddie?"

"Just seemed right." There was a long pause and then he said: "You know, Jennie, when I think of home I remember a day — I must have been about ten or eleven — when I was tagging along behind you and Jack. It was your birthday and we walked along the railway line to the Halt."

So Freddie remembered it too. The day it had all begun.

"I remember the heat and dragonflies and the wild flowers," he continued. "Now when we get to the railheads and I see those chaps on stretchers, laid out in rows, I hang on to that day. That footpath by the line, and the lane going down to Applemere." Freddie seemed miles away. "And Anna, of course, seeing her riding off in that cart down the lane."

Anna? Why "of course"? Jennie wondered.

"That keeps me going when we get to the platforms. You'll see."

She did. Next morning after a fitful sleep and seemingly endless stops and starts and shuntings into sidings, they at last reached the nearest railhead to the front: Guillemont again. The smells, the sounds of gunfire, the haze over what should have been clear sky. It all came back to her. even though there were no Serbian mountains here, only what should have been green fields and gentle hills, all now scarred by trenches and the material of war.

The station was a hastily erected shack with a French stationmaster, if that was the right word — certainly he wore French railway uniform. The platform was already laid out with stretcher cases and more were waiting to be brought off the waiting ambulances. Jennie leaped down from the train, and a small part of her brain watched in amazement that she could be so calm while she talked to the stationmaster, lists in hand. Freeze the heart until she had time to weep at what she saw. The quicker the train was loaded, the sooner the wounds could be attended to and the quicker the train could reach Boulogne and return. The casualty clearing stations were overwhelmed, Paula had told her. The boxes of comforts were being unloaded on to the platforms even as the orderlies were preparing to lift the stretchers aboard, after she had checked them off against her lists. She was suddenly distracted by a pleading voice from one of the stretcher cases.

"Give us a fag, love."

What to do? Delay her job while she found and unpacked a box, or carry on with her job in order that the stretchers could be taken aboard the more quickly. She had no choice. "Later," she said gently, desperately looking round for someone to do it for him. A male orderly appeared from behind her, casting her a scathing look from cold blue eyes.

"Don't you have a heart?" he said.

Not *again*! Her heart sank. It was Dr Dobro-Dobro. What on earth was he doing here? "Don't you have a head?" she retorted, sure of her ground this time, no matter what he thought. Every minute she wasn't doing her job, seriously wounded cases could be worsened. Then she forgot Dr Dobro-Dobro in the more immediate need to carry out her job here.

As the last stretcher disappeared into the train, she heard the whistle going — Freddie's signal for all aboard. Then she realized to her dismay that the numbers did not add up. Paula had given the signal too early, assuming the last stretcher meant there were no more.

Jennie alerted the stationmaster and rushed to the footplate.

"Wait, Freddie. There must still be one ambulance to go. I'm six short on the list."

"Can't wait, sis. The paperwork must be wrong."

"Give me five minutes." She rushed back to the shack. If she were wrong, five minutes wasted on the green signal could mean a long delay.

When she ran back through the station building, the station-master was in a high state of agitation. "*Il arrive*," he shouted. On the road she could see a cloud of dust, which was turning into the shape of a motorised van, and she hurried back to alert Paula and the orderlies. One of them was Dr Dobro-Dobro and she thought he glanced at her as though to admit he'd been wrong. Or perhaps that was her fanciful imagination. There had been a *depannage*, the stationmaster explained to her, and those aboard had been seriously shaken in addition to their existing wounds.

When at last the train was off, a great cheer went up, and Jennie felt her legs trembling as she began to relax. Ambulance Train No. 31 was a different place now, with serious nursing and medical care going on. In the coaches with the sitting-up cases, the air was thick with smoke and an overpowering sense of relief that they were leaving the front, perhaps with a "Blighty" wound that would take them back to England.

The journey back to Boulogne took even longer, but Jennie felt she had won her spurs, and as the days passed she became accepted as an essential cog in the team. After two weeks she would have a seven-day break at Boulogne, but otherwise staff lived on the train. Paula had explained the rules for getting off the train mid-passage, but so far she had only tried it for short walks.

"We can leave the train at our peril for two hours' maximum, but not alone if you're a woman. We can go into the villages for a meal or drink in pairs. If the train leaves, though, you're stuck. It's your responsibility to get back to it somehow. Beg, borrow or steal a bike. The train goes so slowly, though, you can probably run to catch it."

As the days passed, Jennie caught glimpses of Dr Dobro-Dobro from time to time, and did her best to avoid contact with him. Her plan worked quite well, until one evening she was working her way along the swaying corridor to the lavatory and washbasin in the women's section, and ran straight into him as he passed through. Or, to be more correct, she swerved quickly to one side to avoid colliding with him. Unfortunately he did the same with the result that she was thrown right against him and his arm shot round her to prevent their both being thrown backwards.

"Shall we waltz?" he suggested, grave-faced.

"I prefer the tango."

"Difficult in this corridor. But we can try."

His arm tightened around her, he swung her to his side and then backwards, leaning over her in mock ardour, until forced to release her by the arrival of more passers-by. He picked up her hand and kissed it. "I'll book the supper dance next time," he said as he proceeded on his way. Had he recognized her from Serbia? She was almost sure he had. His aloofness had certainly vanished, she realized with amusement. How extraordinary, when his demeanour was usually so remote. She even began to wonder whether she'd misjudged his attitude to her. Her hackles had certainly risen on seeing him, but his arm around her and his nonsense jig made him seem entirely different.

On several evenings she watched him playing a battered, out-of-tune cottage piano in the sitting-up coach, where staff sometimes joined the patients in the evenings. At first it had given her a shock, for Jack's piano had been identical to this one, and seeing Dr Dobro-Dobro playing it had almost been too much to bear. Now she was used to it, if only because those who could sing, and even the cot cases, seemed to get great pleasure from the sing-songs. "Carry Me Back to Dear Old Blighty" was naturally a firm favourite, and so was "Keep the Home Fires Burning", but after that the choice ranged wide, until she almost forgot the thick fog of smoke and the smell of beer. He even sang as he had in Serbia — he would, of course, would Dr Dobro-Dobro, and Jennie admitted he did so amazingly well. Once, when he sang "If You Were the Only Girl in the World", she listened so hard that at the end she felt her skin prickling as though he were singing it for her, although he hadn't even glanced at her.

Of course he didn't intend the song for her. Why on earth should he — even mockingly — be singing for her? She was simply an orderly he had rapped over the knuckles in far-off Serbia and danced with in a corridor on a train in France. Her lips began to twitch at the stupidity of her thoughts.

"Beautiful dreamer, wake unto me," he was now singing. "Starlight and dewdrops are waiting for thee."

On a French ambulance train on the Western Front?

"Who is that man?" she whispered to Paula when her curiosity could be restrained no longer.

"His name's Richard Pencarek. He's a Red Cross orderly. I think he was a medical student before the war. Anyway, he's a tower of strength here."

"He would be," Jennie muttered wryly.

Paula raised an eyebrow. "Don't get interested, duckie. He's another Don't Even Think About Me. Probably has a fiancée back home. I wouldn't know. Pity though. I made goo-goo eyes at him until the cows came home at first. He didn't even notice."

As the days passed, Jennie became more armoured against the ordeal of seeing the stretchers carried aboard. The Somme offensive continued, even though it was now early October, but with pitifully small gains from what everyone said. She had had a week's break by now and had managed to visit home, where she was thrilled to be able to tell them about Freddie's great doings. Dad almost burst his buttons with pride. Oddly, though, she found herself impatient to get back to Ambulance Train No. 31. The Station House seemed holiday, not home, at the moment. Back on the train, she felt part of the team once more.

With so many staff aboard, Jennie rarely glimpsed Dr Dobro-Dobro, and she was relieved, for she was able to relax, without feeling judged by those steady blue eyes. One late afternoon, however, in a siding near Albert, she had arranged to go into the nearby village of Mericourt with Paula, but Paula felt too tired to go. Jennie immediately offered to stay too, but Paula replied: "Don't. I'm better off collapsing here alone. Anyway, I've found someone to go with you."

She had. It was Richard Pencarek. Typical of Paula's sense of humour, Jennie fumed. He looked as surprised as she did, though not, she noted somewhat to her pleasure, displeased.

"I get my supper dance after all," he commented.

"Not along this road," she retorted, stumbling for the second time in a few seconds over the uneven pave cobbles. "And not supper." It was only five o clock after all, even if they had been planning to eat a meal.

"Dancing is a state of mind."

"And difficult on a war front. How can..." Jennie stopped. She wanted to ask how he could look so calm day by day, as he loaded and unloaded dying men. Perhaps she looked calm, too, she thought, after Serbia. Perhaps it was inside that her stomach and mind raged with the futility of slaughter.

"Cope with the job I do?" he finished for her. "Do you want an answer to the question or just a reply?"

She sensed she was being tested, and it annoyed her. "Neither. I shouldn't have asked."

He took this placidly, and they walked along in silence into the village. Jennie fumed. Once again she had put a foot wrong in the great Richard Pencarek's eyes, if not her own. Not that she cared, but it was irritating nonetheless. The "good-good" doctor was strolling along looking completely unconcerned, even bending down to stroke a cat that had marched out to meet them.

Mericourt was not large and it was easy to track down the *estaminet* from the noise level. The smell of garlic and the smoke put her off at first, but a sudden hunger for a "real" meal forced her to face it. The bar was packed full of French workmen, some in berets, some in caps, and all apparently fighting the war from inside a glass of brandy.

There was a sudden silence as she, a female, walked in, and she was glad someone was with her, even if it was Richard. She was the only woman there, and despite the inadequacies of sanitation on the train they suddenly seemed preferable to what she might find — or not find — here. She decided not to drink too much, although that might be difficult considering the large carafe of red wine that had been plonked on the table without their asking.

"Safer than drinking the water," Richard pointed out when she looked dubious. "And choose the stodgy stuff to eat, not oily." They weren't given much choice in fact, for having assured a beaming moustachioed *patron* that they wished to eat, food began to appear.

"I think," Jennie inspected this carefully, "even Serbian stew looks better than this."

"I suspect the ingredients are much the same. Horse or goat." So he did recognize her from Serbia. No doubt now. At least he didn't have his disapproving look on. Inside he might well be mentally rewriting Shakespeare, or planning how to push her off the train, but all his face displayed was polite attention. It was his eyes that were so remarkable, she decided, and they betrayed a different picture sometimes to that his whole demeanour suggested.

"Jennie," he said at last. "Or should I call you Miss Trent? For Freddie's sister that sounds formal. Do you mind?"

"No. After all, we met before." Take the bull by the horns.

"In the train or in Serbia?"

"The latter." Get it over with.

"Palanka," he said matter-of-factly, but did not comment further. Let him think what he liked. "And your aunt is Eileen Harkness, alias Mrs Dellon."

"Yes." She couldn't stop the words. "We are all so worried about her. She is in Montevanya, and now that Roumania is under attack by Germany — "

"Montevanya too," he said, gently interrupting her. "It was overrun by the Central Powers. Hadn't you heard?"

"No." She stared miserably at her plate. "I haven't had much chance to read the newspapers."

"They've a puppet king now, needless to say friendly to Germany and Austro-Hungary."

"King Viktor." So the worst had happened. "What has happened to King Stephen?" she asked anxiously. "Is he dead? And Prince Max?" Max had been so anti-German. Had he stayed to fight? Was he dead too? A cold hand seemed to reach out at this possibility. Ruritania vanished for ever.

He glanced at her. "You sound as if you know them."

"I met them once." Once in another land, another place, another time.

He must have picked up on her anguish. "There's a rumour that the King managed to leave the country by travelling down the Danube in disguise, and that he reached the Serb forces at Salonika. There's a lot of movement on that front now. The Serb army has joined the English and French to fight the Bulgarians. They've taken Monastir again."

Jennie was suddenly full of hope. "My aunt and Max might be with the King too?"

"Yes." He seemed to pick up on the lack of the "prince", for he gave her a curious look.

She was so relieved, overjoyed. "And Prince Georgius could be with them?"

"Knowing your aunt's determination, I would say that was highly likely. I'd hate the world to run out of conjuring tricks while it's coming to its senses."

Time for *her* curious look. "How do you know about his magic?"

"How did you come to be outside that tent at Palanka?"

She gasped at the speed of the retort. Perhaps it wasn't malicious, merely a warning to keep her distance, but she didn't need it. He could keep his secrets. As for her, there was no way she would ever tell him the whole truth about that night. Jack was her memory to cherish. Surely there must be some mote in Richard Pencarek's eye that wouldn't bear inspection?

If there was, he bore no sign of it. His eyes gazed at her as assuredly as before.

Just as they emerged from the restaurant, again in continued silence, on her side at least, there was an ominous double toot from the train and Richard gave an exclamation. "That's the final call. We must have missed the first. We'll have to run."

He seized her hand and pulled her, stumbling, over the cobbles until, out of breath and panting hard, he pulled her up to the train, which was already moving.

"I haven't paid you for my share," she managed to gasp, but he hadn't heard. He was already walking to the men's staff coach, without a backward glance. He was back in his own world — whatever that might be.

CHAPTER XIII

Freddie had leave at Christmas, but Jennie was not so fortunate. The sniping and shelling carried on, regardless of the date. And that meant work aboard the Applemere Halt did too. Two years earlier, during the first Christmas of the war, there had been an unofficial armistice on parts of the line, but there were no such respites now. It seemed to her ironic that fraternization with the enemy was a military crime, but killing as many as possible could gain the Tommies a medal.

She resolutely put all thoughts of Christmas at home from her mind, and concentrated on trying to make it seem like Christmas here. Fortunately it was at least warm on the train, thanks to the steam heating. The Soyer stoves, under the stalwart kitchen orderlies, produced a Christmas dinner of sorts, including some tinned fruit and custard, a great treat. Packets of cigarettes and biscuits were handed out courtesy of the Soldiers' Comforts Fund. There was a carol service of sorts, too, which was the highlight of the day. There was a hush after they had sung "Silent Night" and a lump presented itself in Jennie's throat. It was quickly dispelled by "Good King Wenceslas", though she wondered whether he would be quite so "good" today. The Good King would have his work cut out playing politics, with little time to worry about cutting pine logs for peasants.

Richard wasn't playing the piano at the service. He had vanished on leave early in December and had not yet returned. In a funny way Jennie missed him, wondering if he had been posted to another train. She hoped not.

As soon as Freddie returned, she demanded to know every last detail about Fairsted. But Freddie had had other things on his mind, not least how his beloved Great Central 2-8-0 locomotive was faring in other hands. At home, everything they had once taken for granted was now scarce, he eventually told her. Voluntary rationing was all the thing nowadays, including meatless days, and now that Lloyd George was prime minister the Ministry of Food was even more zealous in keeping its stem eye on what the nation should eat — or not eat. He also told her that some folks at home were under the impression that they were the only ones suffering from food restrictions and that the troops were having a high old time compared with them. Jennie laughed, thinking of the endless tinned meat stews and irregular supplies of vegetables.

"Aunt Win's got some splendid recipe for wartime Christmas pudding. Got carrots in it, she said, but didn't taste too bad," Freddie told her.

"Is she still in the ticket office?"

"Loves it. In her element, bossing the whole village around." A tide of homesickness swept over her, especially when Freddie mentioned Aunt Eileen.

"*She* was there?" Jennie cried incredulously.

Freddie grinned. "For an hour or two. Apparently you spilled the beans on her domestic life, and she wasn't too pleased, but then she and Aunt Win had a good laugh about it."

She knew better than to ask what Eileen was doing there, but she could ask about Georgius — and did so.

"He's in Corfu with the King and other Serbian leaders, and so, officially, is Queen Zita, but Eileen seemed to think she might still be in Montevanya. Isn't she German herself? Max has been blazing away on the Salonika front. He did well at some mountain peak the Serbs recaptured from the Bulgarians in September, and won himself a Serbian medal or two."

"Good for him." Jennie could imagine how much that had meant to him. "Is Eileen going to Corfu herself?"

"She said something about nursing at Monastir."

Jennie's heart sank. Of course that's where Eileen would go. Then she realized how ridiculous she was being, as she herself was constantly travelling to the front line. Although Salonika was at last an active war front, it was still a long way to Belgrade.

"And Applemere?" she could not refrain from asking.

"Just the same comings and goings of the military."

The war itself was also just the same. No invasion, no victory, no armistice even in sight. All they could do was to cling to the belief that war was *not* normal and that normal life would one day return.

"What will you do after the war, Freddie? Carry on driving?" she asked.

"Yes, but I'll be doing it through the green fields of Kent, not these godforsaken battlefields," he vowed.

To Jennie, Kent was Ruritania now, not Montevanya. There was a great distance between the girl who had roamed these green fields with Jack, the girl who had wondered what lay beyond the tunnels of the Fairsted loop line, if only she could leap aboard the train of life. Now she and Freddie knew what lay beyond, and longed for the journey home.

*

Spring 1917 did its best on the Western Front. Incongruously, blackbirds still sang; robins hopped around and wild flowers did their best to bloom where the soldiers' boots had not yet trodden them into the ground. But the coming of spring also meant new offensives, each side struggling to break through the others' lines: the Germans to the Channel and the rest of France, the British to push the Germans back into their own country, and the French endeavouring to drive them into retreat on the River Aisne, despite the exhaustion of the French troops after the long and bloody Verdun offensive last year. Former optimism and patriotism had given way, in generals, officers and Tommies alike, to a grim determination to finish the job. The train had become Jennie's second home, and somehow the staff of Ambulance Train No. 31 stayed together, with only incidental changes, such as Richard, who had never returned. Perhaps the semi-permanent staffing was on the basis that if it worked well it should be left alone. The train had become well known, and the Applemere Halt had changed its name to the Applemere Flyer as a result. At last came the news they had been expecting.

"We're moving northwards," Freddie told them. "Hold on to your hats."

Paula and Jennie had worked out from the railway maps and the station names that they were moving north towards Arras by a roundabout route that took standard gauge trains. By the time they arrived at the nearest railhead there had been heavy casualties at Monchy-le-Preux. The only comfort was that the British troops had actually advanced, and some ground was being held. It was a spurt of encouragement, and spirits, even amongst the wounded, began noticeably to rise.

In Salonika, too, the news had been both good and bad. A British offensive was taking place against the

Bulgarians, but an attack by German aircraft in February had left three hospitals bombed and two British nurses dead. Fear had hung over Jennie for two weeks until a letter came to tell her Eileen was safe.

She and Paula quite often strolled into the nearest village during stops now that the weather was warmer, and Jennie often thought back to her evening out with Richard. He had left the train with ill feeling still between them, and she would have liked to put that right, to understand him better. That was war; it brought people together and it swept them apart. Individuals were ants in the great chain of command stretching from England to the war front. There must be similar ant chains all over the fighting world, and what did two little ants count in those millions?

The Railway Operating Division was quickly laying new track to the fronts, which didn't suggest there'd be a speedy end to the fighting, even though the news that at long last America was entering the war to support the Allies gave everyone a fillip. The British railway presence in France was now huge, and the war was changing everything in the railway world back home too, Freddie had told her. Civilian traffic was severely curtailed, with all cheap tickets abolished — no seasons, no tourist tickets, no cheap day or weekend tickets, in an effort to make room for troop trains and ambulances. Jennie found the thought of no more seaside specials sad, even in war.

At Monchy she had to discipline herself to bear the sights of the stretchers all over again, for it was the first heavy fighting she had seen since the Somme offensive ended in November. It took two hours of checking numbers and clearing each stretcher for loading before she had steeled herself once again not to get drawn into the horror of what she saw.

At one point Paula rushed down with a query over a missing diet sheet. "Looks as if the Flyer will be an Applemere Stayer for a while yet," she threw at Jennie.

A sudden movement from one of the stretchers caught Jennie's eye, but she could see nothing amiss, and the orderlies from the train began loading. Something made Jennie glance over again, and she caught a glimpse of a soldier with fair hair and finely chiselled features. His hands were lying on the one blanket, but as the stretcher disappeared into the train his face looked straight at Jennie.

Only it wasn't a man. It was Anna.

The whole of Jennie's stomach seemed to turn over, and this time she really had to force herself back to her job, which seemed interminable. Anna — here, *wounded*? How on earth could that be? Eileen had told her about Flora Sandes, a British nurse who actually enlisted in the Serbian army to fight with them, and had done so during the retreat. But surely Anna could not have done the same here on the Western Front?

Half expectant, half fearful, she went speedily in search of Anna as soon as the Flyer began its slow journey to the coast, but failed to find her either in the cot wards or the sitting-up carriages. Had it been a hallucination? She had been so sure it was Anna, but yet another careful check also failed. Eventually she found that Anna had been given a corner of the pharmacy to herself as she was the only woman patient. She was suffering from leg wounds, but wasn't seriously hurt.

"This time," Jennie said gently as she pulled aside the curtain, "you can't escape. Not like Rome."

Anna stared back at her in apparent amusement. "What can you mean? Do I know you?"

"I believe so." Jennie hadn't changed that much. "Tell me what's wrong, Anna. What are you doing here of all places? I assumed you were in Italy."

"I'm not," Anna snapped back. "I'm an ambulance driver with the FANYs. and I'm not going back to England whatever your blessed lists dictate."

Jennie side-stepped this. "But why come here?"

"We're here, Jennie. Everything else is irrelevant. Anyway."

She tried to sit up and Jennie stacked pillows behind her. "I might as well do something useful."

"But your parents — " Jennie could have kicked herself. Trust her to wave a red rag at a bull.

Anna looked at her scornfully, as well she deserved. "That was another life, Jennie. I'm not Anna Fokingham anymore."

"You've married?"

"Oh, Jennie, do you have to be so stupid? Of course not. I'm using another name, that's all."

Anna's face was lined, and looked as though it had endured much. The once fragile hands now looked as if they had an iron grip. "Do leave me alone, will you?" she finished wearily.

Thwarted and hurt, Jennie smarted by herself for a while, and then, deciding that Freddie might fare better than her, made her way to the footpath.

"Guess who's on the train," she shouted, wiping off specks of dirt from her face.

"Lloyd George?"

"Anna."

Once over the shock, Freddie agreed to talk to her, and when Jennie passed through the pharmacy coach later she could hear Freddie's voice and Anna's laughter, and Anna only briefly paused to acknowledge her arrival. All was well while Freddie was there, but as soon as he left the barriers came up again. Jennie tried everything to break them down.

"When did you learn to drive?"

"I didn't. I just did it, it's simple enough. I did learn to nurse though."

Another new side to Anna — and an even more surprising one. Anna used to faint at the sight of blood.

"I learned in the Swiss hospital. Once the war broke out," Anna continued offhandedly, "it became part of my new plan. I did some training — not much, but enough so that I could go to the front as a nurse. Then I found that I liked driving more. So here I am. Does that satisfy you?"

"No," Jennie retorted, sure that there was more to this, if only by the hard glitter of Anna's challenging eyes.

"If there is, you'll never know it. It's unfortunate our meeting, but it won't happen again."

Jennie was suddenly angry. Patient or no patient, she wasn't accepting this. "You owe me the truth, Anna."

"I owe you nothing."

"You do, and whatever you think I've done to offend you, nothing wipes that out. I took the blame for your outburst in Dunosova."

"Ah, yes. That was fun. And I gather darling Viktor is now King of Montevanya. Much good may it do him. You must admit I was right," she crowed. "If I'd married him, look where I'd be today. Not here in an ambulance train, but a vassal of Kaiser Billy."

Her voice was rising, and Jennie recognized the signs. Anna was getting into one of her hysterical moods. "So tell me what I've done," she asked quietly. "We were friends once."

"Were we?" It was almost a sneer. "How's dear Jack?"

She had asked, so Jennie would tell her. "He killed himself." She deliberately exposed the wound to the air. "He thought I didn't want to marry him."

"And did you?" Anna barely reacted.

"I wasn't sure. What I *was* sure about was that I couldn't break my promise to you to help you with your plans that autumn. So I told Jack I couldn't marry him till December. He didn't understand, naturally enough. I was your willing puppy dog then, but I'm not now."

"I can see that." Anna sounded a little more amiable. "What were you doing in Rome? You looked as if you'd come out of a cesspit —"

"And you looked as if you were a kept woman."

They caught each other's eye and began to laugh. The barriers were down at last.

"Jennie, don't worry about me. Don't tell my parents where I am. Perhaps Michael if you have to."

"But they love you, they're grieving for you."

"Rubbish."

"Not from what I've seen."

"And you've seen plenty. I'm sure. I always thought you were my parents' stooge."

"I'm no one's stooge and I never have been. What were you doing in Rome? You might as well tell me."

"Closed book."

"Open it," Jennie commanded. "I promised you I'd help you that autumn, but you never came. It changed my life and partly because of it Jack died. What *was* your plan, Anna? Tell me. I have a right to know."

Anna was silent for a moment. "Does Tom know about the babies?" she asked at last.

"Yes. Michael told him."

Much to Jennie's relief, Anna seemed not to mind. "Of course I had a plan," she said bitterly. "I was having a baby — two as it turned out — and I had every intention both before and after they arrived of keeping them with me."

"But they were adopted."

"So my mother thought. If I'd told her what I planned, my chances would have been nought. I paid the staff at the home to tell me who the adopted parents would be. Then I went to talk to them, and offered them lots of money just to take the babies so Mama would be satisfied. Afterwards I would meet them and take them back. I told you I had money of my own. It was all agreed. They didn't mind. There were lots of other babies for adoption."

"So what happened? The war?"

"Human nature." Anna rested her head back against the pillows, looking drained, struggling not to display emotion. "We arranged to meet in Rome where they said they lived. I reached there, having escaped darling Mama, as she no doubt told you, only to find they'd double-crossed me. There were no Monsieur *et* Madame Roc living at that address, and never had been. It took me weeks to tumble to the fact they'd betrayed me. I thought I'd made a mistake in the address or name. They simply disappeared and I spent over a year looking for them. Hopeless. They'd gone for good."

Simple words, but the agony was written on Anna's face. Jennie put her arms round her and hugged her. Anna was rigid in her arms, then gradually began to relax. "It's good to tell someone at last," she admitted. "No one else though. Not Tom — not even Michael."

"I won't, though he suspects something like this. You have to promise me something though."

"I've made enough promises I haven't kept."

"Then keep this one. Keep in touch with me, no matter whether you go back to the front or whether you return to England." Anna thought this through. "That shouldn't be difficult," she agreed. "I'll think of a plan."

Jennie half laughed, half wept. "Oh, Anna, *not another* plan."

*

A day later Anna had gone, transferred to a hospital near Boulogne, but with the offensive at Arras beginning anew in May, Jennie was too busy to think other than fleetingly of Anna, especially since Paula was on leave. A week later Paula returned beaming with happiness.

"I've news. I'm engaged!"

"He's a doctor?" Jennie asked after her excited congratulations.

"No, a pilot flying SE5s up near the Belgian border." Jennie was dismayed, knowing the short life expectancy for pilots, but schooled herself to look delighted.

"And before you say anything," Paula continued calmly, "Peter's going to survive. He says he can shoot down the Red Baron himself now he's got me." She enthused on the wonders of Peter for some time, before adding casually: "Oh, and by the way, your Richard's coming back to us."

Before Jennie could ask more, Paula proceeded to launch into an account of the wonders of London life, the dance craze, the songs, the theatres and the fashions until Jennie began to feel like the Flying Dutchman condemned to sail the world in his ship, except that in her case it was the Applemere Flyer.

"Your Richard" had been Paula's words, but there was no "my" for Jennie any more. She saw single men all day long, and yet except in pity none of them touched her heart. It seemed frozen. Someday, long after this war was over, she supposed she might meet someone else and marry. Or perhaps she wouldn't. The slaughter resulting from this war meant a whole generation was dying. She might live on, dreaming of what life might have been if she had married Jack, or if she had never been to Montevanya. Or perhaps she would become an Aunt Eileen, striding through foreign lands. No, she no longer wanted the world, only a settled place to view it from. That was what she was fighting for, just as all these Tommies were. Dad and Aunt Win weren't going to live under the Kaiser's rule if she had anything to do with it.

All the same, she was pleased that Richard was coming back.

*

Although she'd barely exchanged two words with him since his return, life had clicked into place again. When Jennie heard Richard's touch on the piano or his voice in song, the train became a secure refuge for the staff as well as the patients. So long as Freddie kept this train going and Richard kept on singing, so Paula claimed, there was hope the war would end. All over the word there were thousands — perhaps millions — of Freddies and Richards, but Ambulance Train No. 31 depended on these two, her brother and now — according to Paula — *her* Richard. If only Paula knew how far that was from the case.

Then one day she found him in the pharmacy when she was delivering supplies. Good. She would reopen hostilities with a gentle burst of fire. "Why did you desert us?" she asked airily.

He grinned as though well aware of her motives. "Lloyd George needed my advice."

There was no more time for conversation, but at least a peace overture had been made. This was confirmed when after the train reached Boulogne he asked her out to dinner. She was flattered, and decided in honour of the occasion that she would wear her "best" dress, in fact the only non-uniform one she possessed, a bright-flowered print with a modern-length skirt. Such pleasure to be able to view her legs, though what Aunt Win would think of this she shuddered to think. Especially if she knew Jennie had long since abandoned corsets.

She was glad she had made the effort because they went to the Restaurant Streletski in the Grande Rue, which clearly had pretensions to status. When she'd expressed her amazement at the vast range of vegetables, many of which she'd never seen before, he replied idly: "England has lots of vegetables too — normally."

"Yes, and they're all called cabbage," she retorted with the old joke.

"I like cabbage."

She was suddenly homesick for Station House and Aunt Win's cabbage and sausage stew. "Odd to think that England's just over there, twenty or thirty miles away," she remarked. "We travel farther than that in a day, and think nothing of it, yet we can't get back home without a vast amount of fuss."

"Where's your home?" he asked. "In Kent, isn't it? Eileen mentioned it."

"Yes. Where's yours?" she asked politely.

A hesitation. "I don't have one. My father lives in Cornwall." She decided not to press further. "Are you back permanently on the Flyer now?" Conversation was going to be difficult if it went on like this.

"So far as I know."

She could not think of anything else to say and nor apparently could he. Well, she thought in desperation, no harm in forging straight ahead. "Why did you invite me out tonight, Richard? *Really*, I mean."

He answered immediately. "I misjudged you."

Well, she'd asked for it. "You had right on your side."

"I know now how you felt," he answered nevertheless. *How could you?* she wanted to retort, as he continued awkwardly, "The same sort of thing happened to me. I've realized I'm not cut out to be a doctor or surgeon. I'd been studying in London before the war and was nearly at the point of qualifying." He hesitated. "Can I go on?"

Jennie nodded.

"When war came, I volunteered my services to the Red Cross, which is how I landed up in Serbia as a medical orderly. On leave at Christmas, I found my conscription papers had caught up with me. By that time I knew I was a good orderly, and that I'd be no use as a soldier, so I asked for a non-combatant role in the Royal Army Medical Corps. There was a mix-up and, to cut a long story short, I found myself before a conscientious objector tribunal. It wasn't pleasant. While the mix-up was being sorted out I found myself in prison, doing hard labour. At last I was cleared, and then of all things I failed the medical for the RAMC as unfit. Ironic really. So here I am back again, hoping I don't collapse."

Jennie reached out her hand, and said the only thing she could. "Welcome back, Richard."

He took it. "I kissed this once," he reflected. "Do you remember?"

She caught his eye. "Yes."

"I was so dismissive of you. Can you forgive me?"

She picked up his hand and returned the kiss. "Does that answer your question?"

As they were walking back, she made up her mind. Richard had made amends by telling her his story, and she had to do the same, hard though it was. "There was more to that episode in Palanka than you saw," she forced herself to say, "though it didn't excuse what I did. The stretcher case I ran away from — the man was dying and he looked like Jack. The man I was going to marry."

Richard was very still. "Where is he now, this Jack?"

She tried to speak and couldn't, then tried again. "He died just as war broke out. He killed himself — because of me."

"Oh, Jennie." He stopped in the dusk and took her into his arms. "No one kills themselves entirely because of someone else. That's the spark, not the reason. Search for the reason, Jennie, if it's still needed."

"It's not," she managed to whisper, aware of his arms around her, and that this felt natural and comforting, a moment of warmth in the dark of war. "It's gone away."

Then she was aware that his lips were on hers, gently, lovingly and undemandingly.

"War makes many orphans, Jennie," he said at last. "But the lucky ones find homes again. Are we lucky ones, do you think?"

CHAPTER XIV

"Have you heard the news?" Paula fleetingly paused as she whisked by with a trolley-load of patients' dinners. Jennie wasn't aware of any. She'd been too busy; two of the three kitchen orderlies were ill and she and Paula were helping out. When their presence wasn't needed for feverish cooking, they were delivering or collecting plates. The special diets were Jennie's nightmare. If the wrong diet was given, the results could be fatal. Fever, diabetic and diarrhoea diets, steamed dishes, stews, beef teas, arrowroot, broth: all had to be dealt with in this tiny kitchen space. Any news, including this apparently important item, therefore had to wait until they were able to eat their own meals.

"Goodness, how delicious," Paula declared. "Steak Chateaubriand, I do declare."

Jennie looked at the unappetising mess on her plate — perhaps it only looked so because she'd had a hand in cooking it — and tried to be enthusiastic. "What was this news?"

"We've all been given an extra seven days' leave."

"By the Angel of Mons?" Jennie snorted with disbelief. An extra week's leave for everyone was a tarradiddle not to be taken seriously, like the angel who was supposed to have appeared to save the troops at Mons earlier in the war.

Paula insisted it was true, however. "Freddie says the train needs refitting and the engine overhauling, and instead of doing it piecemeal the ROD have decided to do it in one fell sweep so that we…"

Jennie met her eye when she broke off. "There'll be another offensive soon. We all know that. The only question is where." The push at Arras had not achieved the expected breakthrough, and 1917 would not pass without another.

"Wherever they're busy laying track and the Germans don't have observation balloons or aircraft up. Anyway," Paula cheered up, "let's enjoy the leave."

"Will Peter be able to get some too?"

"It's too short notice. I can go home and break the news of my engagement to my parents. They always thought no one would ever want me, so they'll be delighted to know I'll be off their hands."

Jennie laughed. The idea of no one ever wanting Paula was ridiculous — her golden hair and cheerful manner lit up the train as brightly as the electricity. As for the leave, Jennie decided to check its truth with Freddie before she rejoiced too much. To her pleasure he confirmed it, although he told her he couldn't come back to Fairsted this time, because he was needed for the overhaul of the locomotive in Boulogne.

The leave was due to begin almost immediately, so there would be no time to let the Station House know of her arrival, and Jennie happily imagined Dad's surprise when she walked in. By the time they reached Boulogne next morning she was agog with anticipation at the thought of June in Kent. Then she caught sight of Richard. She had hardly seen him after their dinner together, for it had been a busy few weeks with heavy casualties. Now there was a lull, though the news from elsewhere was soberingly bad. Gotha aeroplanes had replaced Zeppelins as the terror fleet to scourge England, and the terrible news had reached her that nearly eighty people had been killed and a hundred wounded when bombs had rained down on Folkestone. She knew the town so well and couldn't bear to think that it had been devastated.

Richard was standing on the platform with his luggage, and she suddenly remembered what he had said. *I don't have a home.*

"Where are you off to?" she asked brightly as she stepped down with her own luggage.

"I'm not sure yet. Rouen perhaps — it has a wonderful cathedral there."

"Alone?" she asked blankly. That sounded the worst word in the world. "But you can't," she added impulsively when he nodded, looking somewhat amused. "Come with me, you must come to see the real Applemere Halt." Never had she been so certain of anything. He must see Kent. It must be more beautiful than Rouen.

"You can't escape the war entirely," she rushed on. "Not from the front windows anyway, because of the troop trains, but out of the other side you'll see fields and cows. I know there are shortages and now there are bombers but —"

He was laughing now. "Front windows of what, Jennie?"

"Why, the Station House, of course, where I live." Hadn't she said so? "There's room there for you."

"I can't come at this short notice."

"Don't you want to?" She was full of dismay. Of course he must want to — who would not? Kent would be lovely. But then she realized it might be that he didn't want to spent time with her. After all, why should he? "I'm sorry," she began to stammer. "It was a stupid idea."

He put down his luggage and took her hands. "It was the most wonderful idea I've ever heard, Jennie. The Kent countryside and you, too. But your parents are hardly going to want a stranger foisted on them at the last moment without warning."

"You mean, they might think I'd brought you to force a shotgun wedding on you?" She spoke without thinking, and his lips twitched.

"No, that wasn't what I meant. You wouldn't need the shotgun anyway. But it's hardly conventional for a stranger to arrive and announce that he's come for a week, and do they mind?"

"Convention flies out of the window in war," she replied seriously, "even in England. Refugees arrive and doors open everywhere. I saw it at the fall of Belgium. People take in orphans of the storm." Did he mean that? Not need a shotgun? Of course not. It was a joke.

"Is that how you see me?" He looked troubled.

"No. But they will. And anyway, it's not parents, it's Dad and Aunt Win. And Aunt Win is Eileen's sister — you know Eileen, so that means they know you, and that settles it."

He nodded gravely. "It does indeed."

*

Despite the endless stoppages in the sidings, and the delays that getting an extra travel warrant had incurred, they were on their way, even if that did mean standing in the corridor jammed up against each other. She was increasingly impatient to be home. The roses would be adorning the Pretty House, some sort of cake would be brought out for tea, and most importantly Dad and Aunt Win would be sitting at the table with her. She gave a deep sigh of happiness.

"Regretting my being here?" Richard whispered in her ear.

"No. The opposite. Before the war nothing ever seemed perfect. I'd long for this and long for that, then get it perhaps, only to find that it wasn't so perfect after all. When the train actually went through the tunnel it wouldn't be the paradise that I'd expected on the other side. But now I know there can be, if I make it myself. Does that make sense?" she asked anxiously.

"Everything you say makes sense," he informed her.

"I doubt if Dad would agree with you."

"Is your Aunt Win like Aunt Eileen?"

Jennie considered this. "Before the war I'd have said they were as different as Queen Victoria and Florence Nightingale. But now I'm not so sure." She thought about Aunt Win in the booking office. That to her must have been a step as far as Eileen took on the Silk Road to China. "Aunt Win was disappointed at Omdurman," she added impulsively, and felt him shake with laughter. "It's no laughing matter," she said seriously. "Her fiancé died."

"I'm sorry. It sounded so quaint. Does she laugh despite it?"

"Not very much. She loves though. The family, I mean."

As the train steamed slowly through the last tunnel, she felt her heart beat so strongly she thought Richard must hear it. The first doubts were creeping into her mind. What if he did not see the Station House as she did? What if he did not like Fairsted? What if Dad and Aunt Win didn't like him? Impossible. Perhaps she should make it clear he was free to go elsewhere for some of the leave if he wanted to — but if she suggested it he would think she didn't want him at Fairsted. And she did. She was surprised how much. Because of that kiss? Other men had kissed her, either in earnest or in jest, but she had felt no compulsion to bring them to Fairsted. Richard was different.

As they fought their way to the door to alight at Fairsted, she spotted Dad in the doorway of the goods office, and called out to him.

He went quite white. "Win!" he bawled. "Wm! Look who's here!"

In the muddle of Aunt Win's exclamations and Dad's pumping Richard's hand up and down, Jennie remembered Richard's fears that the meeting might be difficult. It wasn't. A friend from Freddie's train was a friend of theirs, they declared. There was immediate talk of beds being made up, apologies given for cocoa butter instead of the real thing, and the necessary small portions of meat. But today there happened to be carrot cake for tea. Made from *new* carrots. And there were early cherries. Of course there would be cherries, even in war. This was Kent.

*

"And over there is Applemere," Jennie pointed across the hopfields. "You can just see its chimneys through the trees."

"I came hop-picking in Kent once as a child," Richard said. It was the first time she'd seen him wearing anything but uniform, and the flannels and blazer made him seem less Dr Dobro-Dobro than she had ever seen him, and more comfortable to be with.

"Did you enjoy it?"

"No. I liked Kent though." He said no more and Jennie did not ask.

"Don't associate Kent only with hops; you should see it in apple-blossom time, when the bluebells are out, and wait till you've tasted its cherries, its damsons —"

"Rose time is beautiful enough for me."

Tom's room in which Richard was sleeping overlooked the garden and she longed to share his thoughts when he looked down on to it, now ablaze with flowers and flourishing vegetables. There was no lawn now that every spare inch of ground had to be given over to producing food, but the roses still bloomed. In the heat of yesterday evening, their scent had floated in through her window, making her restless and unable to sleep, eager for the day ahead.

"Tell me more about Applemere," he said, when at last that day came.

Jennie obediently described how Applemere had come into her life, and the part Anna had played in it, together with a little about Montevanya, including her shock that Aunt Eileen had turned out to be Prince Georgius' companion.

"I like that word," Richard commented.

"So would Aunt Win. I could hardly say mistress, and in any case Eileen's not a kept woman. She belongs to herself."

"She's remarkable. Is she still in Monastir?" When Jennie nodded, he added casually, "Do her comings and goings ever seem strange to you?"

"Everything's strange in war," Jennie replied guardedly. "What in particular do you mean?"

"She does too much. She's in Montevanya, she's in Serbia, she's in London, she's in Fairsted — "

"She's entitled to go where she likes," Jennie replied somewhat indignantly. "She's not under military rule."

"No." He smiled at her, and she had the annoying sense that as usual he was holding back.

"Do you want to see Applemere House at closer quarters?" she said crossly. "We can walk across the fields and look at it from the lane."

When they did so later, he stared at the house for some time. "A house with secrets," he said at last. "A sad one, too."

"Is that how you see it?" Jennie was surprised, it must be the war, now that it's not lived in all the time. Before the war it was a happy place, with beautiful gardens — "

"And yet Anna ran away. Applemere seems to me," Richard added thoughtfully, "a house in waiting."

"Houses are what you make them," she said, annoyed that he did not instantly fall in love with Applemere. The house was merely slumbering, not sad. And one day after the war it would awake.

The following day Jennie nerved herself up to visit Folkestone, explaining to Richard why she had to go there, but that it would not be a happy visit. She was right. Many of the bombs had fallen round Central Station where she had worked, and Tontine Street in the centre had been completely demolished.

"Fifty-one bombs," Dad had said. "That's what the official count was. And one of them nearly caught the fast from London, only the driver saw the devils in time and pulled up short."

"Those poor souls," Aunt Win had lamented. "To think I used to go to Stokes Bros for my Seville oranges every January, and there's nothing left of it now, nor of poor Mr Stokes and his son. Such a nice young man. Nowhere's safe now, they're building shelters — "

"After the horse has bolted," Dad grunted.

"Those horses will be back, you mark my words," Aunt Win replied.

After a sobering walk through the devastated area, Jennie was relieved to find that Sandgate Road seemed to have escaped unscathed. Lady Pelham-Curtis was pleased to see her, casting sharp glances at Richard. So did Joey, the housekeeper's son, who clearly resented Richard's presence, although she couldn't think why. She and Joey had worked together, but there had hardly been a close friendship between them. Nor did Richard take to Joey. "A nasty piece of work," he pronounced afterwards.

When they reached home, it was to discover that Aunt Win was right. The horses had returned. Margate and London had been heavily bombed, with sailors and soldiers among the dead as well as a heavy toll of civilian casualties.

*

"Kent isn't Kent unless we have a picnic," Jennie said firmly as she and Richard carried the basket down to the riverside. The river was little more than a stream here, but it was a place she had shared with Jack, and now she could remember him while enjoying it with Richard. It had been a wonderful week, apart from another clash with Tom, and an inexplicable niggle that something was missing. Inexplicable, that is, until lying awake last night, aware of Richard's movements next door, she realized it was simple. He had not kissed her again, and that must mean the first time had only been a friendly kiss, and not one that promised anything more. Yet now she knew that was what she wanted. She had assumed one kiss would lead to others, but they had not, although she was certain he was enjoying his time at Fairsted. Indeed he seemed almost as at home in the Station House as she was, taking his turn with washing up, setting the tables, lighting the boiler, anything that came along. He had even liked Tom, although it wasn't reciprocated.

Tom had come to tea together with Mary and his lively ten-month-old son, Alfred. He had eyed Richard carefully and "He seems all right" had been his grudging verdict — quickly followed by, "You don't understand people, that's your trouble, Jennie." Then, right out of the blue, he'd asked, "How's Anna?"

She'd retorted quickly to that. "You've a wife and child now, Tom."

"Having one child doesn't make me forget the others, do it?"

He seemed still to be blaming Jennie and she couldn't understand why. Anna, she thought crossly, was still causing problems, even though she'd probably never see her again. She couldn't talk to Richard about her, or to Tom, or even to Eileen. No one — except perhaps Michael. She put Anna out of her mind. She wasn't going to spoil this wonderful day with Richard — even if there was a problem with the sandwiches.

"I was sure you said you liked egg and cress," Jennie said, crestfallen to find Richard avoiding them. It was hard enough making sandwiches with imitation bread, let alone discovering that Richard didn't like hard-boiled eggs, even mashed up — especially since they cost sixpence each now.

"I'll have all the fish paste ones instead," he told her placatingly.

Then she found she'd left the second bottle of lemonade at home. "There must be *something* I've done right," she muttered, even more crossly.

"Being here?" he asked politely.

She had to laugh then, and turned to him to apologize. The moment she caught the look in his eye she knew she had been wrong. Whatever the reason he hadn't made one move to touch her in the days he'd been at Fairsted, he'd wanted to. He must have seen the recognition in her own eyes, for he took her in his arms and brought her towards him, lying down with her on the grass. His lips were on hers, and this time most surely not as a friend. They needed a response and she gave it with all her heart, aware that her body was aching for him as years ago it had ached for Jack. What she had been missing was his body touching hers. *Now* it was perfect.

"Jennie," he whispered. "Oh, Jennie."

There were rainbows at last, in her eyes and in her dreams, as she felt as his hands moving over her light summer dress, holding her, caressing her, until her body arched into his. Then suddenly there was a distance between them again, as he rolled aside from her.

"Not allowed by the Company book?" she asked after a moment. *Not until we're married, Jennie.* Jack's voice came out of the past. When he nodded, Jennie longed to explain that she didn't care about the book, but he didn't come back to her, merely squeezed her hand as he lay on his back staring up into the sky. "A penny for them," she ventured.

"They're worth more."

"Can't afford them on a VAD's pay."

"Then I'll present them to you for free. I'm in love with you, Jennie." He rolled over to look at her. "More than that, I love you. And I shouldn't."

"Why not?" She was trembling with happiness, love and fear all rolled into one. "Do you have a mad wife in the attic like Jane Eyre's Mr Rochester?"

He sat up abruptly. "No," he replied seriously. "But I don't have an attic."

"You mean you don't own a house?" she asked, puzzled.

"Partly. The other part is that Fairsted is your attic. In it you're storing all your treasures from the past: your father, Eileen, your brothers, your memories, darling Aunt Win…"

"But you have a father."

"Yes, but he didn't give me an attic. My mother might have done, but she died when I was eight."

She sat closer and put her arm round him. "Can't I give you an attic?"

He swallowed, then kissed her again. "You have already."

"I'll fill it full of love." She was happier now. Surer of herself.

"Will you, Jennie?"

"Always." Always was a path that stretched out through summer lands towards a certain happiness. Always wasn't just an oasis in a desert, it meant for ever.

"Would you marry me, Jennie? Not now, while the war is on, but afterwards?"

"Now, after, whenever you want." She was filled with great joy. It didn't matter when, except for her body's impatience.

"That's if — "

"I don't like it's." She tried to make it sound a joke, but she meant it. It was a terrifying word.

"You don't know anything about me, and I have to explain why there's an empty attic."

"Very well," she said quietly, tensely waiting.

Richard did not speak for some moments, restlessly tearing at a piece of grass in his hands, and she guessed he never normally spoke of this.

"I told you my father lives in Cornwall, and that's where I was born, too. A poor but magical and mysterious place. But we lived in Helston, a gloomy, grey mining town, though the industry was fast declining even then. My father has a grocer's shop but, more importantly for me, he is strictly Chapel. No Church of England for him. His life is dominated by puritan spectacles glued on so tightly he can never take them off. The answer to everything is no. New clothes, dances, fairs, games, everything except the mere mechanics of living is unacceptable. Even books were frowned upon, although they became my lifeline. They still are. They're the path of freedom whether in Cornwall or France. Fear of sin and hellfire rules his life, yet I think him the greatest sinner of all. He wore my mother down, beating her if she resisted, and she died, I'm sure, of loneliness and despair. I had a sister, and she died too, when I was thirteen. She was five years older than me, and she made me promise I'd escape what she'd been through.

"When I was five, and she ten, there was a terrible shipwreck off the Lizard coast on the Manacle Rocks. The *Mohegan* was on her way to America, and over a hundred people lost their lives — men, woman and children. The bodies were brought up to the nearby village of St Keverne and laid out for burial in a mass grave. St Keverne was twelve miles away from us, down twisty lanes, and yet my father dragged us all there by wagon to see the bodies. "The wages of sin," he thundered. I was just a child, but even I thought this odd. It was a terrible sight, all those drowned people, many of them gashed by the rocks, just children like me, some of them. How could they have sinned so badly? I think even then I could see that it would be better to help people than condemn them.

"The moment I was fifteen and school was over, I left home for good, and took a job on a steamship in Falmouth port. I ended up as a steward on one of the big passenger liners to America. On one of them I met a professor of medicine, and noticed he was always reading. It made me realize that I'd missed out on book learning, however much I was learning in other respects, so I asked him how I could learn. To cut a long story short I became a medical student in his school when I was nineteen but the war broke out four years later."

"In order to help people." Jennie thought she understood now.

"Yes, but there was more to it. One day I went to his study and found him reading a William le Queux spy novel. I teased him about it, and he was quite annoyed. "I enjoy them," he told me. I was a pompous juggins and said it was a waste of time. Nonsense, he retorted. He felt better after reading them and who was to say that that was any less worthy than reading a medical book. Because medicine helped others, I replied, amazed he couldn't see the difference, much as I loved books myself. Well, he rounded on me. Some books mended bodies, some mended souls, some mended the human being, and who was I to declare that a William le Queux novel didn't make him a better and happier human being for reading it? So I began to realize that medicine wasn't all that patients needed. After all, if books had helped me, they could help others."

"Hence your singing to the patients and the piano playing. And the reason they called you Dr Dobro-Dobro."

"Perhaps." He flushed. "I don't feel very good. I try, that's all."

"So why do you need an attic full of the past, when yours is full of the present?"

"You have a past so different from mine."

"It's the future we'll spend together, Richard."

The years ahead stretched out before her, along her Golden Road to Samarkhand.

*

Jennie walked through the front gates of Applemere, imagining she could hear the house calling to her as so often before, despite its loneliness during this war. She had come alone, hoping to find Michael so that she could tell him about Anna. There was no answer at the door, so she went through the side gates into the gardens. There seemed to be no one around, until she spotted a rare sight for these days: a gardener. The Fokinghams had been lucky to find one, even an obviously older man, such as he was.

She hurried up to him. "Do you know where Lieutenant Fokingham is today?"

The old man looked alarmed at even being spoken to, and she tried to reassure him. He was shabbily dressed with a panama hat on his head against the sun, and he looked vaguely familiar. Could he have worked here before the war? She tried again but he just shook his head, still looking terrified. And *still* familiar. Then startled recognition came to her. Surely she must be mistaken. It didn't make sense. But then she had no doubt.

It was King Stephen of Montevanya.

He turned and ambled away. If he had recognized her he showed no signs of it and shaken she began to walk back to the gates, only to see someone bearing down on her. She was shocked and delighted to see it was Aunt Eileen herself, who was supposed to be in Serbia. Eileen gripped Jennie hard by the arm.

"Never, never," she said grimly, "tell a living soul about this."

No need to ask what "this" was. *This* was King Stephen, who was supposed to be in Corfu. Jennie was taken aback. What had she done wrong *this* time?

"What?" she began.

"Don't ask, Jennie. *I* don't know, *you* don't know, you don't *want* to know. Is that clear? Most of all, you have no intention of telling anyone about today, not your nearest and dearest. *No one!*"

*

Jennie returned to the Station House stunned, but she saw nothing more of Eileen until she suddenly appeared in Boulogne early in August.

"We need to talk," Eileen said forbiddingly, and took her to lunch. They sat at a corner table well away from anyone else.

"Spies everywhere," Jennie had said lightly and won herself a glare.

"Let's settle this, Jennie. I've been away or I'd have come sooner. Whom did you think you saw at Applemere in June?"

Jennie knew the answer to that. "You. No one else."

"Quite right." Eileen was obviously relieved, "I hear you're to marry Dr Dobro-Dobro."

"I don't call him that. He's Richard to me. I only love Richard."

"Then love the Dobro-Dobro too, is my advice." Eileen's tone became less brisk. "Now, let me tell you why it is fortunate you met only me last June. Do you know what's been going on in Corfu?"

"No." Jennie had been so full of her own happiness that there had been even less time than usual for reading newspapers.

"There have been plans afoot for years about a Greater Serbia after the war. Now it's been agreed at meetings in Corfu that there should be a formally named Kingdom of the Serbs, Croats and Slovenes."

"There won't be room on the postage stamps for all that."

"Be serious, Jennie. There's a possibility it could be called Yugoslavia or some such name instead."

"It's wonderful news, then." Jennie couldn't yet see how this applied to her seeing King Stephen in Applemere.

"If you're a Serb, yes. Not quite so wonderful if you happen to be a Montenegrin, since the new nation is to be a constitutional monarchy under Serbia, which means Prince Alexander will be king. Montenegro was annoyed, since she has a perfectly good king of her own. The Croats don't want to find themselves split racially between Serbia and Italy, yet the Allies have to be nice to Italy since they promised her all sorts of goodies if they came into the war on the Allied side. And more. Do you see?"

"No," Jennie said truthfully. Her head was reeling.

Eileen sighed. "*Montevanya*, of course. If Stephen were in Corfu, he would be steamrollered by the Serbs into joining Montevanya to this new Serb kingdom after the war."

"And what about Viktor?"

"Naturally he's hoping the Central Powers will win and that he will remain king within a German-Austro empire, like Hungary. If they don't win, then he certainly doesn't want his father marching back to take over the country. He believes Stephen to be in Corfu, and has his spies out there with a death warrant for him. The Serbs believe him to be under the Allies' thumb in London. The powers that be in London believe him to be in Corfu. They too would have their motives to remove him from the scene, though one hopes not so drastically as Viktor. That way Montevanya is in their power to dispose of as they choose at the end of the war. Only five people in the world know he is at Applemere, including myself — and you."

"And Max?" asked Jennie, amused rather than awestruck by this responsibility.

"He's still with the Allied forces, but sees Stephen as the rightful king. We intend to keep him alive despite Viktor's little plans."

Jennie thought this through. "Eileen, you say "we". Who would that "we" be?"

Eileen looked at her. "Go on wondering, little Jennie, but don't think too hard, will you?"

CHAPTER XV

1918

Inside Jennie's heart was a deep core of happiness. Often in the midst of this terrible war she would examine it to give her strength for her job. It sprang from Richard and her memories of Christmas 1917, even though she had had leave but he had not, and even though the celebrations were carried on with the signs of war all around them.

"Twice up and down and we have to draw the blinds," Aunt Win assured her blithely as the gas lighting suddenly lowered. "It's the signal for another air raid."

"Once," Dad had grumbled, helping himself to another helping of smoked haddock — the government's recommended Christmas lunch now that fowl were so scarce and so expensive — "signals meant good decent trains. I'll be glad when this war's over and we can get back to normal."

Everyone had laughed at this understatement, even Mary, though she hadn't much to laugh about now. Tom had gone into the forces — kicking and screaming as Win had privately said to Jennie. He had just finished his training, and had left for France to join the 7th Battalion of the Royal West Kents.

Jennie longed only to marry Richard, whether the war was over or not, and she had finally persuaded him that waiting served no true purpose.

"If," he had agreed, "there's no breakthrough this summer. I couldn't stand another winter without you, even if waving at each other in the staff coach most of the time will be a funny sort of marriage."

There were no married quarters on Ambulance Train No. 31. By unspoken agreement they had not discussed their life after the war. Surely it would end this year. Despite the terrible slaughter at Passchendaele in the mud and rain, Ypres itself had not fallen to the enemy. If it had done, then so might the Channel ports, and what future might lie beyond that was too frightening to contemplate.

Ambulance Train No. 31 had had a regular route to the battlefields of the Ypres Salient, since new light railways had been constructed by the British last year both to replace those bombed by the enemy and to get closer to the fighting. Since the new year, the Applemere Flyer had been re-routed to a quieter stretch near Arras when the line had been extended to Vimy Ridge. Their job was always busy, for the fighting never stopped entirely, but any moment now new offensives would begin. It was hard seeing Richard every day, but only being able to snatch the odd kiss or word, or enjoy the occasional trip to a village if they could arrange it together. But Paula was envious of Jennie's luck.

"At least he's here," she grumbled, "not up in some aircraft somewhere."

*

The Germans wasted no time. On the first day of spring they had launched a massive offensive on the Somme, pushing the

Allies back to the point where it seemed that Amiens might fall.

They can't do that!" Freddie had yelled in fury when this frightening news reached them. "I won't be able to get the Flyer to Le Havre, or Rouen."

Perhaps the Germans didn't hear him, for the French too had been forced back across the River Marne and Paris was under threat again. The Americans hadn't heard Freddie either, despite the Allies pushing them to persuade their General Pershing to allow some of his precious troops actually to fight, rather than just train as they had been doing for a year.

However, Amiens held, and Freddie took this as a personal triumph. Even so, the Germans had advanced so far in the Arras area that the engine drivers scarcely had time to withdraw their engines and trains before the Germans had overrun it.

After that the Applemere Flyer was re-routed so often that Jennie found it hard to keep up. Every day meant more wounded or yellow-faced gassed patients, and the constant coughing up of irreparably scarred lungs made the Flyer a more sombre place than ever before. Even Paula's normal ebullience deserted her. Boulogne became a haven of peace — except in May when it was broken by a familiar face.

Anna again. She grinned faintly when Jennie answered her knock at the door of her lodgings. "You said you wanted me to keep in touch," she said airily.

"I did," Jennie agreed. "Where are the trousers?" Anna looked the opposite of last time. Her hair was trim, her civilian clothes immaculate.

Anna grimaced. "I was sacked. There were a lot of WAAC girls coming out from England, all wanting to do my job, and someone realized I wasn't enlisted. So here I am, with my services on offer."

"We're short of staff," Jennie said doubtfully. Was this wise?

"Splendid," Anna agreed. "After all, the train is named after my home."

"I'll take you to see Paula. You remember her?" Jennie refrained from pointing out that she had disowned Applemere.

Anna did, but then failed to turn up the next day, as expected, and the Applemere Flyer had to leave without her. Typical Anna, Jennie fumed.

A few days later, however, Jennie seized a brief moment to visit Freddie on the footplate, squeezing past his new fireman. When she turned to leave, she found herself staring straight into Anna's innocent-looking eyes.

"Meet my new apprentice, Jack Cole," Freddie said casually.

"What," Jennie groaned, "are you doing here?"

"Don't make a fuss, Jennie." Anna seemed to think there was nothing odd about her new job. "There's so much work needs doing out here, you should be only too grateful to whoever does it. So should Lloyd George, particularly as I don't have to be paid."

Looking at Anna's slight figure, the cap over her hair, filthy face and clothes, Jennie had to struggle hard to believe that Freddie could have been so daft.

"I can't be bothered to enlist properly," Anna continued. "Besides, if I can drive ambulances I can drive trains. Freddie won't let me do that, but he agreed I could be a fireman instead."

"No I didn't," Freddie retorted. "I said you could be my board boy to get supplies, and check coal, and perhaps stoke the boiler from time to time."

"Same thing."

it is not," Freddie said patiently. "Firemen take years to learn the trade, and it's a man's work anyway."

"I always wanted to be a suffragette, didn't I, Jennie? I believe in equal rights." Anna was not perturbed.

"The right to vote is hardly the same as stoking boilers," Jennie pointed out.

"The next thing I knew," Freddie continued gloomily, "was that she had a shovel and the fire gloves on and that was it. She's not bad, actually, and I don't let her go inside the fire box."

"Ah, but you're not watching all the time, are you, Freddie dear?" His new apprentice grinned.

*

Jennie supposed she should not be too horrified. The majority of war work was done by the regular military and other services, but enterprising individuals had their place too. There were the two women of Pervyse, famous for their frontline cellar hospital in the Ypres Salient, and Dr Inglis who wouldn't take no for an answer when the Admiralty refused her plans for hospitals in war areas. And Eileen herself, of course. So why not Anna on the Applemere Flyer?

The days dragged though, and Jennie longed for an end to the death, disease and fighting, despite the odd moments of relief with Paula or Richard.

"Why don't we get married on my twenty-third birthday?" she'd suggested impulsively to him, and he had looked lovingly at her.

"We'll try for leave and get a special licence. I agree. Why wait and wait and wait?"

It sounded blissful. Only weeks to go until August 1st, and her life would begin once more. The cramped train was claustrophobic. She had been travelling in it for over a year and a half and, despite the frequent breaks, she was beginning to dread getting back on it, even though that seemed little enough compared with returning to the trenches as soldiers had to, or climbing back into an aeroplane as Paula's Peter did. She had met him once and liked him. He was ideal for Paula and Jennie wondered why they, too, were waiting for a time that never came.

"Suppose the war doesn't end for years?" she pointed out to Paula.

"It has to. Both sides are exhausted. Anyway, God can't be so unkind as to stop us getting married after this."

Jennie pinned her dreams on her birthday as she counted the diet specials on to the right trolley, double-checking the lists time and time again. She could do her job walking in her sleep — and sleep now was a blessed event in this cramped space. This had been a quiet run. Although they were nearly full, the patients were those who had been recovering at a casualty clearing station and there were more sitting-up than cot cases for once. Nevertheless she'd be glad when they reached Etaples and distributed their load destined for the camp hospitals lining the coast or the officers' hospital.

At last in the late afternoon Etaples came into sight after a ten-hour journey from the front. Jennie had glanced at Richard while she was checking the lists during the loading process, every time feeling a tug at heart and body as she watched his thin, lively face, now grinning as he passed a joke with a patient, now full of gentleness as he spoke to another. She watched his hands and thought longingly of their marriage ahead. The unloading wouldn't take long, and then they would be free to have their own meal, and relax for an hour or two.

But they never reached Etaples. Jennie was in the staff room with Paula while the orderlies were getting the patients ready for unloading, when the train juddered to a stop so suddenly that she was thrown against Paula as the room swayed and furniture toppled around them, pushing them to the floor.

"What on earth's that?" Paula said shakily as Jennie began to disentangle herself. There was a droning overhead but the words were hardly out of her mouth when the crashes that followed and the sudden darkness made it instantly clear what it was. An air raid — and a big one. There hadn't been one for ages, and certainly not here behind the lines in Etaples, even though it was where troops as well as hospitals were congregated. Fear took over Jennie's mind. Were their red crosses on the train large enough? Those crashes sounded very close by. No sooner had the thought come than there were two more crashes, then the floor shifted and the whole train began shaking again. Was it falling? Everything was at an angle.

Jennie was choking with dust and smoke, and the noise of the crashes still rang in her ears. After a moment's eerie silence the screams began. Began and never ended. Jennie levered herself up, choking, trying to clear the fog from the air. Others in the carriage were doing likewise, including Paula, who was now pulling herself painfully up. She too was covered in dust. They looked at each other for one split second, then with one accord they helped pull fellow staff from underneath furniture and baggage, accounting for them one by one. All present.

Outside she could hear Freddie's voice yelling for everyone to jump down on the bank side of the track, and not to move, not to move anywhere. *Now*.

"I've got to find out," Jennie shakily said to Paula.

Her head was pounding. The bombs must have hit the train directly. But which part, oh which part? She had to get through to where Richard had been working in one of the sitting-up wards, two — no, three carriages ahead. She managed to scramble through the next two carriages, one of which, the pharmacy, was now a mess of shattered glass and supplies, but then the corridor was blocked. Sick at heart and stomach, she ran back to the open door and jumped down into someone's arms by the track side.

"Richard!" she cried in relief, but it was Paula.

"I'm sorry, Jennie," Paula kept firm hold of her. "It looks as if carriages eight and nine have been hit directly. Is that where — ?"

"Yes." But the word didn't seem to have come from her and she began to stumble along the side of the track towards the pile of wreckage where she could see orderlies and doctors gathering. The train seemed to be just in front of the Etaples railway bridge, but somehow it had managed to stop in time. In time, she prayed, for Richard. She had training, she knew what to do when — *if* — she found him.

But there was no sign of him in the tangled mess that was all that remained of the two devastated carriages. The roofs had vanished and bodies were lying half in, half out of the wreckage, torn apart and lying all over the track. There was smoke, and the slow movement of doctors and staff picking their way through to search for any signs of the living. She took only a moment to look, then she began to search frantically for Richard.

Shouted orders. Stretchers. Blood, limbs everywhere. And no Richard.

He didn't seem to be among the living on the stretchers, or among the dead, as she forced herself to look. But he must be there, the alternative was too terrible even to put into thoughts. She helped the orderlies pulling aside wreckage with their hands. She could do that at least, heart in mouth at what she might find. Ambulances were already appearing at the side of the track. Then she caught a glimpse of something, heard an exclamation from an orderly, and they both tore frantically at what remained of the piano. Under it was Richard.

Fear gripped her every nerve, every vocal chord. She heard someone call for a stretcher. His face was intact but the rest of his body was bloody and distorted. "He's alive," said a voice.

"Just," said another, then saw Jennie and mouthed the word "sorry".

Why? Amongst so much carnage only truth could help. Tourniquets were applied, then bandages, splints. She watched herself detachedly helping, trying to forget that this was Richard, whose tenuous grasp on life might be extinguished at any moment. So could that of all the others here. She could see that these carriages were a tomb. So even the Applemere Flyer was not impregnable. Pain tore her apart inside. If she lost Richard — no, she couldn't, she *wouldn't*. He was a good man, he tried to do good. Surely that must count for something. But it seemed to mean nothing in this never-ending war. It took whom it pleased.

He's alive — just. She had to cling to these words. She forced herself not to linger as the stretcher left. There were others that needed her. Her love was with Richard, her will was with Richard. With all the strength of her being she willed him to live.

*

Had it not been for Freddie, the Applemere Flyer would have been lost as it crossed the Etaples bridge, which had been the raid's target.

"I remembered something Dad told me about the Zep raid on Folkestone," he told Jennie. "About that driver on the London down train seeing those aircraft ahead and pulling up short. Didn't take much brain to realize these Gothas were heading for the bridge."

It hadn't just been the bridge that had suffered. A hospital had been hit, killing nurses and patients, and the Flyer had lost nineteen to death, including three staff, and twenty-nine wounded further to their original injuries.

"Jennie, I'm so sorry." Anna came to sit with her in the staff carriage, which they had put into some kind of order again. "How is Richard?"

Jennie had no answer for her. She didn't even know to which hospital he had been taken, and she had spent the next two days tracking him down. How badly wounded he was, no one knew. Freddie was determined that the Applemere Flyer should be repaired immediately to continue its job, and she forced herself to support him.

"It's going to go on," he told the authorities. To those who said it should break up and the staff be posted elsewhere, he patiently pointed out that this wasn't necessary. He harangued anyone who had any kind of authority at Boulogne and eventually won consent through sheer persistence. The train would continue and so would the staff, even though it needed more equipment and carriages and it needed them quickly. Freddie and Anna were taking care of this at Boulogne while Paula and Jennie concentrated on getting the pharmacy and stores re-equipped by begging, borrowing and stealing from every hospital in the area.

"Don't let's take no for an answer," Jennie told Paula. "We must get them." *I can do this much for Richard*, she told herself. Wherever he is.

At last she found him in the nearby village of Camiers, at Camp 21 hospital, the first one she had visited. He had given his name as Richard Dobro, the sister explained.

"Is he…?" Jennie could not frame the word.

"No, but it's still touch and go. Are you — ?"

"His fiancée," Jennie supplied. "He has no parents." It was more or less true.

"We've had to take a leg off, and there are other injuries. Shock is the least of them. Even if he pulls through, he's going to be ill for a long time."

"He's not going to die though," Jennie told her calmly. It was a statement, not a question. Even so, she had seen enough death and illness to know that the sister was right as soon as she saw Richard.

"Jennie?" His lips framed her name though no sound came out.

"Darling, you're going to get better," she told him gently. "We're going to get married in two months' time, and I can't get married alone."

A tear trickled out from under his closed eyelids, so she knew that he heard what she said.

"You're going to pull through, Richard. Fight. For me." Later, when she was alone, she would think about what the sister had said. Now was not the time. Think of our wedding." She had to force herself to continue. "Once we're married, Richard, our life is going to be dobro-*dobra*."

CHAPTER XVI

"You're going home, Richard."

There was sudden fear in his eyes and Jennie blamed herself for her stupidity. Of course he would think by "home" that she meant Helston, whereas she had been thinking of Fairsted. He had been in the Camiers hospital for nearly three months now, and he was well enough to be moved across the Channel. He needed more recuperation time, and Eileen had arranged, with Jennie's heartfelt gratitude, for this to be spent in the manor convalescent home.

This was one of Richard's good days, and there weren't many of these that coincided with the days Jennie could manage to be in Etaples. It was late August, and at last the tide of war seemed to be turning with the Allied forces on the offensive and the Germans falling back in retreat, startled at the strong opposition from forces whom they had assumed were spent. Even so, there seemed little hope of the war ending before 1919, since winter would soon be an obstacle to that final necessary push.

On his bad days Richard didn't recognize her, and such blank periods, as the sister called them, could continue for some time. It was heart-rending, and Jennie dreaded coming to the hospital only to be faced with the look of politeness he wore throughout her visit. He didn't want to offend anyone, especially those who thought they knew him; it was just that he didn't recognize them — even Jennie, whom he had been going to marry on August 1st.

She had come to visit on that day, casually mentioning it was her birthday in the hope that it might jog his memory, but he merely wished her a pleasant day with no recognition in his eyes, even when she gave him the books she had brought with her. It was her great fear that his memory might falter and then never return, but so far it always had.

They're sending you to a convalescent home in Fairsted at first. Then you'll be ready to travel to Roehampton for the leg to be fitted." She saw him flinch but she knew that the more she talked of this as being the natural course of things, the more chance there was that he might accept it. So far the crutches remained little used, and on days when he was well enough to sit in a chair — as today — a blanket covered the lower half of his body.

"There's no point," was all he replied.

The black mood was on him today. That was almost worse than the blank days.

"Of course there is," she said sharply. "However could you work on the Flyer without it?" He did not reply, and she felt her feeble attempt at encouragement had been trite. "Or get up to the attic in our house when we're married," she persevered. "We'll never fill it full of dreams if you don't."

The black mood softened. "Jennie, you know we can't marry now. Not with me like this."

Here it came at last, her great fear spelled out for her. "Why not?" Shock, misery and determination all mingled within her. How could she reach him and explain that nothing had changed?

"I'm only half a man now."

"The half I want to marry. All that's wrong is your leg — otherwise there's nothing to prevent our marrying, is there?"

He did not answer and she was scared in case there was something else, something he had not told her. No, she could not believe that, for she had seen his medical records. The leg and shell shock were the major problems. So what was worrying him?

"There's more, Jennie. It's what I *am*. I can't see the way forward."

He looked at her in mute appeal. What did he mean by that? And then she thought she understood. "You know medical work

isn't right for you, but you don't know what is. And now you feel that even if you did know, you wouldn't be able to do it." He nodded, though she wasn't sure whether this was through agreement or just to satisfy her.

"Suppose you find out first what it is you want, and then we'll see if you can achieve it."

"Not *we*, Jennie," he interrupted. "Find someone else, someone you can roam the world with."

"I don't want to roam the world!" she cried. "I've seen the world, and people are just as they are here. No different."

"But the suffering is."

"Remember what your professor said — who are you to judge the depth of need and whether one person's suffering is harder than another's," she said in an attempt to reassure him. "No one can help everyone, only some. You could fail to help a thousand but succeed in helping one. Isn't that one worth it?" He slumped back in his chair.

"I don't know, Jennie. I don't know."

*

As the weeks passed, she was relieved to know he was safe in Kent, even though the Applemere Flyer was still in the thick of the battle. She still nursed to herself her despair that Richard no longer wanted to marry her. His blank periods were fewer now, and he was more cheerful, or so Aunt Win reported. Did he realize he'd have to face Aunt Win's wrath if he deserted her? Jennie struggled to make him laugh in her letters home, but it was hard to do so when the ache in her heart made itself felt so agonizingly.

By September the Germans were retreating so quickly there was an upsurge of hope that the war would soon be over, whether because of the Americans, who were now actively fighting, or because of the enemy's loss of morale. Jennie tried to think of each journey to the front line and back as a trip nearer home. Nearer Richard, nearer his love, which surely must still exist — if only she could connect with it.

*

As swiftly and unexpectedly as it had begun, the fighting ended with the November armistice. Although no peace treaty had yet been signed, no one could believe hostilities would begin again. The news had spread quickly, and nurses, staff and patients gathered to share the moment together. At eleven a.m. a cheer went round the train, followed by some singing of the national anthem. Then weary relief took over as they realized that the struggle was finally finished. So many lives destroyed, so many disrupted for ever. And for what? For something good — but what would that good be? Jennie wondered as she helped to hand out cigarettes and drinks.

Paula was crying, the first time Jennie had ever seen her give way to tears. "What's wrong?" she asked in alarm. "Not bad news, surely?"

"No," Paula sobbed. "I've just realized I can get married now."

*

By Christmas, Richard was in Dover House, the military officers' quarters of Roehampton Hospital, for the eventual fitting of his leg, but it was not going smoothly. He had caught an infection while at Fairsted, which had necessitated another amputation higher up the leg, and this had delayed his departure. Jennie suspected that Eileen had had to go to a higher authority to get him the privilege of staying in Dover House, but could not thank her as she had gone to the Salonika front again. During the autumn this had pushed forward and most of Serbia had been recaptured, with many of the enemy being satisfyingly expelled over the same mountain passes as Jennie had travelled in 1915.

The Applemere Flyer remained in service despite the armistice. Not only did the Allied forces have to ensure the German armies did indeed return to their own land, but disease was still rampant among the troops, and France and Belgium had to be rebuilt. Those who might have thought that with the war over they could all pack up and go home were wrong. Nevertheless, aboard the Flyer they had a new sense of purpose now: they were steaming towards an eventual return home, and there was a rumour that at least some of the ambulance trains might be withdrawn by the end of February.

Christmas itself was a spartan one, which Jennie, Freddie and Anna celebrated in Lille, which was painfully sorting itself out after being retaken by the Allies in

October. Paula had Christmas leave and was spending it with Peter, who was hoping to make a career in flying for the new Royal Air Force. Paula seemed happy about this.

"I thought you wanted to get away from war? Haven't you heard enough about aeroplanes?" Jennie asked.

"Haven't you heard enough about trains?" was Paula's retort, and Jennie laughed. Paula was right. It wasn't aeroplanes and trains that made war, it was people.

Lille still showed many signs of the siege and bombardment by the Germans in 1914, and the food shortages were still critical. Nevertheless it was a free town again, already overflowing with returning POWs, menfolk sent for slave labour, and those dispossessed by war. It was a city of passage, of which the Applemere Flyer was part. They dined, if that was the word, at the Brasserie Armentieroise opposite the central railway station, where the patron proudly produced a bottle of wine that had somehow been saved from German hands.

"What now, Freddie?" Jennie asked, curious as to how his new-found fame — he had been awarded a Military Medal for halting the train at Etaples — would affect his future.

"Driving trains," he replied laconically. "Back to the old company, I expect."

"And you, Anna?" Jennie had been longing to ask, and with the mellowing effects of wine was bold enough to do so.

"Don't worry about me, Jennie." Anna's eyes glinted.

"But I do," Jennie said firmly. She could hardly ask about the babies in front of Freddie, but Anna herself had no such restraint.

"I'm not going in search of the twins, if that's what you mean. If I couldn't find them two years ago, what chance would there be now when there's going to be utter chaos in Europe?" For all her words there was pain in her eyes.

"You won't just disappear, will you?"

"No. I can promise you that."

Jennie was instantly suspicious. "Do you have a plan?"

"Yes."

"That means trouble."

But Anna only laughed.

*

Spring would soon be here and the tall trees lining the path between Dover House and the fitting room at Roehampton Hospital would be showing signs of greenery. Signs of hope. But today they were barren and stark under a gloomy sky. February was the worst of months.

"Did the fitting go well?" Jennie asked Richard.

"Much better. I've been going to the Red Cross clinic for whirlpool baths. It does away with the pain you feel after the amputation. The new amputation, in my case," he added bitterly. "The fitting looks hopeful now."

"And you — are you hopeful?"

"Of the leg, yes."

Her heart sank. Richard was in one of his polite moods. "You'll be leaving here soon," she tried again. "Will you come back to Fairsted? You can stay with us."

"It wouldn't be wise, sweetheart." He stopped, leaning heavily on her arm. "Look at me. This arm would be dependent on you for the rest of our lives, metaphorically if not physically. I can't do that to you."

"What about what I want?" she asked miserably.

"It's the same thing. It would come between us."

"Won't anything make you change your mind? Richard, you're breaking my heart. I love you." There had to be a way to convince him, there just had to.

"It's because I love you so much, Jennie, that I won't do it. Not unless…"

Instant hope sprang up in her. "Unless what?"

"I can see an answer to how it might work."

The misery returned. "But you'll be leaving here soon. Where will you go?"

"My grandmother — my mother's mother — lives in Bexley in north Kent. I'll go to her when the time comes." He squeezed her hand. "Don't look so glum. The address is River Cottage. Now tell me what you are going to do. Go back to the booking office?" She could not even bear to think about it. If there were no Richard, there was no star to guide her.

*

"You have a walk along to the Halt, Jennie. It will do you more good than moping here," Dad said.

She had only been home a month, for the Flyer had been running in France till early April, and now that she was back, she could not settle. With Richard in Roehampton, she felt a bird of passage, and yet Fairsted, she had once declared, was where she wanted to be for ever. She began to walk along the footpath by the railway track, and remembered that summer's day so long ago on her twelfth birthday. Now she walked here alone. No Tom with her. He'd just returned from the trenches, behaving as though he'd won the war all by himself. No Freddie trotted behind her. He was still driving trains in France with the ROD, who were staying on to help rebuild the French and Belgian railways. No Jack and now no Richard. Just her,

Jennie, to wrest what she could from the wreckage of her dreams.

Applemere itself had not yet reverted to being a family home again. Eileen had stayed there when she paid a fleeting visit two weeks ago, and had walked over to the Station House to see Jennie.

"Is the gardener still with you?" Jennie had asked solemnly.

"He's left our employment. However, it's good news for him," Eileen had replied equably. "He's back in his own country and, amazingly, with his wife. Zita suddenly saw the light when the Allies took the upper hand. Viktor and Eva shot off to live in Austria, and Montevanya remains neutral, by the grace of God and the skin of its teeth, as before. Max had a hand in that. He persuaded the Allies that all hell would be set loose if Montevanya lost its neutrality. If the Allies awarded it as a gift to Roumania, the new kingdom of the Slavs, Croats and Slovenes would be extremely annoyed. If they gave it to the new kingdom, Roumania would be annoyed, and if they gave it to Hungary — as I suspect they would like to have done since it's now independent from Austria — *everyone* would be annoyed, except, presumably, Hungary. So for the moment Montevanya remains neutral under Stephen and Zita."

"That's splendid." Jennie was delighted. Not many countries could have managed to retain the status quo from before the war, especially one that Viktor had joined to the Central Powers. "So you and Georgius can return to your home."

"Indeed we can. Georgius is there already. He's a great unifier in his own way. He's one of the placators of this world. not a threat, so he's generally popular there, if only because he cheers them up. No harm in that. Sometimes I wonder though…" Eileen stopped, but when Jennie looked questioning, she reluctantly continued. "I wonder whether the days of the small monarchies aren't over. If there's one thing this war has shown everyone it's that when roused, the people will come out and fight. And once out they may be reluctant to go all the way back in."

"And will you go all the way back in, Eileen? Settle down?"

"What a horrible phrase."

"Very well. Will you keep on your job — whatever it is?" Eileen thought for a moment. "That can't be defined, so my answer is whatever I make it to be. Let's say that before the war and during the war I considered my allegiance lay both with this country and Montevanya. I always made it clear, however, that their interests should never clash. Roger understood that, and they seldom have."

"By Roger," Jennie asked politely, "do you mean his employer?" That was the king, of course.

"Sometimes, Jennie, you ask too many questions. Let us say, his employer, and a certain gentleman we refer to as C. And it's an erstwhile job I should make clear."

"I'm sure it's not completely erstwhile."

"That," Eileen said reflectively, "remains to be seen. And now, Jennie, tell me of your Richard."

Thus encouraged, Jennie had poured out the story, and her own bewilderment at what to do, when in practice she could do nothing. Eileen had not agreed.

"When he sees his path you must be standing in the middle of it, ready to move with him. So, Jennie, there *is* something you can do. You have to help him find that path, even though the choice must be his."

*

Paths were not to be found easily, however. Richard continued to find it hard to readjust. The classes he attended for training set a four-mile minimum standard, and only when he reached this would he be able to leave. Jennie felt stuck in a limbo from which she could only see one exit, and that was temporarily closed.

Anna, to Jennie's pleasure and relief, suddenly appeared in London and summoned Jennie to meet her. *Not* at Fokingham House, hardly to Jennie's surprise, but at the Charing Cross Hotel by the railway station.

"Suitable," she greeted Jennie, "in view of our working association." She didn't look like a fireman now though. She was elegantly clad in a linen two-piece suit, looking for all the world as though she'd never set a dainty foot on a footplate.

"So this is goodbye again, is it?" Jennie asked with resignation.

"Not at all. I wanted to talk about you."

"Me?" Jennie laughed. She couldn't remember the last time Anna had taken an interest in her doings.

"I wanted to set things right before I take my next step in life. It's about Jack."

Jennie went cold, taken by surprise. "What about him?"

"Tom says you're still feeling guilty about his death."

Even worse. Surely Anna had not been seeing Tom again.

"Relax," Anna said, obviously reading her thoughts. "Freddie told me."

"Of course I feel guilty," Jennie replied in relief. "Wouldn't you?"

"No. Not in the circumstances."

"What circumstances?" Jennie frowned as the old wound began to bleed. "And what's it got to do with you, Anna?"

"Quite a lot, in fact. Now stop being huffy and listen. Tom was furious with you for not telling him where I was or that I was having his children, so he kept back from you the full story about Jack's death."

Immediately Jennie began to remember some of the odd things Tom had said that she had not understood at the time. "He said that you had taken me for a ride, Anna. That I didn't see the truth."

"Wrong," Anna replied. "Tom loved me, so he wouldn't have meant that. He was talking about Michael."

"Michael?" Jennie stared at her. "What did he have to do with Jack? I know he liked signal boxes, but — "

"Oh, Jennie, you must know by now there are men in the world who don't particularly like women; they prefer to love men."

Jennie did know. Vaguely, anyway. You couldn't help knowing on board the train. But it had never touched her directly.

"Michael's always been that way," Anna said calmly. "He told me when we were quite young. Another thing our parents don't know about, incidentally, so don't tell them; it's illegal and wouldn't do his career much good. Anyway, one early pash of his was your Jack who, though he wasn't that way himself, allowed himself to be seduced, if you see what I mean. It stopped, but when we went to Montevanya it all began again, and that's when Tom must have found out. Jack loved you, Jennie, and he thought you'd learned the truth about him and Michael, and that's why you wanted to put the wedding off."

Jennie felt her lips trembling with shock. "I never guessed." Emotions rushed through her head, which she would examine later, but now all she felt was a great freedom, combined with a new sense of guilt that she had never seen Jack's torment.

"Michael has another passion, now," Anna mentioned casually. "He lives in Folkestone, and I confess I don't much care for him. His name's Joey."

This time Jennie began to laugh. She almost felt sorry for Michael. No wonder Joey had been so offhand when she and Richard saw him in Folkestone. It hadn't been Richard's rescue he resented; it was hers.

"On the whole, Jennie, I think you should marry that nice Richard of yours, as quickly as you can," Anna continued.

Jennie nodded weakly. "I'm trying. And how about you, Anna? What's your current plan?"

"Me? I'm going to marry Freddie."

*

Jennie felt she'd had enough shocks to last her a lifetime. She'd even stopped worrying about the unlikelihood of Freddie and Anna as a couple. As Aunt Win had said: "Better that than Omdurman."

But what about her? Richard had left Roehampton for Bexley, and so far Jennie had not visited him there. He had been there for three weeks now, and during that time Jennie

had done a lot of thinking about all they could share if only he could find the right path. *Where the wood ends*...She remembered one of the many books she had given to Richard in hospital, and a seed of hope began to form in her mind.

The following day she took the long train ride to Bexley. River Cottage proved to be large and dilapidated, and set in an extensive garden. His grandmother, although clad in black, had piercing eyes that reminded Jennie of Lady Pelham-Curtis. They sized her up carefully as she was shown through to the gardens. At last then they were left alone.

Richard's greeting was warm as he embraced her, and feeling his arms around her again was almost too much to bear.

"Did you never come here as a child?" she asked. She must be comfortable with him first before she tried her plan.

"Not after my mother died, but not for want of trying by my grandmother."

"And the leg?" she asked after more polite interchange.

"Stomping along," he replied shortly. "I'm thinking of working at Red Cross Headquarters. At least I can be useful on the sidelines."

She fought the familiar sinking feeling of despair that nothing had changed. "Think again," she urged. "If we married

He smiled at her, which was almost worse than his previous doubt. "No. You deserve a hundred per cent, Jennie, and I only have fifty to give you."

Very well, her offensive had to begin. "Is a useful sideline the best you can do?" she asked calmly.

"Well, yes. What else?" He looked taken aback.

So far, so good, she thought. "Reaching into people's hearts, as you used to. Do you need two legs for that?"

He took on his bullish expression. "Forget it, Jennie."

"How can I? You used to sing, to play music, to dance —"

"Dance? Like this?" He was angry now. That was good. too.

"You just need practice."

"You want me to go on the stage? Shall I audition for *Chu Chin Chow?*"

"Why not, if you want to."

"I don't!" He was shouting now.

"Remember that poem by Edward Thomas in the book I gave you? "The Path"?" Remember the path that looks

As if it led on to some legendary

Or fancied place where men have wished to go

And stay, till, sudden, it ends where the wood ends.

"Is that where you want to stop, Richard? Where the wood ends? Can't you see the path goes on to *another* legendary place?"

"Not for me." He was listening though.

"Find it, Richard. The path has to go on."

"They're just words. You know that."

"Your professor didn't think that." He stared at her blankly and for a moment she thought she had failed because she would have to explain, and that wouldn't work.

But suddenly he gave a shout. "Words, books. *Books*! That's the path to this legendary place of yours." He let his stick fall, and seized her in his arms. "I'll be a *bookseller*. Why did I never think of it before? We'll both be booksellers. We'll sell to the whole world what they need to help them. Poems, novels, weighty histories, a path ahead for everyone, not the path behind. A golden path."

"You can do it, Richard."

"Only with you, Jennie."

"Of course."

"And where could we do it?"

She thought fast and furiously. "I know where we'll start. There's only one place to rule the world." She was half laughing, half crying. "Fairsted, Applemere, *Kent*!

"Would they have me?"

"They *will*!"

"You realize what this means, Jennie?" He whirled her round, so excited that though he clung to her, he had forgotten his stick.

"Only that I love you even more."

"You'll have to give up that booking office. The station-master's daughter is about to become the bookseller's wife."

Printed in Great Britain
by Amazon